BEAUTY PLUS PITY

ARSENAL PULP PRESS | Vancouver

BEAUTY *plus* PITY

KEVIN CHONG

"Beauty plus pity—that is the closest we can get to a definition of art. Where there is beauty there is pity for the simple reason that beauty must die: beauty always dies, the manner dies with the matter, the world dies with the individual."

—*Vladimir Nabokov*

BEAUTY PLUS PITY
Copyright © 2011 by Kevin Chong

ARSENAL PULP PRESS
Suite 101, 211 East Georgia St.
Vancouver, BC
Canada V6A 1Z6
arsenalpulp.com

The publisher gratefully acknowledges the support of the Canada Council for the Arts and the British Columbia Arts Council for its publishing program, and the Government of Canada (through the Canada Book Fund) and the Government of British Columbia (through the Book Publishing Tax Credit Program) for its publishing activities.

This is a work of fiction. Any resemblance of characters to persons either living or deceased is purely coincidental.

Cover illustration by Chloe Chan
Photograph of the author by Lee Henderson

Printed and bound in Canada

Library and Archives Canada Cataloguing in Publication:

Chong, Kevin
   Beauty plus pity / Kevin Chong.

Issued also in electronic format.
ISBN 978-1-55152-416-0

   I. Title.

PS8555.H648B43 2011   C813'.6   C2011-903313-5

PART ONE

Beauty

CHAPTER ONE

WHO'D PICK A FUNERAL to meet your long-lost sister? A funeral or the sudden arrival of a family member—either would be shitty enough, but that morning, my head felt encased in bubble wrap, my stomach was a wading pool of bile, and I was sweating booze through my shoulder-stuffed suit like a cigarette lighter before it ignites. All of this was self-administered misery, and yet I still arrived late to deliver my father's eulogy.

My father's sisters, Paula and Mirabelle, scrambled up to me tandem-style, like unhappily conjoined twins, in the foyer outside the chapel doors.

"What took you so long?" Aunt Mirabelle, who lived in Toronto, asked with a nervous burp. Her eyes widened as they worried over my face. She stripped a piece of tissue paper from her purse and tried dabbing away my hangover. "We thought you were— we thought you could be ... Oh. Well." She straightened my tie. "We're glad you're here."

"Your mother could not be acting any worse," Aunt Paula announced in her flat, drag-queen croak. "She came close to leaving, but I took away her car keys. We didn't expect her—that girl—to be here."

I asked my First Aunt who she was talking about.

"We don't have time for this," shrieked Paula, who'd come from Hong Kong. She took my arm and led me into the chapel. "You're speaking next."

The chapel was forested with floral arrangements, which would have made my father double-blink in simmering displeasure. My possessive, wingnutty mother had, in fact, completely disregarded my father's wishes about having a funeral at all. There were several dozen people here, many of whom I didn't know, work contacts, most of them Chinese. Hunched over a set of cue cards, Uncle Charlie, who wasn't really my uncle, but a hulking caucasoid who befriended my father at the Happy Valley Racecourse in Hong Kong, stood apart from them like a mythical forest creature. It was Uncle Charlie who'd gotten me sad-belly drunk last night, but even in his grief, he was crisp and sparkly like a missionary. He stood there crouched over a microphone in front of a borrowed photo of Oliver Kwan—a blown-up and underexposed photo of him next to his bike—and the florists' wares, bloviating in my place.

"Bear with me, I have other thoughts to unload," Uncle Charlie was saying. "Oliver had, uh, exceptional personal hygiene. Yes. I never once saw dirt under his fingernails and, like many Asians, his sweat actually smelled nice, like—like tea with honey in it." He saw me and waved me toward the stage. "Well, that concludes my remarks. Where was I sitting?"

At the podium, my breaths felt like pinpricks. I stunk at public speaking; I preferred to let the bones in my face do the talking. In the front row, alongside my aunts and my cousin Gavin, who'd scored weed at a Starbucks earlier and experienced the day like a volunteer for a local hypnotist, my mother emoted for the deaf and blind. I felt the back of my neck grow warm knowing that I could offer no relief, no diversion to the soggy, disconsolate faces before me.

Patting myself for the speech I'd keyboarded and printed two nights before, I kept my head up. I had no inkling that I'd find Hadley—why should I? I was searching for my fiancée, Claire. We were not getting along, partly because she was stressed from law school, partly because I was trying to become a professional model, but the possibility that she would let me down was too awful to consider.

My father, Oliver Kwan, had died six days earlier, on the afternoon of September 3rd, 2008, with my mother, Eliza Mak Kwan, in the armchair next to his bed. "He was breathing with such effort, then he was breathing less and less, lighter and lighter. I could see his spirit leaving," my mother told me afterwards over the phone. "I threw my arms around him, to hold him here longer—it worked for a couple of minutes. Then I let go." Since that year began, the cancer, which had first roosted in his throat, imposed itself on his lungs. Six weeks before he died, my mother and I took turns—first at home, then at the hospice—watching over him, as he foamed with optimism and cheer for our sake. In reality, it was like pretending there was Santa Claus for a twelve-year-old who refused to believe otherwise.

I'd long accepted my father's imminent exit; I'd braced for it so much that the sting didn't pass through me for months afterwards. Still, from the start, I was bothered that my father would choose to go leaving so much unsaid—and not just the obvious. I was at work when he died because, the night before when I visited, my father insisted that my responsibilities to my part-time employer should be my uppermost preoccupation. I went to work, he passed on. Am I paranoid to think he was trying to duck a goodbye? We had chances to speak in the past couple of months, but he remained taciturn until the end, and I was too timid to force him to speak up.

One visit, a week before my father died, bothered me especially. When I stepped through his door, he was on his cell phone, arranging a visit. He was speaking in English, and I assumed it was to one of his few non-Chinese friends.

"Was that Uncle Charlie?" I asked.

He mumbled something indistinct. I actually think he said, "meow," as though we were cats. On the table by his chair was a copy of the Chinese newspaper, *Ming Pao*. "I never realized the news was so repetitive," he grumbled. "They do such a good job of making you forget the news is old."

His English was imperfect, and he would often switch back and forth from his second language to Chinese in a way that would be difficult for me to relate here—I'm no stenographer. As much as I can, I recall his words the way I remember them. That said, in Chinese and English, he spoke in the same deliberate, lurching manner, and he had a way of drawing out his words so that even ordering a pizza was suspenseful.

The newspaper contained a story about the movie director Edmund Chew, an old friend of my father's and a topic of conversation I strictly avoided. Normally, my father would look away at the sight of his name in print, so I was surprised when he brought him up. "Actually," my father said, "his last two movies weren't so bad. They didn't make much money, but at least he made those action movies personal."

"I read somewhere that he's doing commercials now," I told him, hoping this might please him. Edmund Chew lived the life my father might have had.

My father pressed one hand against his chest as he laughed. "He's always following my lead. Maybe he'll get cancer next."

This made me laugh too. "He's been hired by an Italian car company to direct three 'short films' to promote a new line of sedans."

"Perhaps I'm getting sentimental, but I saw his and my relationship in that last movie of his. The villain is about to fall off a cliff and asks the hero, 'What time is the early show playing?' In the film, it comes out of nowhere—the villain is a kind of Jack Nicholson type who says things that are—what do you call it, you know, when they don't make sense?"

"Non-sequiturs?"

"Right. So, in the film, the remark doesn't make sense, but it was an old joke between Chew and I. One of us would call on the other—sometimes your mother would come along—to watch the late show. We knew each other from school and would pawn anything we owned to get in. We'd call and say in English, because we met in our English class in school, 'What time is the late show?' And whoever picked up the phone would reply in English, 'It's never too late for the late show.'"

I didn't know what to make of my father's anecdote, and waited silently for him to say more, but he said nothing, and we reached a wordless standstill. I stood to leave. My old man was reclined comfortably by the window, wearing slippers I had given him for Christmas years before, cotton pyjamas, and a worn blue bathrobe that was untied and had spilled over the arms of his chair. It was late August, but the morning light was still strong and made each feature of his gaunt face distinct. The light rang off his square-shaped reading glasses, and for an instant he had the head of a large insect. He removed them and stared up at me, his eyes flashing needle points. "Malcolm, you don't look very good."

The obvious was too hard to resist. "Neither do you."

"What I mean is you look tired," he told me. "Why don't you take a break?"

"I don't have anything better to do." I meant that I had no other plans, but he took it to mean that I was a child again, overwhelmed by boredom.

"Go see a movie, go to dim sum with your mother. Spend some

time with your fiancée—what's her name again?"

"Claire," I told him. I wasn't sure whether my father was cool to Claire because we were engaged—he thought we were too young to be married—or because of her personality in general, or some combination of the two. "You know what her name is."

My father refused to acknowledge my frustration. "Okay, take Claire out."

"She has a salsa class tonight." When Claire wasn't preparing for her second year at law school, she was dancing. "She doesn't have much time to spare."

He cocked an eyebrow at me. "Then do something by yourself. When you were young, you used to spend hours playing alone."

"I had no friends."

"Don't say that," he said, waving a hand dismissively. "You were imaginative. You had a wonderful imagination, running your cars along the couch."

I winced as I watched my father mime my race-car zooms. "You want me to go?" I asked.

He tried laughing it off, but ducked his head sheepishly. "I wish you weren't so sensitive."

"Just tell me and I'll leave." In those weeks, we'd been solicitous and overbearing. It was justifiable, even if my father was too weak-willed to say it, to want unaccompanied time. Normally he disliked being alone, not because he was afraid of solitude, but because he felt it a waste of his natural sociability. Leaving him alone was like keeping a light on in an empty house. "I'll go if you don't want me around." Now I was the one trying to laugh it off.

"I don't mean to upset you." He paused as an unpleasant feeling came over him. His face was turned from me, but I could see his entire body stiffen. "You and your mother are so touchy these days.

You tell me—how should I feel? I told you. I feel a little better than I did yesterday. And yesterday I felt better than the day before. Just a little. Of course it's no miracle—"

"I don't understand why you talk like that."

"Like what?" he said with a gentle smile. We could go on like that forever, my old man pretending not to understand me.

"I'll see you tomorrow then," I said, with resignation. "Maybe then they'll be discharging you."

Before I could leave his room, he called out my name. "I couldn't finish breakfast this morning. Too much food." He held out a chocolate-chip bran muffin for me, which I put in my pocket and took home for Claire.

My father had a private suite on the fourth floor of the hospice. When the elevators doors opened, there was a teenaged girl standing there. Later on, I would realize it was Hadley. I remembered her because she stepped back at the sight of me with what must have been some sense of recognition, but at the time I was embarrassed because I'd felt rebuffed.

A couple of days after my conversation with my father, he was making plans for his own death. My mother and I didn't know what accounted for this change of outlook, but we felt something close to relief that he had given up any pretence of a recovery. He sat up in bed and explained his wishes.

"Listen, I want to be cremated," he explained to us in English, so he was sure I understood. "I want my ashes taken to Hong Kong and placed with my parents' remains. When my ashes are returned, you can do something over there. Malcolm hasn't been back since he was a kid." He looked to me, then back to my mother. "Please, I don't want any kind of ceremony. It's too much trouble."

"It won't be any trouble," my mother insisted. She'd spent her high-school years with relatives in Oakland and spoke much better English than my father, and, at fifty-five, was two years younger than him—a short woman with closely spaced eyes, delicate features, and a copper complexion. She stroked my father's forehead, swiping back a lock of hair as though he were her child. She looked gaunt in a grey sweater and dark, skinny jeans. Her own hair was long and greying, and worn up, one chunk flashing in the air like the tail fin of a whale before it descends into the sea. "Why do you think it'd be any trouble?"

"I don't want people to waste a perfectly good afternoon weeping over me," he said, switching back to Cantonese. "Back me up, Malcolm."

I mumbled noncommittally as my mother removed her hand from my father's head. "This isn't about you," she said. "This is about giving us a chance to express our grief. Right, Malcolm?" Again, I mumbled indecisively. "Besides, *everyone will be there.*"

My father chuckled until he hurt himself and winced. "Everyone?"

"What's so funny?"

My father's face settled into a frown. "I don't want any ceremony. Those are my wishes. Respect them."

We didn't say anything more about it and spent another half hour in his room silently until we decided to let him rest. "He doesn't have very long," said my mother. She was a high-strung woman who'd long grappled with depression, but since my father had been sick, she'd become more assertive, practical, self-possessed. "We need to get started on the funeral preparations. I don't care what he says."

Before the elevator had reached the ground floor, my mother was already talking about flowers and catering. Although I didn't speak up in front of my father, I had to side with my mother on this point. Why was he so insistent on not having a ceremony? What kind of man would want to pass into the void and not make sense of his place within his own family—who seemed to keep the best of himself away from his own wife and child?

Apparently, my father was that kind of man. And, upon my mother's insistence, I was the one responsible for delivering his eulogy.

Soon afterwards, I was called to dutifulness. First, I had to pick up my Aunt Mirabelle, who flew in from Toronto with my teenaged cousins Anson and Gavin. (Uncle Don, her husband, an oral surgeon, had too many impacted wisdom teeth to wrench out.) The next morning my Second Aunt, Paula, arrived from Hong Kong. Both my aunts attended to my mother's wishes—vetting floral arrangements, hissing street addresses into their cell phones, tracking food deliveries—unlike at family gatherings in the past, in which they vied for my father's attention with joyless velocity. Mirabelle's sons, snivelling robot-flinging adolescents when we last met, were now sized for rugby and guarding velvet ropes. On the day before the funeral, I found their company a cozy distraction. After we'd been out for dim sum, Anson—a nearsighted, disquietingly shy second-year university student—planned to visit a former classmate who'd dropped out of school to play bluegrass and plant trees, activities he seemed to find enviable. Gavin, who was a sixteen-year-old suburban imp with a ferrety smirk, wanted me to take him to a hash bar. Disregarding his request, I dropped him in front of a Starbucks.

In the afternoon, I fetched my suit from the cleaners and the water filter Claire had asked me to buy in mid-August, before returning like a mad scientist to a parcel of resumés and photos—pages from the book of clippings I was assembling for various modelling

agencies. Some of the bigwigs at these agencies I'd queried before—
the image middlemen who'd handed me their cards at the agency
panel in the spring, before I graduated from modelling school.
They'd previously rejected me for valid, if non-specific, reasons, but
I wanted them to realize I could not only accept, but blossom in
the face of criticism. In their unpunctuated, one-line e-mails, I saw
them implicitly challenging me to shrug off adversity, negativity,
and indifference—it wasn't worth their time to deal with someone
they didn't first reject three, four times, because that wasn't how this
world functioned. The new photos they needed to see conveyed a
more natural, less preened-over look. It was what they wanted.

After stopping at the post office at two, I returned home—a
one-bedroom with a den—and typed out my eulogy for my father, which I had written out longhand, all soulful-like, on a legal
pad the night before. It was the worst-possible speech and could
only have been more wretched if I'd used a laser pointer. My father
didn't want a funeral, I suspected, precisely because he'd correctly
surmised what kind of ear-stuffing presentation I'd deliver. Still, I
printed the speech and put it in an envelope. Because I'm absent-
minded in the morning, I made sure the envelope was tucked in the
left-hand jacket pocket of my suit, which hung from the doorknob
of our bedroom door.

At four, I retrieved my cousin from Starbucks, where he'd still
managed to get high, deposited him at my parents' house, and returned home again to wait for Claire. Last week, she'd reacted to my
father's death with loud sobbing. Her reaction was unexpected; my
father had been polite, but never made much effort around her—
and she'd taken note of that. She wiped her eyes and poured herself
a glass of water before going into our bedroom, closing the door,
then sobbing again.

When the phone rang, I was ready to hear Claire's voice, calling me from the library. Instead it surprised me that it was Uncle Charlie. Given the choice between eating alone or meeting my father's best friend, I gobbled down a banana and left a note for Claire.

Uncle Charlie was a Cadillac-sized man with a head of inky-black corkscrew hair and a nose that had been broken so many times—from errant footballs, he told me—that it resembled a piece of ruptured sausage. He sported a gold Rolex and a ruby-encrusted pinkie ring that sat on his hairy finger like a daisy among weeds. When I arrived, he was already drinking at the bar, extending his patented leer—top lip curled over his bared teeth, obscene in combination with his unnatural tan, bottom lip dangling, left eye twitching—at a waitress.

Decades earlier, Charlie Branca left Brooklyn for Montreal as a draft dodger. Then, taking a job as head of security for a large financial house, he lived in Hong Kong for a decade, where he met my father. After taking early retirement, he and his then-wife, Ling, moved to Vancouver to open a bed and breakfast. Uncle Charlie, however, found the hospitality business involved too much ingratiation. Meanwhile, Ling, a slight woman from Hong Kong with a downtrodden aura and wire-framed glasses, joined a start-up religion on Vancouver Island whose leader commanded her to divorce Uncle Charlie and become his sixteenth common-law bride. Charlie, who returned to security work for an Internet gambling company, pronounced himself a freelancer for life.

Over the years, between girlfriends who drank vodka from paper coffee cups and tattooed their knuckles, Uncle Charlie routinely appeared at my parents' house, boiling shrimp balls and shredded jellyfish in the hot-pot or watching Westerns. When I was a teenager, his apartment was flooded and he slept in the guest room for a month, during which time I would occasionally find him in the kitchen in his underwear fixing ham-and-cheese croissant sandwiches.

Uncle Charlie's local was a sports bar where waitresses wore jerseys emblazoned with their first names and lucky numbers: on our side of the room was "Chelsea," number sixty-nine. As I took the stool beside him, he dragged a finger at our neckbearded bartender.

"Two," he said to him.

The bartender poured two shots of Crown Royal. In Uncle Charlie's hand, a shooter glass looked like a thimble.

"Mac, what can I say?" he said. He put a hand on my shoulder and patted my head. "I did my best to be outlived by him."

"He couldn't ask for more."

He raised his glass, tilted back his head twice, and downed it, then waited for me to follow suit. "Your father loved Crown."

I lifted the rye to my mouth. "You're full of shit."

Uncle Charlie ordered another three shots, which I swallowed without further cajoling. Then I asked the bartender for a glass of water. By the time I finished another two shots and stepped outside, the street was wobbling.

Time spooled out of grasp like a roll of runaway toilet paper. After limbo-waltzing down a back lane to Uncle Charlie's townhouse where he poured me another drink—a bottle of mescal sat on his coffee table—he put a tape in the VCR. The video was entitled *Donut Hut Corporation: Defining Sexual Harassment.* Of the thirty-five training films he'd appeared in, Uncle Charlie said this one, produced for a nationwide chain of donut shops, was the very first. In this video, he played a lecherous shop manager who verbally and physically harasses a female employee in the kitchen by the grease traps.

"The grease traps aren't dirty," Uncle Charlie deadpanned. "But I am."

There were seventeen instances of sexual harassment in that scene, a narrator announced in voiceover. *Can you name them all?* In his taped-up armchair, my father's friend howled at each one of his harassments, every outburst of mirth a cue that I ignored. My reaction to the video was unexpected. I'd heard about my father's corporate training movies, but unlike his ubiquitous commercials, had hardly seen them, and this glimpse of his work made me want to be alone. Of course I was drunk, but I could see my father there. I could sense him in the movements of the camera, the long static shots he used as frequently as he could. My father was in awe of Kenzo Mizoguchi's long takes, and ridiculous though it might be, even in this video I could detect the influence. And I could feel my father's direction in Uncle Charlie's ridiculous deadpan, the very palpable lechery on his face undercut by his silly come-ons—wasn't my father alluding to Bertolt Brecht?

"You need to cry," Charlie said, encouraging me. "It'll be good for you. You need to cry." He put on a VHS copy of *La Strada*, one of those movies Federico Fellini made before he got all weird. As Charlie crouched over his VCR to fast-forward past the copyright warning onscreen, I remembered something my father mentioned to me a couple years before, when I was still in Montreal. He'd called me up because he'd been reading the memoirs of Luis Buñuel, which Buñuel had written in the 1980s just before he died. My father told me that Buñuel wanted to climb out of his coffin every ten years or so and wander around, after he died. He'd get a cup of coffee and read the newspapers. Once he was content to know the world hadn't changed much, Buñuel would climb back into his coffin. My father was already sick at this time, and it was hard to understand his amusement, or even why he was so eager to relay such a whimsical vision of the afterlife, because the story was so depressing.

I now thought about Oliver Kwan crawling out of his coffin, even though he'd been cremated, and couldn't help wishing for it. Then I fell asleep on Charlie's couch.

In the traffic before rush hour, Uncle Charlie lived ten minutes from our empty apartment. Returning in the dewy morning, I worried that Claire was upset with me. I fell into our bed, perpetually unmade, and was startled out of it by the chill of its unslept-in sheets. Changing and primping, I patted my jacket pocket for the eulogy and told myself it would be inconceivable for her to go absent.

Eventually, I arrived at a flat-roofed brick building, solemnly unremarkable, on the east side of the city, by the cemetery where they used to bury the Asians and Jews. In our search for a locale, my mother and I had faltered. We'd thought about the racetrack for the memorial, but my father had lost interest in racing in recent years. We settled for the chapel at the funeral home where he was cremated.

Once my aunts escorted me inside, I stepped up to the podium. Uncle Charlie had left the microphone a little too high for me. I adjusted it with my left hand and with my right hand removed the envelope from my jacket pocket and flattened out my eulogy on the podium. Starting to read, maybe a word came out of my mouth like sleep talk. I froze.

September 14, 2008

Dear Malcolm,

Please, please forgive me for writing this to you at such a terrible time in your life. I decided I couldn't attend the service.

I can't be with you and your mother, knowing in my heart, as I have in the past few days, that we don't belong together. I love you so much, I don't know if you can believe that. I do.

If you like, we can to talk about this later, because I'm not sure I can supply the right explanation for my decision. All I can say is that, in the past few months, you've been pushing yourself away from me. Only recently, I've decided I can't keep pushing myself back to you.

Good luck with whatever you might choose to do. You're very smart and kind and generous—I still feel that way. My only hope is that you find something that suits your talents.

Yours Sincerely,

Claire

P.S. In the next couple of days I'll get the rest of my things. Please have a cheque for my half of the damage deposit waiting. You might have already guessed, but I'll be staying with Seamus …

I read this note twice before finally turning to the eulogy I had ready in my other pocket. My voice trembled as I read over the biographical summary. Born in Hong Kong in 1951, the oldest of three, his own father died when he was only six. A poor student who dropped out of school when he was fourteen, he washed dishes and drove a cab, devoting his spare cash to the cinema.

I settled down for a moment and ad-libbed. "I think my dad, if he could, would have lived inside his favourite movies," I told the audience, which murmured appreciatively. "*Touch of Evil*, *Tokyo Story*, or anything with William Holden. Most of all, he loved *Mary Poppins*. He would drive his Saab like a maniac while humming songs from the soundtrack." I earned a light chuckle there and allowed myself to smile.

According to my mother, he had also been a fan of Charles

Aznavour in *Shoot the Piano Player*, François Truffaut's second film. When they'd met, my father was wearing a trench coat, his shoulders folded together, puffing his Gitanes and stifling his smirk in an effort to shrink himself into Aznavour's melancholic piano player. Aznavour performs Charlie Kohler, a saloon pianist who plays amidst petty thieves and chippy dames in Paris. Charlie has a past. He was a famous concert pianist named Edouard Saroyan before his wife's tragic death. Trust my father, in the course of his adolescent self-invention, to idolize someone pretending to be somebody else.

"My dad wanted to be a great filmmaker himself," I continued. "In order to learn about cameras, he went to every photography studio he knew before finding work as an assistant to a portrait photographer. After work, he'd go to the movie house near his parents' apartment building and would watch whatever was playing. In the early 1970s, he started working in films in Hong Kong, doing camera and lighting work for Golden Harvest studios."

I stopped here again before finishing the story. "His moviemaking dreams were realized, in a way. After emigrating to Canada, he worked at a box factory for three years before he enrolled in a course for industrial filmmaking. For the last twenty years, he made all those commercials and training films that you know about already."

Staring at Claire's letter, trembling as I read it over again, I looked up at the crowd, vainly searching for her, as if out of reflex. "Everything I have," I said, "I owe to my father. I wish I could say this better, but it's all I can say. Thank you."

I stepped down. No more than ten minutes had passed. My mother bounded past the people already streaming out for refreshments, out of the chapel.

"We told *that girl* not to come," Aunt Paula said. With locked teeth, she looked to the exit. "Not today."

"Who?" I asked. They had taken for granted that I knew the person of interest.

My father and his sisters had chosen their own English names as adults, so their personalities, to a debatable extent, were telegraphed in their choices. Prissy and deliberate, Aunt Mirabelle wet another piece of tissue paper with her tongue and resumed dabbing my face. "Don't be so hard on *that girl*," she said to her sister. "We all must be allowed to grieve."

I stepped into the reception area, where my father's friends, all in late middle age, spoke and ate with both comfort and an uneasiness that they felt familiar in these situations. My mother sheltered herself in the washroom, weeping. In her absence, it was my job to thank everyone for coming, and I dutifully received their hugs, accepted their kisses with the furthest side of my cheek, and listened to their kind words as if they were playing elevator music. I pointed them to cake and tea. One by one, I disentangled myself from them.

It took a moment to find the person my aunts had been talking about. She had hidden herself in a far corner of the room and sat on the bench of an electric piano that had been pushed aside, a piece of gauzy tarp thrown over it. On a plate balanced between her knees was a piece of coffee cake. She didn't look much older than sixteen or seventeen, a tall, robust-looking girl with big walnut eyes, a bell-shaped forehead, and a buttery complexion. One corner of her face was curled into a deeply preoccupied expression.

She wore a dark crushed-velvet dress with large buttons running down the middle, green tights, and boxy platform shoes. When she caught me looking at her, the corners of her mouth turned down. Who was that staring back at me?

CHAPTER TWO

I'D BRACED MYSELF SO hard for my father's death, maybe too hard. But with Claire, I felt her absence like a toothache that throbbed and ached throughout the day. I had the same anxiety dream repeatedly—the one where I am driving, and my seat is set too far back. According to the Internet, it was a common anxiety dream; it was also a scene involving Hightower in a *Police Academy* movie. I would wake up before sunrise, unwilling to fall back asleep.

She didn't contact me, and I wouldn't call her. Because she knew my work schedule in the first couple of weeks after her disappearance, she snuck in to remove her things in a cruel, piecemeal fashion. Her winter clothes and her crockery went during my Monday shift; her wall hangings and spider plant were swiped on a Wednesday; and then her espresso machine and her DVD player vanished on a Friday. Suddenly, I felt empathy with all the unwanted tattoos in the world. My place in her life was being scrubbed away by a laser wand.

What I missed most about Claire was the sound of her voice and our conversations. On both counts this was perverse revisionism, because Claire always spoke as though she had a grape jammed in her nose, and the conversations we had felt like the small talk you made during a police sting operation. Our back-and-forth degraded to the point that we'd listen to music over dinner, speaking only to remark on a lyric or bass line that we particularly liked; during breakfast and sometimes even dinner, we read aloud choice bits from the books and magazines we had in front of us. After a while, in fact, it became a point of pride that we could sit through entire meals without an exchange. Chatty couples, in our minds, distracted themselves from the emptiness of their lives by reciting celebrity gossip and errand lists—not that we didn't do that, too. Two or three months before I received Claire's letter, we'd downed margaritas with another couple—he was in medical school, she was an accountant—who couldn't stop talking, who'd fact-check and embroider each other's stories incessantly. The two of them, in fact, reminded me of how obnoxious I'd been with Sandrine, my previous girlfriend. On the way home, we sneered at them.

"They couldn't shut up about their vacation," I told her in the cab home. "I don't think I *ever* want to go to Indonesia."

"Yeah, it was boring," said Claire, who was wearing a periwinkle blue summer dress and had put in her contacts; she always looked better without glasses. "They weren't that bad."

"Talking about your vacation for more than, like, thirty seconds is as bad as talking about your dreams."

"Why is that?"

"Because, when people talk about their travels, it's not about what you saw, but how you felt," I said. "You know?"

Claire nodded. "It's like describing a fireworks display," she suggested. She had that kind of talent, an ability to express things I think better than I can, even when she'd rather not.

Even though Claire and I were never chatty, she was like an emotional credit union in which I deposited my anxieties and aspirations like paycheques. I wanted to tell her about my mother's strangely calm disposition since my father's death, the appearance of my long-lost sister, the new photos I had done, the wino who sang opera while thrashing through our recycling bins downstairs, the *South Park* movie playing on TV. I was watching the fireworks alone.

Even as Claire was deleting herself from our shared life, I carefully inspected the house for traces of her: a stray hair in the bathroom sink or a glass streaked with lipstick. After a while, I found nothing. On her last visit, the day she took her bed and dresser—she must have had help—I found one last reminder: her engagement ring. On the counter was a tiny ruby set on a silver band that she'd found in an antiques shop and for which I'd pawned my beloved American-made 1989 Fender Telecaster.

I met Claire DeSouza in a German Literature class. We were assigned to the same group for a ten-minute presentation on Christa Wolf. Claire was plump but not fat, and wore thick, plastic-framed glasses, black jeans that flattened her ass, and T-shirts under a rotation of cardigans. I sought her out because we sat in the back row together, and she was so studious-looking that I knew she'd do all the work. I'd been apart from my previous girlfriend, Sandrine, for eight months. That relationship ended with me behaving horribly, and I didn't want to date anyone seriously. To that end, I man-whored around the campus, which led to chlamydia and a pitcher of draught beer being dumped on my head. I was desperately lonely. Even in university it was hard for me to make friends.

Leaving class, I asked her to go for a beer. Her face turned red; it was hard to say whether she was embarrassed or angry. "Who put you up to this?" she asked me. She started moving quickly.

I caught up with her. "What are you talking about?"

"You've run out of other girls to have beers with?" she said, smirking. "Yeah, you used to date Sandrine Jennings, right?"

"Um, yeah."

"She's a major nutcase."

I was still a little sensitive about Sandrine and felt protective of her. "Well, you don't know her."

"Not like you, I'm sure. She left town with zero notice six months ago. Totally screwed over her roommates. What a princess."

"Okay, so I guess you don't want to go for a beer."

She stopped. "It's noon. I have class at one-thirty."

"There's time."

She agreed instead to lunch, which I let her pay for because I wanted money for beers. Over that meal, I found out that she had been accepted to Princeton, but had chosen to come here on scholarship to avoid taking money from her dad in Ottawa. She had two part-time jobs, which was why she was taking an extra year. I asked her what her dad did and she glowered at me. "He makes money from cell-phone software," she spat out as though he ran a sweatshop. Her dad had wanted her to get an economics degree. She was an honours English student instead, though she was practical enough to apply to law school. (I was getting a general arts degree, out of indecision.) "I don't want to be someone who needs to figure out their life, you know?" she told me, after she accepted one of my clove cigarettes. (Yes, I know cloves are lame and age-appropriate in the most negative way, but my mother would have slit her wrists—literally—if I'd taken up real cigarettes.) "I mean, I might make the wrong decision, but at least I'll be doing something, and as soon as I realize I'm screwing up, then I'll do something about it."

I took this statement personally, as though she were needling me, so I was surprised when she invited me over for dinner the next night to work on our project. She lived in a fourth-floor walk-up on Rachel Street with five roommates; given the number of people there, the place was remarkably placid and tidy. It was decorated with hippie wall hangings from a roommate who majored in anthropology and another roommate's painting of Frida Kahlo in a Star Trek uniform. I arrived thirty minutes late, in the same clothes I'd worn the day before—I hadn't done my laundry.

"I'm really sorry," I said. "I almost forgot about this."

"Oh," she said. "It's no big deal."

Right away, I knew she was lying. It wasn't Breakfast at Tiffany's, but she had stepped it up. She wore a lacy top under her cardigan instead of a Black Flag T-shirt and had put on makeup. I could smell something cooking on the stove and noticed an open bottle of wine on the kitchen counter.

"You look nice," I said.

"Thanks," she said, quickly turning from me. "I actually got started on the presentation." She handed me cue cards to read over for the next day; they were written in her dense, neat handwriting and included stage directions, like "pause for laughter," and phonetic pronunciations for some of the German names, like "Gert-uh" and "Vit-gen-stine." She might have thought I was brain-damaged. As I suspected, there was no work for me to do. "Do you want something to eat?"

At this point, one of her roommates—the hippie anthropology major—stepped into the kitchen. She seemed sort of startled by my presence. "Oh," she said, sizing me up like an antiques appraiser looking for nicks and other careworn patches. "So, you're Malcolm?"

"Yes."

It unsettled me that I'd been a topic of conversation; noticing this, Claire glared at her roommate, who immediately excused herself. She had made a shepherd's pie that we ate with the bottle of red wine on her tangerine-orange fabric couch. Unlike most people in the world, wine seemed to make Claire less calm, and as she pushed food around on her plate, she yammered on about German literature, her favourite Aki Kaurismäki movies, and her desire to learn the tango. She wanted something to happen between us, but couldn't allow for it. It was endearing, if not altogether sexy.

I took her plate from her lap and placed it on the coffee table. "You need to calm down," I said. "Normally, I'm the nervous one."

"Really?"

"What are you thinking?" I asked.

She laughed. "I hate it when people ask that question. It's like, 'If I wanted to tell you what I wanted to say, I'd tell you.'"

"Yeah, me too."

She shook her head. "No, that came out wrong. To be honest, I've noticed you."

"Really?"

"Yeah, back when you were with Sandrine," she told me. "We were in a Shakespeare class last term—I'm not sure you noticed." I hadn't. "That's where we first met. And I knew Sandrine through friends. I'd see you two at parties and you would ignore everyone around you, like the two of you were the only people in the room. I don't think I liked you so much then."

We saw a movie the next night, a painter friend's vernissage the next day, a band the night after that. Then she came over and beat me at Scrabble. Then I watched TV at her house while she wrote an essay. Then I dragged her along to meet some of the friends I promised to shoot pool with. For the first few nights, we'd sleep together with our clothes on. And then we fooled around, but not all the way. Her shyness was infectious, and while I was impatient, I felt no rush. When we did go all the way, it was like stepping off a plane in a foreign city and feeling immediately at home.

Claire never seemed too preoccupied with her appearance. Rather she sidestepped any opportunity to boost her vanity, rarely wearing makeup, even though she was self-conscious about her looks and the way we looked together. She hated, for instance, the way she walked. She had been born with one leg slightly longer than the other and spent her childhood wearing shoes with customized heels. Then, when she was a teenager, the doctors gave her a choice: an operation to shorten one leg or one to lengthen the other. The first operation would've been less painful, but her father insisted on the second operation because he didn't want her to be a runt. It took her six months to recover.

To be honest, it was easier to be around her knowing that everyone wasn't plotting and scheming to steal her away, as it had been with Sandrine. But then she became possessive. I couldn't leave her side at any gathering; my pee breaks couldn't be overly long. Any female acquaintance was closely vetted. This went on for maybe six months. I rebelled. I started going out without her. When I went over to her place for dinner or to do my laundry, I'd tell her I needed to go home to write a paper, but would meet up with friends instead and play video games. She would find excuses to text or call me. After a month, I accidentally threw my cell phone in the washer with my jeans.

One night, Claire found me at a bar with a girl I'd met playing pick-up soccer the previous summer; our other friends had left and we were finishing our game of darts. It was January, and Claire arrived alone, bringing in that deep chill from outside. As soon as I saw her, she turned back out. I recognized those crazy eyes from my mother; that was enough for me to stay inside.

I didn't speak to Claire for three days. I was sad, I was happy. I was relieved. When I felt safe, I bought a new cell phone. It rang immediately after I'd activated it.

"Where have you been?"

"Hi, Mom."

"Malcolm."

My mother was weeping. "What is it?" I asked her.

"There's no hope."

My father's cancer, which he'd dismissed as an easily remedied inconvenience, had spread from his throat to his lungs and was at stage four. "If we're lucky," she told me, "he'll live another year."

"Do you want me to fly home?"

"No," she said, "you have school."

"I can miss school."

"What good would it do?"

I asked more questions until my mother said she had places to go. Afterwards, I covered myself in a duvet and wept: the world had grown even more indifferent to my well-being. When I was done, I put on my coat and boots and walked over to Claire's apartment on Rachel Street.

One of her roommates answered the door and let me in. Claire was in her pyjamas, lying on her back, reading over the practice logic questions in her prep book for the LSAT. She looked sick and groaned when she saw me.

"Why are you here?" she asked, turning away from me.

"I wanted to see you."

"You should have called."

"Sorry," I said. I never called. I showed up expecting her to be home; I was rarely wrong.

"Have you been crying?"

I knelt down on her mattress so her head was in my lap. She was too sick to wear her contacts, and stuck on one lens of her glasses was an errant eyelash. I remember thinking, at first, that girls really weren't ever as attractive wearing glasses, but the intimacy that allowed me to observe it was itself beautiful. She fixed her eyes on me like a jeweller.

"What's the matter with you?" she asked me. "Is everything okay?"

Claire could have been angry with me. She could have asked me about the girl from the bar. She could have pouted and let me suffer, but she didn't. This was someone who couldn't bear it when characters in bad TV shows were hurt or embarrassed. This was someone who, before university, spent every Saturday for three years volunteering at a nursing home, playing Scrabble with a woman who had dementia. Thinking about the way she would eventually leave me, I couldn't help but feel like I was the one who iced down her heart.

"Marry me."

She coughed. "Don't be stupid."

"I'm serious," I said. She had been the impulsive one pushing things forward; she'd suggested we move in together when my roommate graduated next month.

"You're not joking."

"I'm not."

"But why? It's never come up."

"I don't know why," I told her, and started rubbing her feet.

"We're only twenty-four."

"I know." She removed her glasses and appraised me with unsteady, shifting eyes.

"Do you have a ring?" she asked me. Her eyes searched my pockets greedily.

"Sorry."

"What if I say no?" she asked me.

But I knew she wouldn't say no.

Our friends deemed us degenerate. Like Claire and me, many of them had stretched out finishing their degrees to five years. Some had been together since first-year orientation and were either breaking up or progressing, whether it was relocating together or cohabitating. We knew it would be a long engagement—until Claire finished her law degree.

It was her idea to move to the west coast, where she'd been accepted into law school, to be with my father. I found work at a used record store and sponged off my parents, paying for more than my share because she refused to touch her tainted trust fund. My mother adored my fiancée. In her mind, Claire wasn't only what I needed, but perfect for her. "I've always wanted a daughter," she insisted to her once, her face reddened from two glasses of wine, "because we would be able to *relate*." She placed her hand on Claire's face. "Soft faces age better," she said, turning to me emphatically, as though I should be entering her thoughts into public record. My mother would buy Claire handbags in bulk and tote Asian bridal magazines to our place. The two of them played tennis together. They had long phone conversations in which, at some point, Claire would disappear into our room and shut the door.

My father, however, remained distant around Claire. He regarded her with a mixture of admiration and impatience, like someone at the door stumping for a worthy charity. Over dinner, he would often lapse into Cantonese, pretending he didn't know the right expression in English, and pass over Claire's attempts to discuss *Jules et Jim* or *The Searchers*. On a couple of recent visits, he would claim to be feeling tired and go to bed—something he was normally loath to do, even when he could barely keep his eyes open.

"You'd like her," I said to him once when we were alone.

"I have no problem with the girl," he said to me, being abnormally blunt. "She's fine, maybe a little too earnest for my taste, but perfectly fine."

"Then what is it?" I asked him.

"I don't want you making any rash decisions," he said. "Live with the girl, but why get married?"

"It was my idea," I said.

He tried to laugh it off, but coughed instead. "Who else?"

Around the time I entered modelling school, Claire started studying out of the house, sometimes with other students, mostly apologetic women who would call at ten-thirty p.m. and ask her for study notes. Then Seamus started calling, more and more frequently. They would go on dinner dates, which I was always invited to, but for some reason I knew better than to get in the way of their studies. It was Seamus who got her interested in salsa.

Seamus Henry was a critically acclaimed but commercially unrecognized novelist whose one book, *Eye [I] Chart,* was written using only the letters on the eye-exam chart at his doctor's office. I first met him at a law department orientation party, one of the dreariest social functions I've ever endured. Always resplendent in bespoke suits and studded with conspicuous jewellery, Seamus was between grants and working as part of the department support staff, an assistant to the dean of admissions.

I whiled away the evening listening to Claire's colleagues gather around a bowl of eggnog and fret about school. Most of the talking was done by a fellow whose head bobbed like a springy toy when he spoke. While they nibbled on pieces of a fast-crumbling gingerbread house, someone in her circle of friends brought up the topic of intelligent design.

"A long time ago, there was no life on the planet," Seamus said.

As he looked around the room and began speaking, he gave the appearance of someone confiding burdensome news that he had carried alone for too long. I suspected that some sort of corrosive agent was used to make his teeth such a piercing white. "Most fantastically then, aliens came to this planet and deposited their fecal matter, their shit. This, strictly speaking, was an accident." While Seamus said this, he gestured with his hands, suggesting the grandeur of creation. His English was rather formal and rigid. "Nevertheless, ever since, we have been watched over by these aliens. My good friends, they are responsible for Stonehenge and the disappearance of Amelia Earhart, and so forth—the list goes on. We are like science projects to them. Jesus Christ was actually an alien, as is the Pope, and when we die our consciousnesses become one with the aliens, who function as a collective."

Seamus's face flushed until it was the colour of an eraser. He crumbled into laughter. I was confused.

"He was being sarcastic," said one of Claire's friends to me, wiping her tears. She looked at me only briefly before her loving gaze returned to Seamus. Another person in the group was doubled over in his wheelchair and nearly spat out his gingerbread.

Later on, we drove Seamus home. Salsa dancing came up in conversation. Claire remarked that she was looking for a new studio. For my birthday, my mom had given her an audio version of the latest Michael Ondaatje novel on CD. Seamus picked it up, turned to Claire, then to me. "Do you have no respect," he fumed, "for the written word?" I didn't know then, but I was well on my way to losing her.

I'd come home from work to find Claire's engagement ring. I held it in my palm, closing my hand over it, then opening it as though it were a magic trick. I'd cycled back on one of the few remaining hot days of the summer, and I might have lingered longer in that spot if I wasn't so sweaty or had a chair to sit on. I trembled with the ring in my hand. I wanted to curse her, but she wasn't giving me a chance. I didn't know what to do, I only knew I smelled, so I stepped into the shower instead.

In the bath, the spraying water rang off the metal fixtures of the tub in such a way that twice I stepped out, thinking Claire might have called. The only way that I could bathe with any comfort was if I took my cordless phone into the bathroom and placed it an arm's length away, on top of the toilet. I was lathering my hair for the second time when I heard something. The phone rang twice before I stepped out of the tub, dripping wet, to answer it.

It was a female voice that was too breathless to be Claire. "May I speak to you?" She spoke like she wanted to be rid of all her words at once. "Malcolm?"

I told her she was speaking to him.

"My name's Hadley." She sounded hesitant. "We sort of met recently."

"I don't remember," I barked back impatiently. I was getting shampoo all over the phone and I thought I was speaking to the new branch manager at my bank about my retirement savings plan. "Are you working for somebody?"

"Um, I don't really have a job yet."

I was confused. "How did you get my phone number?"

"Oliver thought you might want to meet me."

"Did he actually say that?" I was surprised that my father had taken the time to speak to my bank.

"Do you need proof that I'm his daughter?"

Now I knew.

"Of course not," I told her. My throat tightened and I could feel my fingertips wrinkling. "I was in the shower when you called. Would you be able to call me back in a little while?"

"All right," she said. "Unless you don't want to talk to me. That's okay, too." She laughed. "Just tell me and I won't call you."

"No," I said. "I'm really in the shower. I turned off the water when you called. Listen"—I held the phone near the bathtub—"can you hear the water swirling down the drain?"

She hesitated. "I'll take your word on it."

I told her to call me back in ten minutes, then finished showering and dressed. I started reading the book I'd been trying to read for an entire month, *Tender Is the Night*, but couldn't get far into it. The phone rang again.

"Hi," I said, as I picked up the phone. "Sorry about that."

It was another woman's voice. "Hello, Malcolm Kwan?"

"Oh, I thought you were someone else."

"This is Vanessa Bryce. We got your photos and your measurements yesterday and we'd like you to come down for a meeting next week."

"Should I bring anything?" I asked, wondering if I spoke differently when I was grinning madly.

"Just your book."

I scribbled the information on the title page of *Tender Is the Night* and thanked her. Shortly after I hung up, the phone rang again. This time it was Hadley.

"Sorry I took so long. I was supposed to call you in ten minutes, but I took, like, thirteen," she said and laughed.

I was in a good mood because of the previous phone call and laughed back. She sounded like she was chewing on something. "Are you eating?" I asked her.

"Mm-hm"—she chewed some more—"I was hungry, and now I'm eating this popcorn stuff covered in caramel. It's kind of gross, because I'm near the bottom of the can, so it's mostly pecans, but I guess it's not so bad. Sorry about my chewing."

"That's okay."

"Just a second." I listened to her chewing sounds for a while before she resumed speaking. "Were you surprised to hear from me?"

"I guess," I said. "I'm sorry I didn't talk to you at his memorial. I was a little overwhelmed."

"Oliver never said much about you, except that you lived in Montreal for a while and that you're getting married soon."

"I'm not anymore."

"Living in Montreal, or getting married?"

"Both, neither."

"Do you want to talk about it?"

I didn't say anything.

"Hello?" she asked.

"Still here."

"I don't have any siblings, just my mom and sometimes a stepfather. Were you ever curious about me?"

I told Hadley I didn't know she existed until a week ago.

"So," she said, "are you curious now?"

CHAPTER THREE

EARLY ON, AFTER MY parents came to Canada, my mother did a diploma in social work and helped find housing for people who'd been recently released from mental institutions, people who would play their guitars at three in the morning and tried to perform their own sex changes, but she gave that up as soon as my father became successful as an industrial filmmaker. She took painting and drawing classes and started dressing less like someone's mom and more like someone your mom would hide behind a mailbox to avoid.

The night before she boarded a plane to Hong Kong to return my father's ashes and fulfill his wishes, my mother stood at an exhibition of her own work in knee-high brown leather boots, denim overalls, a brown turtleneck, a peacock-patterned scarf, and blue-tinted, silver-frame glasses that she didn't really need. There were five other artists showing at the crowded gallery, a converted warehouse space with exposed piping and brick walls, all women my mother's age who painted nudes and landscape portraits. One of them owned a catering company, which supplied the hors d'oeuvres that floated past us at eye level, served by men in purple bow ties, as though we were at a wedding.

"I should have brought you flowers on your big day," I told my anxious-looking mother, who took me by my arm. "I'm sorry."

"At least you're here."

Six of my mother's postcard-sized paintings could be found in the far corner of the gallery. Her landscapes were painted in meticulous flecks of contrasting colour. She liked small paintings, she claimed, because she was too busy as a wife and mother to paint anything larger. Maybe I'm not an objective critic, but from a distance, her paintings took on a sinister beauty; past a certain distance, one couldn't tell exactly what she had painted, and I thought this was how they should be seen. There were a couple I especially liked—one of English Bay at night, in which the sky is a tangle of magenta and the water is black and seething. From six feet away, I thought the painting was a portrait of a jellyfish. A row of fir trees from across a lake near Chilliwack. From the right distance, I thought the painting was of an alligator or some other low-riding reptile.

For three hours, she stood dutifully by her work, hands behind her back as though she were a bank guard. As her friends and some patrons trickled over to congratulate her, including one woman who asked her to repaint one of the pieces in another colour to match her couch, she seemed to swell in their presence, continually turning to me to hand me her empty wine glass, which I would replace. She introduced me to people who gushed over her work; many of them were former students of hers and told me what a confident, encouraging teacher she was. By the end of the evening, she'd sold five of the six paintings exhibited.

I'd waited by her side, even though she told me I could leave early, because I knew she liked having me there as a neutral, bored presence. Until now, it was my father who had come to these shows with her, holding her purse (as I was doing now), only fractionally less ingratiating than he normally was, and with a well-concealed smirk at all the self-important artists who drifted past him.

By the end of the evening, my mother was too drunk to drive and asked me to take her home in her silver BMW. She slumped against the inside of the car door and, as I drove, smiled crookedly as though half her face was held up by a refrigerator magnet.

"Did you really think it was good?" my mother asked.

"*Yes.*"

"I hate thinking of painting as a hobby," my mother said hastily, "but I started a little too late, and without any focus. And yet it was always nice to have something of my own. Your father was never very encouraging."

"I remember."

For the most part, my father regarded my mother's painting and drawing as a helpful diversion, something that kept her afloat and content. He liked some pieces better than others, but was never convincing about whether her work was worthy altogether. "I don't know much about visual art," my father told us. "It would be unfair to offer an uninformed opinion." In reality, my father was someone who had an opinion on all things compositional, from the way flowers were arranged in a bowl to the amount of pink frosting on a birthday cake. His silence was unintentionally cruel.

"There's something I should tell you, Malcolm," my mother said. "Claire and I went for lunch last week."

I glared at her. "What?"

"I'm sorry," she said, her face shadowed with guilt. "It was her idea. She wanted to return some books of mine. If it makes you feel any better, we didn't talk about you once. I think I'll always care about that girl."

I didn't feel better.

"How did she look?" I asked, cringing at how pathetic I was as the words left my mouth.

"She looked—" my mother trailed off. "She looked *happy.*"

"Oh."

"I know it's hard for you now, but it's a good thing. I think we're both afraid to be on our own, but it will turn out well."

"Hadley called me yesterday," I told her.

This was the first time I mentioned the girl to my mother, and maybe I brought it up now, when I was still off-balance from the mention of Claire's name, to rattle my mother back. She swallowed this news slowly, as if it was a raw oyster.

"I mean, Dad's, my—"

"I know her name," my mother said. "What does she want from you?"

"To meet up."

She stuck out her chin. "And what did you say?"

"I said I would."

My mother looked away from me. "You were just a child when she was born. And then there was never a good time to tell you. At least your father never thought there was a good time. This wasn't news to me. Your father told me about his affair when she was born. Of course I was upset. I squeezed a wineglass so hard that it broke in my hand." She held out her hands, which were unmarked. "I was very upset, not only about her, and not only about that woman, that Sheila, about his fling, but because I always wanted another child." We sat in silence for a moment, then she added, "We got over it."

"Had you met her before?" I asked her.

When she turned back to me, my mother's face was wet from her tears. She shook her head. "Not until the memorial service. I didn't know I would react that way when I saw her."

"You weren't happy," I said, unable to avoid the obvious.

"I suppose there's no harm in meeting her. I imagine you're curious. Are you looking for a sister?"

"*No*," I blurted.

"Because you don't have much in common," she told me flatly

as I drove up to my childhood home. "I don't expect you to take my word on it, so I'll let you find out the hard way." She put one hand on the car-door latch. "I'll see you tomorrow."

I made sure my mother had safely entered her home before returning back to my scarcely furnished apartment. I thought about Claire's newfound gaiety and couldn't sleep. The next day, when I came over to take her to the airport, my mother was still packing in her messy room. Half the bed was unmade. On my father's side of the bed, his nightstand was crowded with the pill bottles that reduced his pain and Chinese ointments he'd applied to muscle aches eighteen months before. There was a pile of newspapers on the floor, stacked and waiting to be read. Hoping to flood these images with others, I asked my mother if I could borrow a couple of her paintings.

"Sure, but while you're downstairs," she asked me, "get my black suitcase?"

In their basement, my parents kept the washer-dryer, a neglected ping-pong table, unruly plants that would probably suffer under my care, and a computer room where my favourite painting of my mother's hung. In the centre of the photo was a yolky orange circle above the city skyline. The moon stood disproportionately over the houses, whose lights shone through closed window shutters like stubble. I took the painting off the wall and dropped it into my jacket pocket.

When my mother finished packing, I took the suitcases to her BMW. She waited inside the car, holding a metal container that held my father's cremated remains. "If he had his way," she said, tapping the bronze urn with her finger, "he'd be buried with his parents. I'm hoping they'll let me place the ashes in his parents' mausoleum. But there's so little space to bury people in Hong Kong;

bodies are buried there standing up in the ground."

"Why do you think he wants to be so far from us?" I asked her.

"That's how he was."

At the airport, we checked her bags and shared a cinnamon bun in the food court, watching planes taxi outside. I walked her to the security area. My mother asked me to hold my father's ashes as she dug through her purse for her passport. The urn was about the size of a large teapot. I was surprised by how light his remains felt in my hands.

I was given some money, cash for "watering the plants." It was enough to cover rent for the next month. My mother was the only person I knew who kept all her money in an envelope—it was as though she meant for it to be petty cash, disposable and unaccounted for.

"Are you going to be okay?" I asked her. "I could still come along with you."

Shaking her head, she brought her cheek to mine and whispered: "I wish I was the kind of mother you didn't need to worry about."

In pictures of my mother as a young woman, she affects a vexed gaze and purses her mouth as though nothing could cure her, even if that disaffection looks as true to life as a teenager playing a senior citizen in a school play. My mother read philosophy at Hong Kong University. Her father was a pharmacist, and her mother came from a wealthy family. There, she met scholarship students and Marxists, and grew ashamed of her wealth. At that time, she recalled being caustic, self-important, and standoffish. But like me, she was timid and shy. Afraid to be seen alone, she carried books around with her—translations of Yukio Mishima novels and volumes of Sylvia Plath's poetry—like force fields of prose and verse.

My parents' first run-in was at a demonstration in 1968 in support of the university protests in France. My father, who claimed to be apolitical, said he was dragged there by a friend. Over dinner at a congee house, Eliza grew brave and railed about the Vietnam War and compared the plight of blacks in the United States to the Chinese majority under Imperial British rule. "There was a spark, but it was complicated," my father once recalled to Claire, hinting at some long-ago scandal that he still couldn't bring himself to admit, "and we didn't actually get together for some time."

My mother glowered at him. "You don't have to tell them everything."

When they did hook up, things moved quickly. After dating for two months, my parents impulsively decided to elope, forgoing even a picture from their wedding day, let alone a ceremony or banquet or wedding dress. "Your father wanted to get married," my mother recalled. "And I said I would agree only if it were done as quickly as possible." It doesn't bother my mother that she doesn't even remember what she wore, but it was the main reason why my father's mother despised her.

My mother started feeling unwell after her first miscarriage. "Life had been so simple," she recalled. "Your father was working with Edmund Chew at night, writing that script. And I was at home alone when I knew something was wrong. I couldn't reach him, and the old lady who lived next door had to take me to the hospital. It was terrible. Something had shattered inside of me. I thought the world had ended. I wept for two months."

She would suffer through three miscarriages—each one wringing more of the well-being out of her—before she finally gave birth to me shortly after they arrived in Canada. It was my mother's idea to move; I was to be free of the incoming scourge of Communism, of course, and a more conspicuous form of post-colonialism, and she would have enough distance to separate herself from her old pain.

Now that I knew about Hadley, I questioned my recollection of my parents, but the recollection, for the most part, held up. My parents might have argued a lot, but they always made up. They spent time apart, but were often together. They made rice porridge together on Sundays and always danced together at weddings. When my dad left on a work trip, he made it a point to kiss my mother on the lips, almost intentionally to make me squeamish. I felt no less squeamish those times when I came back home from university, and I would hear my mother's stabbed-mouse noises as she and my father had sex in the morning; they seemed to have grown careless about the noise since I left home. Was my father unhappy with us? He did make it clear that he immigrated to placate her.

"It's a nice place to live," my mother would insist.

"But you're not really alive here," he would say in the sardonic tone that he used to voice awkward truths. "This is the place you go *after* you live."

To move to Canada, he gave up working in the movie business, just when his friend and rival Edmund Chew started directing. The first feature Chew directed, *Shakespeare's Revolver*, was a police procedural based largely on a script my father had co-written with him and for which he received no compensation or credit. The first inklings of Chew's style, which he later exploited to less effect in Hollywood, were there: the static pauses, the slow-motion shots through billows of gun smoke, the meandering voiceover soliloquy. He made the kind of movie my dad loved.

My father railed about this theft for years, but never did anything to assert his claim. "Who would believe me?" he would mutter. "He's a big shot. What have I accomplished?" He tried instead to make his peace as a kind of exile, taking up golf with Uncle Charlie and finding pleasure in his life outside his family.

For the front half of my childhood, I was sheltered from my parents' neglect by my grandmother, who served as my personal valet. My father's mother would cook for me, knit me ill-fitting sweater vests, and play cards with me—all while grumbling lightly about what a flighty, neglectful mother I had.

A couple of months after my grandmother died when I was eleven, my dad took me out for chicken fingers and told me that I had to watch over my mother. Even though it was a chilly day, we sat outside on the patio so he could smoke. "This might be more than you can handle," he said. "But I don't know what else to do. I need to work and, well, I'm not good at this. I wish I didn't have to force this on you. I had to support your grandmother and your aunts when I was your age, and you're twice as smart as I was. There's a Chinese saying: 'Tall ships find ways to fit under low bridges.' Do you want a hot chocolate?"

It wasn't so bad at first. My dad came home at a plausible hour. My mother painted every day in the backyard studio she'd had built, popping in to see if my school work was done. We ordered pizza. My parents let me adopt a pound dog. We were all miscast in our roles, although we seemed to be making the best of it.

But within a couple of months, everything good turned bad. My father burrowed himself into another project. My mother, who'd bounce back and forth from anti-depressants, decided that she had no talent and stopped painting altogether. Maybe it was the toll from her miscarriages, but she would as often look at me with cold disdain as she would with boundless affection or apology and sorrow. She yelled at me for talking too loud on the phone, for leaving towels on the floor in my room, and for looking at her with such resentment.

I got sick of pizza. The dog died unexpectedly.

One day, I returned home from school to see a fire truck parked on the street outside my house. There was a burnt rubber smell in the air. I felt my heart catch in my throat, and I remember running to my house and seeing smoke in the back yard. I crept into the back yard, afraid of what I would see: my mother in her nightgown, in front of a small, newly extinguished bonfire, and two stern-looking firemen. My mother hadn't noticed me yet, and I could see her as those firemen did—a wild-eyed nuisance. She looked like a TV evangelist, intense and angry. "I didn't know I was doing anything wrong," she said, patting the back of her head as though she were her own pet. "Suddenly all my paintings, all my drawings, became sickening to me. I had to get rid of them as quickly as possible. Can't I even do that?"

I shrunk away before anyone noticed me and hid in my room. When my father came home from work, there was an argument. The weeks that followed were crammed with hushed accusations in their bedroom that I could barely detect.

My mother came and went for a couple of months, departing for workshops on islands or for quick visits to my other grandmother in Hong Kong. My father tried to stay home more often, but on many nights just left money for me to order in. I'd pocket the money, eat macaroni and cheese, and buy more video games. My mother would always return with hastily purchased gifts—homemade peanut brittle from a bakery outside Ucluelet, or just a postcard—then disappear into her studio.

The first time I had to call an ambulance, I was fourteen. My mother had not been out of bed in thirty-six hours and didn't respond when I tried to rouse her. I called my father, but got his office voice mail and left a garbled, hysterical message. Then I called 911. I explained the situation and read the names of the pills to the operator. After making me check that she was breathing and on her side, the operator asked me how old I was. I told him I was fifteen. Then I lied again and said my father was on his way. I sat in the ambulance as they took my mother to the emergency room. My father showed up four hours later, after my mother's stomach had been pumped and her condition had been stabilized. He looked relieved that my mother had survived, but couldn't help glancing at his watch. "You did really well," he said, before taking me home. In the car, he explained that my mother wasn't hurting herself because she didn't want to be with us, but because she couldn't help herself. "It's like she feels things extra hard. Everything is stronger, richer, smellier than it is for you and me. So her reactions are more powerful." I started seeing her as an endangered species of one.

When I called 911 again six months later, I wasn't nearly as rattled, and I was surprised by how practiced my answers were. The third time it happened, when I was sixteen, I was frighteningly close to indifferent. Puberty had been kind to me. I'd grown up and filled out, and my skin wasn't nearly as bad as other teenagers', and one day a girl named Cindy Arau, who liked hip-hop dancing and horses, invited me to her house to watch TV in her basement. After that, I basically joined her huge Catholic family. Her brothers became my best friends. Her dad taught me how to drive. Her mom would sew buttons back on my shirts.

On a rare night when we were at my house, Cindy and I were making nachos when I had to call the ambulance. "It's okay," I told her. "It happens." She was shocked that I was so even-minded. I called my dad and suggested I get a ride home from the hospital with Cindy's mom. It gave me another excuse to stay over at their house, even if it was in a sleeping bag on the floor in the room shared by Cindy's two younger brothers.

My mother settled down over the years, with the exception of an occasional outburst, but the biggest boost to her mental health was, ironically enough, my father's illness. For the first time, she became my father's guardian, researching his illness and all the treatments, forcing him to eat flax seeds and drink chamomile tea and take his medication at the right time. She found strength in my father's illness.

The used record store where I worked was close enough to Hadley's water-polo practice for her to meet me there. The not-exactly-cool store, wall-papered with concert posters no more recent than 1983, was run by Earl, a guy with bushy clown hair who would go on regular, sustained monologues about the worthiness of black musicians. "Some musicians, you know, had *feel*," he would tell me at the end of my shift. "Keith Moon had feel. Those guys in Rush—all chops, no feel. Coltrane had feel, so did Rick Danko. Hendrix had that black-guy feel, you know. His hands were gigantic—he could palm a beach ball. Let me tell you something about black-guy feel. Clapton had a little of that when he was in Cream. He used to roll back the tone knobs on his guitar and call it *woman tone*. But he was no Hendrix. What he had was different. His hands were *gigantic*." You could turn your back on Earl while he talked—most of us did out of necessity and self-preservation—he didn't seem to mind.

It was about fifteen minutes before the end of my shift, the time-killing portion of my work day. I'd spent the past half hour coming up with my weekly staff picks for the board next to the new releases when she appeared, with her mouth hanging open like she'd run here. She was wearing a grey overcoat and a pair of sweatpants, and her wet hair was tied in a ponytail. Her face was flushed and her ears were entirely pink.

I had the same throbbing in my head that I did when I first saw her. I felt something like the opposite of déjà vu, a persistent suspicion that I had selective amnesia, because she felt so recognizable to me that someone must have performed an operation on me and removed our years of acquaintanceship. Yet, in spite of this sense of familiarity, when she tried to hug me, I threw my hand out at her. Then I tried to hug her as she held out her hand. In the end, we patted each other like we were searching for weapons under each other's clothes.

"Hey," she said. "Are you ready yet?"

I reached for my jacket. "Pretty much."

She looked around. "So, do I get a family discount?"

"Well, it depends on what you want," I said, laughing nervously at her joke.

She shook her head. "I was just kidding. I don't want to take advantage of you or anything."

"What kind of music do you listen to?" I asked her.

Hadley shrugged. "I sort of like classical music, like Beethoven's piano sonatas or Schubert."

"I don't think we have much of that here. Do you like anything more contemporary?"

She thought about it with her face buttoned together, then burst out laughing. "My boyfriend plays black metal. I'm not so into music."

"Oh," I said, and this rapport I imagined having with her vanished. Having bad taste was better than having no taste at all. My dad had felt the same way. For both of us, holding opinions on movies and books and music was an obligation—like voting. When Earl came out of the back room, I introduced Hadley as my friend.

I followed her onto the street. Outside, the pale blue sky had the same depthless uniformity as in the summer, but there was already a chill in the wind. The onset of fall reminded me of everything that had passed in the last few months; it was depressing. Walking briskly, she put one hand up to her neck, pinching the collar of her overcoat together. On her wrist were half a dozen rubber bracelets of different colours.

"What do you want to do?" she asked me.

I shook my head. "I don't know. I only graduated last year."

"I mean, today."

"Oh."

We walked aimlessly, drifting farther away from my workplace on a busy street, as she prattled on about water polo. "We just started practicing," she was telling me as we passed a construction site for the upcoming Olympics. "The season starts in October and the provincials are in April. I'm graduating this year, so it's my last shot. Two years ago we made the quarter-finals of the provincials."

"Oh," I said. "That's good."

"Do you play any sports?"

I shook my head. "I have a bike that I ride." I needed to improve my fitness, according to some of the modelling agents I'd met with. "Do you want to see a movie?"

"Sure."

We could've backtracked to my car, but the seven o'clock shows wouldn't even start seating for another hour, so we had time to walk downtown. Neither of us cared what we saw. There was a lot I wanted to know about her, water polo aside, but I didn't know where to begin. After a while, it occurred to me to ask her what her last name was. "I mean, do we have the same last name?" I asked her.

Hadley shook her head. "It's Wallace," she told me. "My mother's father was English, which was why I'm named Hadley—it was my grandmother's name—and her mother is Scottish. I never thought of myself as Asian, as half-Asian, even though I looked different. It's funny, I guess." She laughed. "For a while, my mother wanted me to take my stepfather's last name, Linstrom, which is Swedish. I think my mom thought it would save her marriage if we all had the same last name." She rolled her eyes. "She has such stupid ideas. She and my step-dad argued about everything. Plus, my mom's the jealous type—she calls it *being attentive*. They separated this spring."

I tried hard to see her jealous mother in her, but then I grew queasy thinking about my father's affair.

"They were together since I was a child but married for only a year," Hadley continued. "He still calls my mom every day to plead his case. The phone rings and rings. My mom won't get a new phone number. I think she likes it—whenever the phone rings, she jolts up from where she's sitting."

"So you knew my dad," I said to her. I tried to correct myself, even though I got it right the first time. "So you *knew* him."

"Yeah, though only for the last couple of years. Only after he got sick. He called my mom and asked if we could meet. You know, I always wanted to know him. She didn't want us to get together, but I insisted. It was really cool seeing him." She paused. "It was also strange, you know?"

I nodded.

"Do you miss him?" she asked.

"Yeah, of course."

"I think I do, too." Hadley's big brown eyes began to moisten. "I've never even seen his movies."

"They're commercials and industrial films."

"I'm sorry I ruined his funeral."

"The service was very difficult," I said. "We were all so emotional."

"You looked so upset, standing up there when you gave the eulogy. I was worried you might faint."

"Yeah."

Hadley walked faster than I did. If she resembled my father at all, she had his wide cheekbones and maybe his laugh. Otherwise she had a collection of traits—abnormally straight posture and big teeth that she flashed often, a chattiness and cheerfulness—that must have come from her mother's side of the family, or perhaps belonged only to herself. I knew people like her in high school, even in university; perfectly contented, well-adjusted types whose adolescent selves were only a few degrees off from their finished adult versions. Unlike me, they had little to apologize for or feel embarrassed about. I wanted to know more about this girl's relationship with my father, but I lacked the nerve to force the issue, so I did some more biographical sketching. As she listened carefully, I told her about how I was trying to find work as a model, about going to school, and my recent split with Claire.

I had just mentioned my broken engagement when I caught sight of Claire. She was across the street, walking in the opposite direction toward Seamus's apartment. She had her book bag slung around one shoulder and was wearing dark jeans, her favourite pair of boots, and a pea coat I'd never seen her in. She looked like she was in a hurry and didn't notice us. I stopped.

"That's her," I said, turning around and covering my face with my hand.

"Who?"

"Claire."

I pointed her out to Hadley, who made an incredulous expression. "But you'd just mentioned her—"

"I know, but that's her."

With Hadley a step behind, I trailed Claire two blocks to a supermarket. We stood across the street as Claire went inside, grabbing a basket before stepping out of view.

"When was the last time you saw her?" Hadley asked me.

"Uh, a week before the funeral."

"Why don't you just talk to her?"

I shook my head. "I don't want her to see me like this."

"You don't look so bad."

"I could look better."

"Why are we following her then?" she asked me.

"I want to know how she's doing," I said, my voice cracking. "I saw her every day for the past year and a half. And then she left, with only a note. I haven't heard from her. And then my mom had lunch with her."

"Why would your mom have lunch with her?"

"My mom's kind of weird."

"So is mine," she said, as though to console me.

"My mom says Claire's happy."

"Do you want me to go inside and follow her?" Hadley asked me.

"Inside the supermarket?"

She nodded. "I could see what she buys," she said. "That could tell you how she's doing. If she's buying TV dinners and pints of ice cream, then maybe that means she's missing you."

"But what if she's picking up a giant box of magnum-sized condoms?" I asked her. "Or a pot roast?"

As I waited around the corner at a bus-stop bench for Hadley to return, I realized I wasn't off to a good start as an older brother. For the first time that day, I wondered what she was hoping to find in me and what I could offer her, besides ridiculous, belligerent errands. In my head, I started to think of things I could do for her. If she needed a ride, I could drive her places in my dad's car. I could tell her more about my dad. I could teach her the few words of Cantonese that I knew. I could make her some CDs. I could buy her liquor. I could be another version of my dad—ironical and distant, aloof. And, if she really needed it, I could follow *her* boyfriend around.

I was still compiling my list when Hadley arrived with a bag of chips. "Sorry for the delay," she told me, taking a spot next to me on the bench. "I was hungry."

"Did you find her?" I asked.

Hadley nodded. "Yep. She bought a roll of toilet paper, some bananas, yogurt, and a can of chickpeas."

"She hates chickpeas—I wonder if Seamus likes them," I said.

"And, um, she also bought condoms."

"Oh."

"Is it okay I told you that?"

"Yes."

"I don't like lying. I hate myself when I lie."

"That's okay. Condoms?"

"But only the regular size."

I closed my eyes for a second and thought I would faint or barf. "Did you notice anything else?"

Hadley offered me a chip; neither of us had had dinner. "Not having met her before, I can't really say if she's happy or sad," she told me. "She's cute, though."

"Thanks," I answered. "Thanks."

A bus pulled up in front of us. We had to tell the driver that we were just sitting there. He glowered at us.

"Do you still want to see a movie?" I asked her.

"Sure."

"Is there anything you want to see?"

Only someone related to my father would have picked the new Edmund Chew movie.

CHAPTER FOUR

THE NIGHT BEFORE my appointment with Vanessa Bryce, I met up with Charlie Branca, who said he wanted to check in on me. I'd hoped to ask him about my half-sister, but when I arrived at his local, he wasn't at his usual place by the bartender but in a booth with two women who were wearing a lot of makeup. One of the women scooted over to allow me to sit, moving a flavoured martini along the table with her.

"There he is," Uncle Charlie announced. "Mac, meet Krystal and Rayelle."

"Mr Unpunctual," said Krystal, the older of the two, who had dirty blonde hair. She slurred her words, so they came out like, "M*ish*ter Unpunk*chew*-el."

"The Tardy Boy," Rayelle piped in. She had thick arms and wore a dress that looked like it was made out of a blue checked tablecloth.

"We're the Tardy Boys," Charlie joked. He turned to the waiter: "Get this man a crantini!"

Krystal and Rayelle worked for a catering company and had been in a threesome with the playboy owner of the company Charlie worked for. They'd met Charlie when his boss thought they'd stolen his expensive watch and had Charlie—whose job roughly approximated that of the one-armed man in the Harrison Ford adaptation of *The Fugitive*—break into the condo the two women shared to retrieve it. Krystal attacked him with a lacrosse stick.

"It turns out the watch fell under the bed when we tied him to the bedposts at the Holiday Inn," Krystal said. "What a shithead."

"And the plasma screen TV he gave us isn't big enough," Rayelle added.

"And he was a lousy lay."

Rayelle whispered in my ear: "She wanted him to save it for her."

"Hey, it wasn't a complete loss," said Uncle Charlie, hoisting his glass. "You girls met the Tardy Boys!"

The women cheered.

I sat through two rounds of cocktails, which I now recognize was far too long for me to realize that Uncle Charlie had tricked me into a double-date. Simmering at this, I couldn't laugh at any of his strange, sort-of funny observational humour—even the jokes I couldn't normally keep from laughing at.

"You girls know how they say, 'Sex is like pizza—even when it's bad, it's still good'?" Charlie was saying.

Rayelle and Krystal looked at each other, nodding solemnly as though the pizza analogy was a law of science, then waited patiently for the punch line.

"But have you ever been raped by pizza? Have you ever been made to eat a slice of pepperoni by a guy you thought was your friend?"

"You're so funny!" Krystal said, but she didn't laugh.

"And have you guys ever noticed the difference between how Chinese and Japanese restaurants are named? Japanese restaurants use Japanese names, like Tojo's or Kintaro. Chinese restaurants, at least the fancy ones, are all named after abstract concepts, like the Regal Meridian or Grand Honour. The other day I called up a Chinese friend for dinner and said, 'What do you think about Blind Justice? They've got really great deep-fried shrimp.' 'The last time wasn't so good,' my friend said back. 'I've heard good things about Uncommon Valour.'"

Rayelle turned to me. "Why are you so quiet?"

"He tells that pizza-rape joke all the time," I said, worried I was being impolite.

She placed her hand on mine; her fingernails were the colour of grape drink. "Is something on your mind? Are you thinking about modelling right now?"

I nodded sombrely.

When the two of them left to powder their noses, I glared at Uncle Charlie until he slid to the edge of the booth, his face vibrating between phony indignation and apology. "I can't believe this," I told him. "I can't believe you sucked me into this."

"They wanted me to bring a friend," he explained, mixing his drink with his pinkie finger and then licking the tip. "They didn't want me to think they only did three-ways. You can leave before anything happens." His eyes darted away from me. "This is about something else?"

"No. No, it isn't."

"What's this really about?"

I figured I needed to say something soon before those women came back. "Did you and my dad go out like this?" I asked him. "Did you take him trolling around for trash?"

Charlie leaned back against the seat and stared up at the ceiling. "Oh, God. No. Your dad—no. He would never. I didn't mean to give you that idea. Your dad wasn't like that."

"He wasn't?"

He took a slug of his crantini and swirled it in his mouth. "When you're playing golf with friends, you make a lousy shot and get to call a mulligan every nine holes. And that means it doesn't count, you know what I'm saying? Well, your old man had a couple of mulligans."

I wanted to ask more, but by then Krystal and Rayelle had returned. "We totally get that pizza joke now," Rayelle said. "It's hilarious."

It might be conceited for me to think I wasn't your typical aspiring male model; it might be the very same attitude that marks me as your typical aspiring model. But with the parents I had, I could aim only to be an artist or, failing that, someone who at least swung honourably at that designation. They expected it out of me the way other Asian parents wanted their children to be surgeons—if not a surgeon, then a dentist. At school, I took drawing and writing classes. "As long as you try," my mother said, "it doesn't matter if you end up a graphic designer or a director of commercials."

"You look the way I do when I talk to my mom on the phone," Sandrine said to me once, in the middle of a weekend wasted writing the script for a short film that I hated from the outset. She'd come by my apartment with coffee.

"No one likes this part."

"I know what you're saying, but I don't think you hate being a writer the way real writers hate writing. Why do you want to do this?"

"What else is there to want?" I asked her.

"Maybe you're one of those people who'd rather have a normal job."

I turned away from her to the window and scowled at the moon.

"I didn't mean to offend you."

Sandrine was a fashion student in the city. She was deliberately kooky, and maybe it was an affectation, and perhaps her cocaine habit contributed to it, but I was at the right age to be charmed by her efforts to enliven the mundane. She would paint my toenails pink while I was sleeping. Or, should the ladies' room be occupied, she'd run into the men's room at a bar without a microsecond of hesitation. For some reason, she took to me. Her friends, by contrast, regarded me as though I were a yokel who'd just stepped off a farm, wiping off the chicken blood from my hands on my pleated jeans and plaid shirts.

"How would you feel if I told you to stop designing clothes?" I asked her.

"Yeah, but I like fashion. I like trying to do it. You're writing because it's expected of you."

"Stop talking," I told her. "My head hurts."

"You want to go shopping?"

"Yes."

To my great shame, shopping for clothes was what made me happy. This had been a recent development. Until I was a teenager, I allowed my mother to buy my clothes—dark turtlenecks and indoor scarves. This wardrobe made me a middle-school punching bag until Cindy Arau, who wanted me to look like the lead in her favourite teen soap opera (played by an actor who later appeared in a Internet video in which he snorts coke from another man's erect penis), took me to the mall to help me buy designer jeans and sneakers with money I earned working for her dad.

It was Sandrine's fault that I grew to love wearing clothes. She had a way of infecting you with her passions. She would patiently educate you on colour coordination, the way a shirt should hang off your shoulders, the little filigrees of tailoring that set apart an item of clothing. You simply enjoyed things more because of her— or with her. I grew to love clothes the same way I became fond of watching the sun rise with a bottle of cassis or listening to Frank Sinatra or giving a cab driver twenty dollars and asking him to take us to his favourite place in the city—even when the smirking cabbie dropped us off a block up the next street.

Neither of us had much money. We would scavenge the thrift stores in the Lower Plateau and Mile End, buy what we could, and then trade in the things we didn't love to get more clothes. Sandrine patiently taught me how to knit that winter, and I made her a tea cosy and one oversized scarf for Christmas. She made me a pair of pants that I only stopped wearing because Claire, who felt I never got over Sandrine, would cry when she saw me in them.

Sandrine's school had an annual student fashion show every spring; that year, some of the cooler students decided they would have a secret show in a converted warehouse space for the pieces their instructors hated. The cool students were supposed to find their own models, normally friends or people they recruited online who needed the experience. I was at Sandrine's house drinking the last beer in her fridge when her best friend at school, the one who encouraged her after an instructor made her cry, called to complain that she'd lost a male model. The show was in two days, and her friend said he was no longer able to dull his panic with weed and poutine.

"I don't know," I heard Sandrine saying. She was looking at me sceptically, as though I was morbidly obese and at the foot of an alpine trail. "I mean, I could ask."

"What's that?" I asked. I held out my beer: "Do you want a sip?"

"I need you to do me a favour."

Sandrine explained what the show entailed, and I initially declined. I didn't want to embarrass myself. I was an artist. I wasn't good-looking enough. Sandrine couldn't be bothered to persuade me, so we dropped the subject. We went out for pizza, cycled to a party across town, then changed our minds and rode our bikes back to her house where we drank one roommate's Pimm's with another one's iced tea while listening to Frank Sinatra.

"This is a perfect night," I said to her.

She laughed as though I'd made a joke.

"I think it is."

We were on her couch. She yawned and stretched out, resting her head on my lap. "I'm sleepy," she said.

"I want to be in your friend's show."

She smiled. "I'm glad."

"I don't think I want to be an artist."

"Even better."

The theme for the show was metamorphosis. A stylized cockroach was projected onto the back wall. The public address system was blaring chirpy dance music as I moved out of the crowded, sweaty dressing area and sauntered down the runway and back. People by the stage rose out of their chairs; flash bulbs went off like fireflies. I wore a tight white shirt with the outline of an AK-47 on it and a leather jacket she'd studded with paper clips. The experience was a pleasant blur. I don't remember how I walked or turned, if I smiled, or whether I knew I shouldn't have smiled. I didn't expect it to go so quickly, and I didn't think being the centre of attention would be so intoxicating.

In the audience was a friend of Sandrine's who needed a model for some portfolio photos. He came to my apartment the next week and we strolled around the neighbourhood taking photos. I stood against a crumbling brick wall, my right arm draped across my chest and clutching my left shoulder, and watched with a suspicious squint as a cat crossed the street. I lay along a park bench and smiled into the light of noon. I walked down St. Laurent in a scarf with a debonairly ambivalent reaction to the street traffic. We did some serious shots, some smiling ones. The photographer called me a natural when he e-mailed the images to me.

I hadn't been semi-professionally photographed before. I was surprised by how easy it was being in front of the camera. Sandrine said I was being shallow. I couldn't exactly disagree with her, but I wasn't so deep to begin with. I saw myself as the opposite of the Amish, who believe that having your picture taken steals a part of your soul. Photos gave me soul, or at least a complexity I didn't necessarily possess; they infused my vacant expressions with ponderousness. As much as I wanted to be an artist, I had never had any ambitions to be an actor or a performer; I never wanted an audience outside of the person holding the camera. That was enough.

When I was nine, I pleaded with my father to let me accompany him to a shoot for a Ninja Pizza commercial, a local Japanese-themed pizza chain that appeared in the early nineties and was founded by a guy who owned several karate studios. I was the right age and it was the perfect moment in time to love both ninjas and pizza. It took an entire week, but I wore him down.

"This is going to be boring," my father told me as we drove to the set. "I don't want you to complain or interrupt me if you don't like it."

"I've got my Game Boy," I said defensively. "When do I ever interrupt you?"

My dad smiled. "You're right. You could even be louder."

"How loud?" I asked, raising my voice.

"Louder."

"Louder?"

"A little louder."

"THIS LOUD?" I said, screaming.

My dad winced. "Good, good."

We pulled into the Ninja Pizza restaurant in a strip mall outside the city where the commercial was being filmed. I was given a chair on which to sit behind my father as the lighting was set up. Later on, I came to understand that my father did "retail work": advertising for places with cash registers, like local supermarkets, restaurants, or gas stations. The accounts for international brands like car companies or shoe manufacturers, the ones with bigger budgets, special effects, and celebrities who commanded attention, were usually handled in bigger cities. A commercial on a smaller budget could still be good, even win awards, my father insisted, but it had to be based on a clever premise and a strong script.

To my dad's chagrin, the Ninja Pizza spot was conceived of and written by the restaurant chain's proprietor, a karate instructor with a Polish surname and a carefully groomed, winged moustache. Wearing jeans and a leather jacket with Ninja Pizza written on its back in bamboo script, he hung tightly to my dad as the crew set up and the cast lingered by the pizza ovens.

"This has to go a very specific way," he told my dad, pointing to the script.

My dad scratched his nose, the kind of gesture he'd make when he was impatient. "Of course," he said.

In the commercial, an Asian man in a black hood stood in front of a pizza oven brandishing a sword and speaking in broken English:

NINJA:

Since imperial time, Ninja pizza bring hungry people best two-for-one pizza with faster delivery. So fast you don't see us.

EXT. DOORWAY OF HOUSE. NIGHT

Ninja Pizza delivery man appears from the bushes, rings doorbell, then gives the hungry customer a pizza. The delivery man throws a smoke bomb on the ground and vanishes.

INT. NINJA PIZZA. DAY

A montage of different Ninja Pizzas.

NINJA:

(v.o.)

Ninja Pizza make best pizza, use flavour from east and west. Try eel and pepper flavour. Dare to survive blowfish pie with Okinawa deep crust. Enjoy squid-lover special. For extra two dollar, Ninja Pizza give you Ronin bread with choice of teriyaki or wasabi dipping sauce.

INT. NINJA PIZZA BAKERY. DAY

Ninja stands next to Ninja Pizza chef in white hat. In front of them is a flattened piece of dough.

NINJA:

Ninja Pizza promise you delivery in thirty minutes or your pizza free. No honour in late delivery!

(Ninja disembowels himself with sword. Tomato sauce spurts out of his stomach and lands on the flattened pizza dough.)

The actor playing the ninja, who wore a tube that spat out tomato sauce, performed the ritual suicide half a dozen times with escalating degrees of bombast.

My dad directed the cast and crew in whispers, leaning into the ears of the actor in the lead role and the extras playing restaurant-goers, looking into their eyes until they repeated back his direction and nodded.

"He's doing it wrong," the karate instructor said, pulling my father aside. "It's supposed to be funny."

"I think it's funny."

"People are supposed to *know* it's funny. The way he's doing it, he looks as though he's in actual pain."

"The situation is *already* absurd, Tom. If he mugs into the camera, then it becomes too campy."

"Listen, I know exactly how this commercial works."

"All right, let's try it your way."

"One more thing: the accent he's using isn't right. Why isn't he mixing his Rs with Ls?"

"The accent he has is more believable," my dad said. "Don't misunderstand. I'm not someone who likes to take offence. I don't mind accents. I think my own accent is pretty funny. But, you know, Mickey Rooney in *Breakfast at Tiffany's* came out a long time ago."

"Follow the script."

My father mumbled something, then called a break and walked out of the restaurant with his cigarettes in one hand. After a quarter of an hour passed, the people on set, most of whom had worked with my father before, began murmuring and glaring at the karate instructor, who broadened his chest defiantly. Even then, I knew he wasn't a bad guy, just someone who felt he knew what was best for his own business as the person who cared the most about it. He disappeared into the kitchen and came back with a slice of the blowfish pie—which was just bologna.

"Eat this," he said. "You've been here all afternoon, just sitting there. You need something to eat."

I shook my head.

"You don't want it?'

I shook my head again.

"At least say, 'No, thank you.'"

My dad returned five minutes later and struck a deal with the karate instructor. He would do the commercial the way the instructor wanted it, but the instructor would have to leave. The chastened karate instructor apologized, insisting that he'd only wanted the best commercial possible, and then went for coffee next door. The shooting resumed, with my father completing the commercial without any consideration for the director's notes, but the actor who played the lead ninja was tense.

"Sorry," the actor said. "I mean, *saw-lee.*"

The cast laughed nervously.

"Do you want to take a break?" my father asked.

"I can do this."

My father turned back to me. I lifted my nose from my Game Boy. He asked me to show the ninja actor how I would perform the scene.

He led me to the mark in the front counter and placed me on a foot stool, then handed me the prop sword and stepped behind the camera.

"Swing at the pizza," he told me, looking into his monitor.

I lifted the plastic sword above my head and swung at the pizza.

"Now scream."

"Yeeaaahhhh."

"Louder."

"YEAAHHHHH!"

"Louder!"

I didn't act on my desire to become a model until years later, shortly after I returned to Vancouver with Claire. We'd been back for about a month, and the excitement of the return, the flurry of friends to see, and the frenzy of relocating had waned, and what was left was an aftertaste of disappointment. Being in my hometown only exacerbated the sense that I had no traction.

One day I was in the mall, headed toward the dollar store to replace a French press that I'd broken and buy some ice-cube trays. By the public library, I passed a man—a neckerchief-wearing, professorial, stylish, vaguely Middle European man—sitting at a booth. He was handing out pamphlets for the Modelling Institute. I approached the booth and looked over the pamphlet. The cover depicted three handsome men in suits. On the back page was written:

How do you know if you should be a model?

Do you have an interest in the fashion industry?

Do you set high goals for yourself?

Do you enjoy feeling great?

If you answered "yes" to even one of these questions, then you should consider the Modelling Institute!

"So," said the man in the booth. He was wearing tinted glasses and spoke with an accent. "Are you interested?"

"I modelled a little before."

"Then you are."

I shook my head. "It's too expensive."

"You don't even know how much it costs," he told me.

"I don't have too much spare money. I'm out of work."

He looked up at me, his hands locked together. "So, you're telling me that you have a career that fulfills you?"

"Not exactly."

He nodded as though I'd agreed with him and said, "My father wanted me to come work with him in the family business. It would have been so easy for me to become a Formula One race-car driver. But I wanted to do something exciting, I wanted to model fashion."

"Race-car driving is pretty exciting."

"Mm-hm." Then he applied some logic on me. "You're heritage is, what, Chinese?"

I nodded.

"What do you think the ratio is of Asians to the general population in Greater Vancouver? Have a guess?"

"One in ten?"

"One in nine. And what do you think the ratio is of male Asian models to the total number?"

"I don't know."

"One in twenty-five. It's a good time for you."

I was still not convinced and was about to turn away to the food court when he tried another line of argument.

"How do you rate yourself on a scale of 'A' to 'F'?"

"What do you mean?"

"'A' for gorgeous. 'F' for ugly. 'C' for average. Which one are you?"

I thought about it for a moment. "'C-plus?'" I waited for him to respond to my joke. "Am I right?"

"There's no correct answer." He looked me over, his starchy eyebrows drawn together and perched in a show of optimism. "But I'd say you're a strong 'B,' possibly a 'B-plus.'"

I edged around the booth. It had been only a year and a half since I modelled in Sandrine's show, but I felt much older than I'd been then. There was my father's illness, my break-up with Sandrine, my engagement with Claire, and now, my move back to Vancouver. All of that had been so exhausting; my life had been folded and re-arranged, origami-like. Holding the brochure, I felt opportunity and possibility returning to me.

That next week, I attended the free introductory classes on "industry awareness" and "photo movement." I sat in a room with fourteen other young men, all of whom betrayed some degree of shame. On the walls of our small classroom were pictures from Gap and American Apparel advertisements. Arriving a few minutes late, the man at the shopping mall booth strode to the front of the room. His name was Martin. He'd been a catalogue model in Brussels and an industry professional for twenty-five years. The first thing he told us was that no one needs modelling school to be a great model. In fact, many successful models have succeeded without it.

"Why enrol in the Modelling Institute?" he asked himself. He counted the reasons on his fingers. "Our school allows you to be in a nurturing environment surrounded by other aspiring and practising models. We prepare you for different varieties of modelling work. We teach you how to prepare yourself for your work—how to dress, how to eat. We make sure you enter the industry with appropriate expectations, because we're realistic. We understand that not all of you—maybe none of you—will be the next superstar. Some people here have runway potential; others are more suited to television work. We provide you with professional feedback and teach you to be your own best critic. In terms of career placement, we bring to class a number of industry professionals you can tap for information and other networking opportunities."

I paid for the classes in three instalments using my credit card, which made Claire's face turn into one pulsing blue vein. The classes took place over a twelve-week period in the spring. I found the photographic segment of the course more enjoyable than commercial acting, and, with runway work, discovered that I enjoyed walking in doubles (i.e., in pairs) happy more than doing singles serious. I was critiqued and heard harsh words about my diet and the condition of my skin, but given praise for my attitude.

I finished classes in June amidst talk of job placement and agency referrals. Had it worked out so far? Not yet. Martin warned of scams, open casting calls from agencies searching for raw, undeveloped talent that wanted to charge you $500 to use "the best photographer in the business" or agencies that offered to "train" you— wait, I already paid for that.

Bryce Modelling Agency was recommended to me by one of their new clients—a friend from school named Clint. Clint was an ex-kick-boxer who decided to try modelling after his fourth concussion. So far, Bryce had gotten him a print ad for an energy drink and a billboard for a chain of fitness studios. According to Clint, Bryce was a top agency that was restructuring and committed to finding new talent. I waited until I got my latest set of photos done before I sent them my C.V.

Vanessa Bryce's office was located in a modest brick building in Gastown above an Indian restaurant, and in the waiting room, the smell of cumin and onions crept through the open windows and the hound's-tooth patterned carpeting. After I arrived (in brand-new skinny black jeans and fitted T-shirt) and introduced myself, Vanessa's secretary told me to wait in her office. I stepped through a door and took a seat in a small room taken up by a glass desk shaped like a kidney bean. On the wall behind the desk were dozens of Polaroids and test shots, most of which seemed at least five or six years old. The men in these pictures, with their peroxide-splashed bangs and sideburns, looked like they were auditioning for boy bands. It was like being in an octogenarian's barbershop, forced to choose between faded pictures of long-ago matinée idols for my hairstyle.

Fifteen minutes later, Vanessa Bryce appeared. An elfin woman in her early forties, she had a heart-shaped face, a shiny forehead, and a long thin nose that ended in a sharp point. Her crinkly red hair fell just past her ears. Her fingernails had a clear finish, and she was wearing a cream-coloured turtleneck and large hoop earrings. Because her desk was high, her feet dangled from her chair when she sat.

"Sorry to be so late," she said. Without looking me in the eye, she shook my hand, put a paper coffee cup on the desk, then began shuffling sheets of paper as though her business affairs were a game of Blackjack. "I was talking to my asshole electrician today." She paused to remove the lid from her coffee and take a gulp. "After some sweet-talk and cajoling, he agreed to fuck me over for only $1,200. Also, sorry about the awful smell of this place. If you don't think curry smells awful, try to sit through a summer of it. I don't even like coffee, but at least it distracts me from the stink of the lunch rush."

She looked at me for a second to soften her remark, then let out a nervous bark. It wasn't exactly a laugh, more like the gasp one made while being strangled.

"What sort of work are you interested in?" she asked me.

"Photographic work," I said. "You know, for ads and magazine shoots."

She flipped through my photos. "*Yeah*, that's going to be *very* easy. In this economy."

"So," I said, my voice wobbling with doubt, "you don't think I've got potential?"

"I don't know. To be honest, while this agency has been long established, my experience with the business isn't as, well, rich."

"But isn't the agency named after you?"

"Actually, it was named after my husband. Then he died, only months before the recession hit, and left me with this business to run. Don't get me wrong, he used to talk about work over dinner, even if we ate together less frequently near the end, but that dinner banter wasn't, you know, *comprehensive*."

"My father died two weeks ago," I blurted out without thinking. "So I know how that feels."

She shook her head with a wistful expression on her face. "How did he die?"

"Lung cancer."

"My husband was hit by a bus," she said, trailing off.

"I'm sorry—"

"On his way to a tryst."

"Oh."

"With his male lover."

"*Oh.*"

We took a moment to consider our respective losses, savouring the curry-scented workplace. I handed Vanessa my book and another copy of my C.V.

"Okay, some of these photos are good, but some are kind of cheesy, especially the arty ones. Not everyone can be Man Ray. Or is it Ray Ban? I have famous-person dyslexia, you know? Burt Reynolds and Tom Selleck are indistinguishable to me."

"I've been meaning to get rid of those photos."

"Good idea," she said. She put down my book and read over my C.V. In order to fill the page, I'd littered my resumé with distortions and fabrications. I watched Vanessa's expression apprehensively as she looked up from the page with a giggle. "So, you say here that you can recite the Lord's Prayer in Latin."

"I went to a private school." I listed the Lord's Prayer as my "special skill" when I figured out that I couldn't climb rocks or scuba dive, and that everyone knew how to play the guitar.

"Let's hear it."

"I'm a little rusty. I was never very good at languages, though I also know some Cantonese and a little German."

She laughed again. This time her laugh made me wince. "Come on."

"*Pater noster qui es in caelis: sanctificetur Nomen Tuum; adveniat Regnum Tuum; fiat voluntas Tua, sicut in caelo, et in terra*"—I recited it the same way I did before lunch at St. Luke's, in the heavy-breathing, lobotomized mumble of my adolescence—"*Panem nostrum cotidianum da nobis hodie; et dimitte nobis debita nostra, sicut et nos dimittimus debitoribus nostris; et ne nos inducas in tentationem; sed libera nos a Malo. Quia Tua est potestas et gloria in saecula. Amen.*" I let out a sigh when I was done.

"Good show," she said, putting my resumé into my portfolio and shutting it with finality. "As your friend Clint may have told you, we lost a lot of clients when Harold—Harold was my husband—when he died. His lover forged his will, and there was confusion about who owned the business. I blame myself for dropping the ball. Now we're actively seeking new talent." She placed her hands flat on my book and leaned toward me. "Let me ask you: why do you want to be a model?"

I'd prepared myself for this meeting, but not this basic question. "My girlfriend dumped me because I wanted this," I blurted. "I've got to prove her wrong, to rub it in her face."

For a moment, I thought she might start clapping.

"Well, you have potential," she said. "There's something about you—you're not 'fresh'—that's not the right word. A better word would be, hmm, 'unlikely.' Yes. There's something about you that's unlikely."

CHAPTER FIVE

"Why do you say, 'hello,' as though you wish it weren't your mother?" the voice asked on the phone. My mother was in Hong Kong. My eyes fixed on a strip of daylight that rippled through the blinds.

"What?" I asked. "I was asleep."

"You know the time?"

"It's a Saturday."

"You were hoping it was Claire," my mother said.

"That's not true," I lied.

"I always thought that Sandrine was the one you really loved."

I got up out of bed. "I didn't answer the phone expecting it would be her. There was nothing wrong about how I said hello."

It was October. I was feeling better, or maybe I was only feeling less terrible. There were fewer instances of spontaneous bawling, wearing the same clothes four days straight, and failed masturbation.

"I found an agent," I told her, looking at blank spaces on my walls where Claire had hung her photos and paintings; they looked like the skin around a wound after pulling off the Band-Aid.

"Nice," my mother mumbled. "Whatever happened to that one-act play you were writing?"

"I gave it up."

"Well, you were very talented with words. Even if you're doing this other thing, I wouldn't give up writing. It could be your back-up."

"Some back-up."

"I'm putting your grandmother on the phone."

I shook my head. "Please don't—"

My maternal grandmother, whom I'd met twice, had had a cyst removed at an expensive private clinic, but was recovering well. In my clumsy Cantonese, I asked my grandmother how she was doing and she praised me for how much my Chinese had improved and said that, though she must have been told I had finished my degree, I should study hard and make good grades. My mother took back the phone.

"Do you miss me?" she asked.

"Sure. I mean, yes."

There was a pause.

"Why isn't it enough for *me* to call you?" she asked through a heaving sob. "I gave birth to you."

"Yes," I said robotically. If I fought back with her, which I have, it only drew things out.

"After everything. Now I'm taking care of your grandmother and listening to friends brag about their grandchildren and the cruises they're taking. What do I have?"

"It's not like you were the one who died," I snapped back, because if I didn't argue at all, she would think I didn't care about her.

"I suffered as much as your father."

"Like sympathy cancer?"

"Oh, shut up. You little bastard. Talk to your grandmother again."

I hung up on my grandmother. Then I showered, changed, and swallowed a bowl of oatmeal. Hadley was supposed to visit that afternoon. I called to cancel, but she didn't answer her phone. Maybe if I'd been in contact with Claire, or if my mother were in town, or even if I had been getting modelling work, I wouldn't have spent time with Hadley. As it was, then, she was the only one around. The second time I saw her, she cut class in September and we had lunch at Helen's, my favourite diner, and watched a discounted matinée. The next week, I met her boyfriend Marco, a seventeen-year-old who rode an electric scooter and played in a band called Four Ounces of Fluid. Marco was stocky, hairy-armed, and bearded.

Hadley buzzed my door—three anxious beeps. I panicked for a moment, then told her to wait downstairs before looking myself over. These days I went everywhere in a threadbare tweed blazer that I bought with Sandrine, some kind of button-down shirt, and one of the four ties I owned and carefully ironed. I resolved to dress up whenever I felt despondent, as a way of forcing myself to live up to my appearance. Sometimes I wore a tie around the house. I headed downstairs.

"Why do you have to make me feel like such a slob?" Hadley said. She was in her water-polo jacket, old jeans, and a pink V-neck sweater.

"I'm dressing to impress," I said with the kind of smirk I used to think was ingratiating.

"I'm not someone you need to impress."

"So, where do you want to go for lunch?"

"Would you be okay with a change of plans?"

Our new destination was Ikea, where Hadley wanted to buy a birthday present for her best friend, Krista. "Krista's kind of weird," she explained, "and she has her heart set on the ice-cube trays they have where you can make ice cubes in the shapes of stars and moons."

"And this is the only thing that will make her happy?"

Hadley shrugged. "It's easier to do what she asks than explain to her that she's being weird. Believe me, I've tried."

We took my father's Saab, which he'd bought three years earlier.

For years he drove an old Toyota mini-van that my mother hated and Uncle Charlie made fun of. "People look at the car and think you're a janitor," my mother would say, swallowing a sigh before turning to me and adding, "Not that there's anything wrong with that kind of work." My dad told me it reminded him of a van he used to ride in one summer he spent on an island outside of Hong Kong.

"We became friends with the village girls and pawned everything we could to hang around them and go swimming every day. They lived on the other side of the island from the ferry terminal and there was a deliveryman who'd drive us across the island. I still don't know why you never learned how to swim." The Saab came only after the mini-van died multiple deaths, but he grew to love his new car, which still smelled like smoke and aftershave, and would speed headily through yellow lights while listening to the Three Tenors.

"My mom wants me to learn how to drive," Hadley told me. "She signs me up for lessons but I keep cancelling them."

"You don't want a licence?" I asked her.

"No, maybe, I don't know. I don't mind taking the bus or cycling. It's better for the environment. Besides, my friends would laugh at me for driving my mom's old car."

"Everyone needs a licence," I said. "You could borrow this car."

She let out a snort. "You sound just like Oliver. We had that conversation in this car six months ago. My friends saw him when he dropped me off and thought he was a sex pervert. They didn't know we were related. He said to tell them he was my acupuncturist. My friends actually believed that! We laughed about it for weeks."

I hadn't visited Ikea since I'd moved back to Vancouver with Claire. We entered through the level for kid's furniture and then the brightly staged living-room spaces for people who wanted to one day replace the cheap furniture they bought here with expensive designer pieces from downtown stores with exposed piping or with antique tea tables and sofas that their children would squabble over after they died.

"You know, you could pick something up here," Hadley suggested. "I mean, since we're here. You don't have to, of course, but since we're here ..."

Hadley had seen my half-furnished apartment the other week, and I'd made an excuse about not being able to shop before finally admitting to her that I didn't want to shop alone; I would need help to overcome my retail paralysis. Taking shallow breaths among the happy couples shopping for their shared beds, I found the same futon that I'd bought with Claire, then found a slightly more expensive version. I told myself I was trading up.

Because she asked me to, I attended Hadley's first water-polo game. To me, it passed like a blur of splashing, wide-shouldered bodies, and I kept my gaze fixed on the scoreboard, waiting for the sweet release of the final buzzer. The game was held at a pool in Kitsilano, so, to celebrate, the entire team went to a Greek restaurant on Fourth Avenue for feta-cheese pizza. We took a long table near the back of the restaurant near a faded photo of the Parthenon and the ladies' room. I sat at one end next to Hadley and her best friend Krista, a gabby, excitable blonde with pale skin and marble-grey eyes.

"When I was in Greece," I told them, "I met a guy from Philadelphia, and we used to eat blocks of feta with wine for breakfast. He had a great accent. 'Nothing is bett-ah than fet-ah.'"

Both of them started giggling.

"When were you in Europe?" Krista asked.

"After high school, for three months."

"Did you have fun?"

"It was great." Actually, my trip abroad with Cindy Arau was marred by a theft and a vicious case of stomach flu, but I was unwilling to sour them on an entire continent. "I'd love to go again."

"That's what Krista and I want to do," said Hadley. "We applied for this program."

"If we get in, they're going to send us to a developing country, like in Central America or Africa, and we get to help a village build schools and wells. But first we have to fund-raise and save money on our own."

Hadley took a bite of her pizza, her chin tick-marked with sauce. "But that's only if we get in."

"Wipe your chin," Krista said before turning to me. "Hadley's always so pessimistic."

Hadley swept her face with the side of her thumb. "Wouldn't it suck if they selected us but we couldn't be part of the same project?"

"No!" Krista yelped, as though it had already happened. Then she covered her mouth at the thought of a far-worse outcome. "What would suck more is if one of us was selected and the other one *wasn't*."

"That would be terrible. I don't want to think about it."

"I'm only saying it out loud so it won't happen."

"Because you're no psychic."

"Right."

"Still," Hadley continued, "I'd be jealous."

Krista played along. "Yeah, if you got picked and I didn't, it would really suck. It would totally ruin our friendship. I'd see you on the street and pass by you without saying a word, and then I'd turn to my new best friend and say, 'Hey, Francesca, that was

Hadley; she used to be my best friend, but then she helped some villagers in a developing country build a dam, and now I hate her guts.'"

"Who's Francesca?"

"I always wanted a best friend named Francesca."

Hadley laughed. "Don't be a goof."

"You are."

They noticed me watching them pretend to argue and found this outrageously funny.

"But, seriously, I had a dream that we didn't get into the program," Hadley continued. "Both of us didn't get accepted into the program, so you shaved your entire head and dropped out of school, and I became an angel, like in that German movie about the angels, and talked to sad people and helped them out."

I actively despised people who described their dreams in minute detail, but Hadley was young enough to be indulged. Krista, on the other hand, followed her story with her mouth scrunched in concentration.

"Did you like those Ikea ice-cube trays?" I asked her afterward.

Krista seemed puzzled. "What?"

I looked to Hadley, whose face had become waxy and stiff. "The ones for your birthday."

"*Oh,*" Krista said sharply. "Oh yeah. They were very nice."

One of the boys on the team, who was shaped like a yield sign in a track suit, glided over to us from the other end of the table. He leaned against the table and put his hand on Hadley's shoulder. "Hey, Had."

There was something about him that triggered, for the first time, an impulse in me to protect Hadley, even if it was unnecessary. Scowling, she jerked her shoulder away from him.

"It's Hadley," she told him. "Two syllables."

"Good game."

"You, too."

The boy was single-minded. "Hadley, I was wondering whether you had an extra slice for me."

Hadley pointed to the half-finished pizza in front of her. "It's all yours."

"Thanks," he said, taking the largest slice.

"Well, what are you waiting for?" Hadley asked him when he continued to linger.

He looked at me in disbelief—what had just happened was so unlikely that he wanted a witness—before returning to his end of his table.

"What was that about?" I asked.

Hadley made a puke face.

"That's Liam," Krista said. "Our coach loves him. And all the scouts from the American schools are drooling over him. Everyone loves him"—she laughed—"except *maybe* Hadley."

"I was so stupid," Hadley said with a guilty expression. "We used to go out last year."

Krista agreed. "Marco is way better for you."

Hadley looked at me sheepishly. "We dated for six months, then last summer he became a jerk—he was really full of himself. All he ever wanted to do was tan. I broke up with him. For a while we talked about getting back together, but then I met Marco."

"Liam still acts like you two are a couple."

Hadley groaned. "Does it get on your nerves as much as it does mine? All boys think they own the world."

"They do," Krista said.

I let out a pointed cough.

Krista, who flirted the way I lathered bug repellent on myself when I went camping—no spot was uncovered—turned to me with an overly sly smile, and asked, "So, Malcolm, do you own anyone?"

I shook my head.

"He just got dumped," Hadley said.

"It doesn't matter who broke up with whom," I insisted. "We grew apart."

Krista nodded with vigorous condescension. "Maybe we can set you up with someone."

I politely declined, but they picked up on my embarrassment. "Krista has an older sister named Trish," Hadley said. "Guys love her."

"How dare you!" Krista yelped. "Yeah, Trish is like a doorknob—every boy gets a turn."

Hadley groaned. "You are *so* beneath contempt."

Even then, I noticed her poise was obscured only flimsily by her teenage awkwardness. She could be gossiping freely with Krista and then glance back at you to make sure you were present. Her eyes had a stillness—a cheery fatalism, which was like my dad's.

After dinner, we walked to my house along a side street in Kitsilano under damp and yellowing elms, passing the neat Edwardian Builders with their inviting porches and herb gardens. The occasional rusting Volkswagen microbuses sat in their driveways. Joggers passed us, heads bowed to the pavement, huffing in their shorts and long johns.

"You were bored to death today, weren't you?" she asked me.

"Not at all."

"My mom would come to my games, but she'd get too involved and make suggestions about my play. She doesn't know *a thing* about water polo. I had to ask my coach to ban her. She says if we get to the finals, though, she's coming anyway. She's so busy these days. She says it's to distract herself. She's been taking an accounting course at night for the past year."

Because Hadley lived on the East Side—she took a bus every day to her school in Point Grey—I insisted on driving her home. I'd walked to the swimming pool and, as we approached my apartment building, Hadley wanted to see where I'd placed my new futon. The large windows of the living room faced south and looked out onto the street. The windows trapped hours' worth of light during the day and made the living room, where my new futon sat like a majestic zoo animal released to the wild, oppressively stuffy throughout the summer. The apartment was still bare and littered with outdated free weeklies and empty cracker boxes.

"I didn't know you had such a big place," she said, staring out of the den window.

"It's too expensive for one person. But I don't think I can move without a mental breakdown."

"Who did the painting?" she asked. Above the desk, which I bought at Ikea after purchasing the futon, was my mother's post-card portrait of the moon.

"My mom."

"It's beautiful—so beautiful."

I was surprised anyone else felt the way I did about my mom's paintings.

We stood by my desk, looking at the big orange moon in the night sky and the tiny houses in the background. "My mom does a lot of landscapes," I told her. "Her paintings remind me of all the stuff I like about her, and not the stuff that annoys me."

"I like it."

"I'll tell her you thought so," I said, knowing I never would.

"She's in Hong Kong right now to see her mother. Plus, she's taking his"—again, I wasn't sure what to call my own father in front of her—"ashes, so she can bury them with his parents."

Her eyes stayed on the painting, but words began to form in her mouth slowly. "For the past year, I saw Oliver every couple of weeks," she told me. "He picked me up from the house, so I never saw where he and your mom lived. He took me to the movies, whatever I wanted to see, all the movies my mom wouldn't let me go to. Once, we even went for dim sum with my mom. I knew he was sick, but he would tell me how much better he was feeling. Then, for a couple of months I didn't hear from him at all. I called his cell phone. I sent him e-mails. Eventually, he called me one morning and told me to come to the hospice."

My father appeared in my head that day I had walked in on him, speaking on the phone, before he shooed me away.

"I didn't want to tell my mom about it—she can get so emotional," Hadley continued. "So I let her drive me to school and took the bus to the hospice."

I nodded.

"I saw him lying there in his bed; I couldn't help it, I started crying. I know I should have behaved. He called me over to him and I started sobbing on his chest, on his hospital gown. He looked so frail. I asked him to tell me the truth. I never want people to lie to me, even when the truth is something I don't want to hear. I wanted him to admit to me he was dying. He didn't want to say it, but I kept crying, and finally he said it. He told me that he was dying and he started crying, too. And then he said he wished we could have known each other better. The nurse came in to check on him and she started crying, too. Oliver introduced me as his daughter."

I knew then that she was the person my father was talking to when I walked into his room—that time when he was so impatient for me to leave. And it was only after her visit that my father started planning for his own death.

"Did I meet you in the elevator that day?" I asked her.

Hadley nodded. "I probably should have introduced myself."

"I wouldn't have believed you."

Her eyes had grown wet. "I wanted to spend the day with him, but he was getting tired," she continued. "I asked for something to remember him by, but he didn't have anything. So before I left, I gave him something of mine instead. I took one of my bracelets"— she touched the coloured bands of rubber on her right hand—"and slid it under the wristband the hospice gave him."

"He was waiting for you," I told her. "He wanted you to release him."

She shook her head. "Release him from what?"

My father had told me about Werner Herzog one night when we were watching *Fitzcarraldo*. "Someone once told me this story," I told her. "Werner Herzog, a German director, likes to walk for days and weeks. He hates planes. He hates cars. Sometimes he'll walk across Europe to get somewhere. A friend in France, another movie director, was dying, and she wanted to see Herzog before she died. Herzog decided to walk to France from Germany. His friends gently suggested to him that he should fly or drive, that there wasn't enough time to walk, but he said no, that she would wait for him. For whatever reason, he knew she would still be alive. He must have walked for days, weeks. When he finally got to France, his director friend was still alive, but she had grown very tired. 'I've been waiting for you so I could die,' she said. 'Please release me.' And so Herzog said that he released her, and she died."

I couldn't tell you if Hadley got the right impression from the story. The way Herzog relates the anecdote, with a guileless, almost saintly whimsy, you really believe that he could send a dying woman peacefully off to the afterlife. Hadley was much more practical-minded than that, but Herzog came to mind because Hadley had been the one who had released my father from whatever false hope kept him from speaking about his imminent death. My mother and I had tried for weeks—directly and indirectly, calmly and impatiently—to get him to admit that he was dying, but we didn't have what Hadley had. It could have been the part of her that wasn't related to me, the part that belonged to her mother—or maybe it was something only inside her.

Hadley was desperate to see the world. Although it involved volunteer work, the program she had applied to was coveted among her friends—something they could be jealous about, for once. She was in a school district with rich kids who drove hybrid SUVs or rode $1,500 road bikes that were computer calibrated to their bodies, the children of doctors and engineers and software designers, while she was the jock who commuted, the daughter of a receptionist/former aspiring actress. Hadley worked—as a lifeguard and a counter-person at a bakery—while her friends completed internships at animation companies and job-shadowed marine biologists. In the summer, while she and her mom were making their annual visit to her grandfather in his crumbling house without air-conditioning in Toronto, her friends went on eco-tours of Patagonia and the ruins in Angkor Wat, or shuttled between the city and their beachside properties on the Gulf Islands.

It didn't take me long to realize that I came from the kind of household she envied. Until I was about sixteen or seventeen, old enough to be on my own, my parents dragged me on their vacations.

There were the obligatory trips to Hong Kong, where I shopped, visited relatives, and ate—so much eating. I mentioned it, offhand, to Hadley, who looked at me as though I'd sprouted wings.

"What's it like there?" she asked me.

"It's bigger. There's a lot of neon."

"What else?"

"Everyone's Chinese."

"Wow. Was Oliver different there?"

"Yeah, I guess. He knew everybody."

"Everyone in Hong Kong?"

"It seemed like it."

I didn't tell her about the time when I was fourteen and we were having dim sum in Kowloon and Edmund Chew walked into the room. I strained to catch a view of him, but he was at the other end of the restaurant, and he'd turned his back to us. My father pretended not to notice his arrival and spoke very loudly instead about how his long-time tailor, the guy who made all his shirts and suits when he came to visit, was retiring. "He was slipping up a bit," my father said. "Last year, I had to get a collar redone elsewhere, but he was once the best. Every year, this place becomes a little more foreign for me, even though it never feels like home over there." We sat in silence with old friends of my parents, nibbling on chicken feet and shrimp balls, until the bill arrived and we left.

And then there was the time when I was seven when my mother spent three days in Madrid weeping. She'd wanted to go to the Prado her entire life to look at the Goyas and El Grecos, but there she was, inexplicably weeping in our four-story walk-up room. Even at that age, I knew my mom would just cry at any time, in any place, for absolutely no reason. My father took me to the museum instead, and I remember feeling as though we were visiting a castle. Later, we went to the other museum in Madrid, the one that has Pablo Picasso's *Guernica*, and the most distinct memory I have from that trip was of a crowd gathering around the painting. I must have thought they were mobbing a fire juggler—something worth seeing—and I pushed my face anxiously through grown-up asses and handbags. My father scooped me up on his shoulders, and I remembered staring at Picasso's mural, at first disappointed there was no fire juggler or Michael Jackson imitator, and then grateful I could share this with the other onlookers. I didn't know art—still don't know it—but I knew that these people were pummelled by beauty. Later, my mother asked me what I'd seen and when I told her, she seemed relieved to know all that beauty, even if it remained unseen to her, was present in the world.

Hadley had been swimming since she was an infant and swam the breaststroke for two years in middle school. She chose water polo because she enjoyed being on a team. In the summer, she had worked as a lifeguard at a public pool. I told her how I took swimming lessons as a kid, but after almost drowning at a pool in a resort in Jamaica as a nine-year-old, I never stepped foot in a pool again.

"You should have gone into the pool the next day," Hadley told me.

I shook my head. My parents were arguing that day. My mother felt my father wasn't paying enough attention to her, and my father grew quiet and started drinking margaritas, which wasn't exactly his style, in the morning. I was lying next to my mother by the pool. "He takes me for granted," she said. "I gave up a better life to be with him." As my mother returned to her room, I edged into the big, busy pool and lost my footing.

"Hey, I could teach you to swim," she suggested.

"I don't know," I said, half-heartedly.

"You could teach me to drive."

"Okay, sure."

She nodded. "We both get something out of it."

It was enough that my personal life was a shambles. I needed to work. With that in my mind, I met Vanessa for lunch at the Indian restaurant below her agency's office. The restaurant, which was darkly lit even during the day and pleasantly shabby, full of frayed bamboo-backed chairs, had a vegetarian buffet lunch special that helped crowd the restaurant in the afternoon. After lining up for our food, we took two seats by the window. The brick streets outside were sparsely occupied and slick with rain. Vanessa ate only a salad and drank cardamom tea with Sweet 'N' Low.

"The food here's not bad," I said.

"Yeah, except that I always feel like I'm eating my job," Vanessa said. "How are you with electrical work?"

I took "electrical work" to be modelling-related term and pretended I understood what she was talking about. "I could give it a shot."

"My doorbell doesn't ring properly. If you ring the door at my house, you'll get a small electrical shock. UPS refuses to deliver because it's a hazard for their couriers." She chewed on a piece of shredded carrot with an ornery expression. "The real-estate agent called it a fixer-upper. And it wasn't a problem with Harold around. He used to be very handy with electrical work. He was so good with fixing things. I ask you—does that sound like someone who preferred the company of men? Me, neither. Fortunately, he had quite a life-insurance policy—his lover hadn't yet convinced him to sign it over. The agency is all I have in my life, but thank God I don't live off its proceeds. I'd be in a cardboard box." Vanessa said this blithely, then took a long sip of her cardamom tea to signal a change in subject. "Are you afraid of heights?"

I shook my head.

"Good, I need someone to re-tile my roof. I'm willing to pay you twelve dollars an hour."

"I don't know how to tile."

"I've got a book."

I sighed.

"What's the matter?" she asked.

"I thought we were going to discuss *modelling* work."

Vanessa apologized. "Of course, of course." She put down her fork and let out a sigh. "The agency working the long-distance account sent me an e-mail. I'm afraid they're going with someone else, but they said they were impressed with your book. Next time."

"Did they say why they chose someone else?" My concern was that my appearance was too "editorial"—too exotic, not symmetrical enough—for most of the mainstream work. Of course, I also knew that certain looks go in and out of fashion. Last year, androgyny had been the rage. Now casting directors were looking for models with big lips.

"They said they needed someone who has more experience with commercial work."

"But how do I get experience if I can't get a job?"

Vanessa pinched together her shoulders and held her palms flat in front of herself as though she were measuring quantities of air.

"Any print work available?" I asked her.

"Malcolm, I told you it's a tough market for magazine advertising right now." Her expression changed, and she bore the face of someone who's had unreasonable demands placed on her. "Now, now, don't get down on yourself. Something will come up. I mean, look at me, I could be down—the business is still struggling, and

I can't trust men—but that's no excuse to quit. You don't think it's hard for me, too? All day I'm at the office, trying to hustle work. This is the first meal I've had in two weeks where I'm seated." She banged her fist against the table. "Promise me you won't quit."

"Sorry, I guess I'm new at this."

"It's okay, but I'm going to need you to be patient," she said. "Remember, it's quality not quantity. If we want work that leads to better work, we'll need to bide our time."

I shook my head, undeterred, and continued pleading. "Anything would be good," I insisted. "I just want experience. I don't need to do a huge billboard right away or get paid thousands of dollars."

"Okay," she said, eyeing me with newfound interest. "You don't care what you do?"

I nodded.

"Desperation is something I can use."

True to her word, Vanessa found work for me the following week in a print ad for a dating service. With opportunity, though, came more anxiety. The night before the assignment I thrashed about in bed, worried that I would have some sort of on-set meltdown or that the photographer would be some creep who would force me to snort cocaine with him in a sauna. Then I grew antsy, afraid I'd get a blotch on my forehead, but when I woke up, it was clear. This I took to be a good omen.

The shoot took place in an industrial area outside the city, past the flashy signs for the Auto-Mall and the Go-Kart track. Three times I had to circle the area in my car before I found the correct warehouse building. The photographer's studio was on the second floor of a nondescript block with a cube van parked in front of a large garage.

After buzzing the entrance, I was met by a photographer named Stuart, a short, olive-skinned man with a widow's peak, a stubbly face, and beefy fingers. He was friendly, if laconic, and soon after our introductions led me to a changing room and told me to put on the wardrobe waiting there for me. In the changing room, a closet with a dressing table and a small makeup mirror, there was a black leather vest, tight black slacks, and an ascot. Also in the room was a bottle of body oil.

I put on the outfit, applied some oil on my chest and arms, and found the set. He was setting up his camera and lights around a black suede couch and a fur rug. Loud dance music was playing from a small boom box.

"This isn't pornography, is it?" I asked, perhaps naïvely.

Directing me to spread out on the couch, Stuart's laugh was abrupt and a ghastly, opportunistic smile spilled across his face. "Not unless you want it to be."

I shook my head and lay on the couch, my feet at one end and my head—propped up by a glistening, oiled arm—at the other.

"Okay, then, it's just an ad for a dating service," he said, taking a couple of test shots and making adjustments to the lights. "Don't worry—I'll make you look really good," he said, returning to the camera and snapping another photo. "Can you feel the music?" The music was more distracting than helpful, and I tried to feel some other music in my head. "Smile for me." Stuart seemed pleased. "Okay, now I want to see you look serious."

Though this was hardly the situation I imagined when we did mock photo shoots as our end-of-year assignment, I tried to follow some advice that Martin had given us: To accentuate your jaw, you should clench your teeth and place your tongue on the roof of your mouth.

"Can I get you to bend one knee?" I bent a knee. "Good, now I want you to look sexy." He snapped some photos. "Okay, too much grimacing. I want it to be a vacant-looking sexy, like you're day-dreaming." He snapped. "Great, that's it." He asked me to kneel on the couch with my hands on my knees, looking over my shoulder. Then he wanted me to take off my vest. I did, and I felt cold. "How long have you been doing this?"

"I just started."

"You're a natural."

Obviously, this wasn't ideal. I tried to remember the advice my father gave me when I received a lousy grade for a class I had no interest in, but was required for graduation. He told me to create my own challenges and to seek satisfaction in meeting my own expectations. At the time, I reacted to his words of motivation with a yawn, but now I know that when my father gave me advice, it came from his own experience. It was his job to create his own challenges for educational films on proper restaurant hygiene or used-car commercials, and he accomplished the tasks with visual flair and wit. And so, I tried to feel the pulse of the punishing dance music. I emptied my head of complication and searched for perfection in the clicking camera.

It was Hadley who eventually calmed me down two weeks later when the ad appeared. In the classifieds sections of both the local free weeklies was a shot of yours truly sitting backwards on a chair, gleaming, oiled legs astride. I wore a frog-like smile and held a telephone in my hands. The caption that ran above it was mortifying:

MANTALK: CALL NOW!!!

He's been waiting to hear from you. He's had a long day

between classes at art school and a shift at the juice bar. Then he ran three miles along the Seawall and washed his Jeep. Now he wants to let loose. Cocktails, sushi, clubbing—and then maybe something AFTER HOURS. You name it. IT'S YOUR CALL.

"You look good," Hadley offered, closing the newspaper. "Like a stunt double for a movie star."

I nodded dumbly. At a table opposite ours, a clutch of girls pretzelled themselves in convulsive shrieks; I promptly ducked, as though these flat-iron enthusiasts were laughing at me. We were at Benny's Bagels—which teenagers preferred because it was open late and the manager let them linger for hours hunched over their smudged laptop keyboards and toast crumbs—waiting for Marco to arrive.

Hadley opened the paper again. "Tons of women would go for this."

"Yet it makes me look so fruity."

Hadley gummed her chin. "Malcolm, complaining does not flatter you."

This made me apologize.

"I asked for *any* exposure, and I got it," I said. "Vanessa took two phone calls this morning. There's interest in me for a winter fashion spread in the newspaper and for a camping-supplies catalogue. That's not fruity, right?"

"Not fruity at all."

While waiting for her boyfriend, Hadley needled me about Thanksgiving. Weeks earlier, my mother had called from Hong Kong to say she couldn't return until she'd hired a nurse for my grandmother. I'd written down her arrival time and made a note to replace her dead plants. My schedule was free of commitments.

"Why don't you come over to my house?" Hadley said repeatedly. "Give me a reason."

As a holiday that my immigrant parents only encountered as adults, Thanksgiving didn't incite within me the hang-ups, disappointments, and grudges that anguished my friends. I'd spent two Thanksgivings with Claire's family at their monstrous, pink-marble estate outside Ottawa. There was Claire's father, swaddling his belly while the plates were cleared. Everything he offered had conditions attached to it. Even I was expected to grovel whenever he visited Montreal and picked up a bill. There was her heavily sedated mother, who spoke as though she were reading aloud from a children's book. There was her alcoholic brother, who disappeared an hour before dinner, then fell asleep at the table. And there was a spinster aunt who resented the exclusion of her aspic from the meal.

"Don't you like turkey?" Hadley asked. "Don't you like creamed potatoes and my mom's ramen-noodle salad? Do you have a problem with the best pumpkin pie ever, that I make from scratch, even the pie crust? Plus, afterwards, we have coffee and liqueurs."

I'd choose having hair on my back over attending that Thanksgiving dinner.

"Maybe next year."

Her mouth cracked in disbelief. "You're going to spend Thanksgiving alone."

"Don't make it sound so bleak."

"You're going to make me cry."

"Don't cry." It was a weak ploy, given how my own mother was the world's uncontested champion crier. Compared to the best, Hadley was a half-hearted manipulator.

"You're going to disappoint my mom. She wants to meet you. Plus, she's less bossy and critical when we have guests over. *Please.*"

Finally she deployed what must have been her weapon of last resort—a pathetic, whimpering noise. It could only be resisted by someone with a pinecone for a heart.

Marco's arrival, in his blue army-surplus jacket and camouflage pants, bought me time. Hadley's boyfriend acknowledged me with a big grin, clapping his hand—hard—on my shoulder. He wore brown leather wristbands and a guitar-pick necklace. I dragged a chair over from an empty table as he pushed up to Hadley.

"Okay, I've got a question for you." Hadley ran a hand up his back, strumming Marco's neck. "Malcolm has two Thanksgiving options. He could stay home alone in his empty apartment eating low-fat chicken and listening to his mopey music. Or, he could hang out with me and eat good food. What do you think he should do?"

"Well, that depends."

He was deadlocked between his girlfriend and whatever dudely obligation he felt toward me, his mouth knotting as he looked for a way out. Then he let out a sharp gasp.

"*Holy shit.* That's you!" He pointed to the ManTalk ad still open on the table and began to laugh. "Dude, you're like a gigolo. You're a Chippendale."

While Marco's laughter filled the room, Hadley kept staring at me with her big brown eyes.

"If you make him shut up, I'll go."

"You promise?"

I had to make a solemn oath—twice—before she put a finger to her lips and Marco quieted down.

CHAPTER SIX

HADLEY'S MOTHER RENTED a stucco bungalow on the east side, hidden behind a picket line of evergreen bushes. The home had an unwanted aura—its detailing needed a touch-up and yellowing grass grew knee-high on both sides of the concrete path to the door. Behind a neighbour's wire fence, a growling dog tried to warn me away.

I arrived five minutes early, dressed in my only tailored shirt (a splurge), a pullover sweater, and corduroys, bearing a bottle of sherry and a box of After Eight mints. I found the doorbell beside a cobwebbed mailbox and pressed twice. I heard running footsteps and saw a grey figure through the frosted pane of amber glass next to the door. Hadley appeared wearing the same crushed velvet dress that she wore at the service, the one with the Oreo-sized buttons running down its front. Her hair fell in a ladder of curls and her mouth was apple red. She received my gifts enthusiastically and welcomed me inside.

"Should I take off my shoes?" I asked.

"If you want," she told me. "It's no big deal. Are you hungry?"

I removed my shoes. "Not starving."

"Good, we're running late," she said. "Plus, my mom has work friends who aren't here yet."

Inside, their house was tidy and warm, with sofas covered in quilts and a gallery of framed pictures of Hadley as a girl. In the front room, an older man who was bald with a fringe of long, wispy grey hair and shaggy, off-white sideburns, sat at the end of a couch watching television. He looked groggy. One of his arms was draped over the end of the couch; in the other he held a can of domestic beer. Periwinkle blue eyes stood out on his pink face above a bulging red nose and drooping mouth. He wore a sweatshirt emblazoned with the logo of the University of British Columbia, rumpled slacks, green socks, and blue velvet slippers. Nodding at me curtly, he set down a newly emptied can of Pilsner on the coffee table next to four other empties, picked up the clicker, and held it at chin level to click.

"Grandfather, this is Malcolm," Hadley announced in a slow, rounded voice. "He's Oliver's son—my brother."

He spoke deliberately, but in a beer-brined slur. "James Wallace, how do you do," he said, which sounded like, "*Change walrus, out chew do.*"

Our eyes met for a flash before his attention returned to the television. Onscreen was a curling match—plump, moustached men glided in their shoes along the ice. He snorted in frustration and changed the channel to an episode of a dating program, the daters now separated and gossiping about each other. James Wallace watched this program for a moment and flipped the channel again. "You listen, tell your mother there's nothing good on the telly."

"Grandfather is visiting from Ontario for two weeks," Hadley said quietly. When she turned to the old man, she had to raise her voice. "Grandfather, you must be reasonable. What can mother do about what's on TV?"

"Very well." He set the clicker on his lap and stared at her in resignation. "Be a love, and fetch grandfather another refreshment."

Hadley scooped the empties from the coffee table. "Grandfather, Malcolm plays darts—don't you, Malcolm?"

"Not so much recently," I said, raising my voice like Hadley had. "In Montreal I was pretty good."

Hadley turned to me, her voice lowered. "Grandfather is obsessed with darts, and he's very serious about his competition."

Her grandfather sat up on the couch to size me up. One corner of his mouth turned up as he grew curious. "Get me another drink, Hadley, and then maybe your friend and I can have ourselves a friendly match."

All the settings were in place at the dining room table. I followed Hadley into the kitchen where Sheila Wallace stood at the kitchen counter tossing ramen-noodle salad.

"Mom, meet Malcolm."

I had thought a lot about meeting Sheila. I approached the counter and held out my hand to her. When Sheila looked up at me, a distressed expression dimmed her eyes before she took my hand. I can't imagine how I must have looked. I thought of my father as Old World, and he never seemed to express much interest in women who weren't Chinese, and here was this very *white* woman. She was a busty, big-haired strawberry blonde in her forties with a pink face like Hadley's grandfather, dark, arching eyebrows, and large front teeth. She wore an apron around a short-sleeved blouse that revealed her fleshy arms and wide hips.

As she checked on the turkey and let her potatoes cool, Sheila spoke in a breathless, excitable tone much like Hadley—and I had thought she would grow out of it—her sentences punctuated by put-upon looks and rolled eyes. "We're running late, but make yourself comfortable," she said. "I was very sorry to hear about Oliver. Look at you. Oh, that must have been hard for you. Look at you, so much like him. He was a decent man, not perfect, I guess, you know, but who is? And I'm so glad that you and Hadley are getting to know each other, not that she tells me much about where you go or what you talk about. But kids need their own space. And better she spend time with her brother—and that's what you are, you need to look after her—better you than with all her boyfriends."

"I have just one boyfriend," Hadley said from the refrigerator, where she retrieved a can of beer. "Do you think I'm easy?"

Sheila ignored her daughter and continued speaking to me: "I don't want her to make the same mistakes I made with men. I see those guys she goes out with, and it's like she's taken a page from my own book." She laughed. "Real deadbeats. Of course, when you're young, you think there's plenty more where that came from. They're charming, but they'll lie to you and cheat. That Liam, for instance. He treated her like crap, cheated on her, criticized her, but still she followed him around for an entire year."

"We're not dating anymore," Hadley said, stomping out of the kitchen. "I'm going out with Marco. And Marco's sweet."

"Oh, Marco—he's not a bad fellow." She waited for Hadley to leave before she said any more. Her voice, lowered at first, quickly grew loud. "She's been such a grouch lately. Do you know why that is? We don't talk as much as we used to. We used to be really close, but now I'm taking night classes and working full-time, I hardly get to see her. Christ, I'm so tired when I get home that I can hardly make dinner." She went to the refrigerator, pulled out two cans of Pilsner, and foisted one on me. "Do you smoke?"

I shook my head.

"Me neither—not anymore," she said, adding a horsey laugh. "Oh, I can't say that I've been the best example. She had no real father growing up."

Having prepared myself for any sort of extreme reaction to the mother of my half-sister, I did not expect to feel relief. I let out a deep breath. Looking at her now, she did not fare well against my own mother, and I was certain my father couldn't have cared much for this woman. Whatever intimacy she shared with my father, whatever secrets she might have of him, had been stubbed out by time. Maybe it wasn't fair, maybe I was wrong.

Sheila was still talking. "The closest thing Hadley had to a father figure was Arnie, my ex-husband," she was saying. "Hadley and Arnie were real close for a while—they're both nuts about swimming, they both love to criticize me—but our marriage was, what's the word, a shambles? I won't bore you with the details or anything, but it was the same old cycle repeating itself. Still he calls me every day, tells me what a mistake he's made, tells me how he can't live without me. I mean, it's flattering and all." The oven timer rang and she removed the turkey. "Okay, let me ask you, sometimes I want to take him back. But do you believe what they say—once a cheater, always a cheater?"

I looked at her uneasily, not sure what to say, and fortunately Sheila had the sense to know this. She laughed her question off and took a pull of her beer. "So Hadley tells me you want to be a model? Did I tell you I used to model? A little acting, too."

I sucked on my lip, waiting to see whether she was joking again. Realizing she wasn't, I opened my mouth to say something polite, but Hadley appeared at the kitchen door with another empty beer can. "Malcolm, Grandfather wants you in the basement," she said. "He's taking his practice throws now."

Before I went to Hadley's house for Thanksgiving, I couldn't stop thinking about my first girlfriend, Cindy Arau, whom I met in grade ten.

From the start, Cindy Arau and I had nothing in common. She was ridiculously pretty, of course, with a klieg-light smile, tablespoon-sized eyes, and shiny, flat-ironed hair that ran halfway down her back. She pretended she didn't realize how beautiful she was, but swung her hips whenever she exited any room with a male in it. I loved the taste of her ginger-mango lip gloss.

And yet I could never get over how girlish and square she could be. She loved horses and country music. She refused to swear and used words like "shoot" and "friggin." When I met her, her life was already planned out. She wanted to live in another city, get an education degree by twenty-three, move back home, teach nine- and ten-year-olds until she was twenty-eight, have three children in rapid succession and, when they were all in school, try her hand at writing cookbooks. Her father owned a successful cement-mixing company, and she insisted I take a summer job with him. I was aware, early on, that I was either going to be part of her plan or out of her life.

The truth was that I loved her family more than her. I loved the Arau's gaudy, oversized house, the smell of fish sauce in the kitchen, the portrait of Jesus Christ over the fireplace. I actually loved working for Mr Arau, who would bring a lunch packed by Mrs Arau for me every day that summer. And I loved playing darts and eight-ball with Cindy Arau's brothers in the basement. When my mother went away alone to Greece to rest and recover after a hospitalization, I spent two entire weeks at their house.

At some point, both Cindy Arau and I knew we weren't compatible, but we stuck together because of my attachment to her family. She took pity on me and kept me around longer than she should have.

Cindy Arau was also obsessed with clothes. There are women who look good in jeans and those who should always wear a skirt, and she was one of the former. She owned two or three pairs of jeans that she loved, including a pair of flares she brought out for special occasions. One Halloween, the last one before we went to university, she decided we were to go as a disco couple so she could wear her bell-bottoms with an Afro wig she'd bought at a community-theatre thrift sale. It was my mother who suggested I go into the back of my father's walk-in closet to dig out a white, three-piece suit that he wore in his nightclub days. I found the suit right at the end of the closet and then looked for the matching shoes in the shelf above.

I couldn't find the shoes right away and had to dig further until I located them at the back of the closet. The shoes sat awkwardly in the box, and after looking at them for a moment, I noticed a stack of letters and postcards hidden underneath a carefully cut piece of cardboard. The correspondence was written to my dad, addressed to his production-company office and dated well over a decade earlier. Each one had the same slanted script, the same double-underlined words in every other sentence, and the same big hearts at the bottom of the page from a woman named Sheila. A couple of the letters even had lipstick kisses imprinted on them, included details of weekends away and other enticements. Some were sad little "miss you" postcards. I read each twice, then put them away. Those letters were why I had so reluctantly accepted Hadley's dinner invitation.

"Nothing goes according to plan," my dad told me once, "even when you don't have a plan." Last I heard, Cindy Arau was living with a pot dealer and swearing all the time.

There were two doors out of the kitchen. One led to the dining room. We went through the other, which faced a hallway lined with more photos that led to Hadley and Sheila's bedrooms. Another door opened to the basement steps.

"God, so sorry about my mom," Hadley said as I followed her down. "If you weren't around, she'd rag me more."

"She's okay," I conceded. "She cares about you, is all."

She shook her head. "I can't wait to get out of here."

"You'll be in university—in not too long."

"It feels like forever. Do you mind entertaining my grandfather? He's kind of cranky, but if he didn't insist that I be named in honour of my grandmother, my mom would have named me—I'm not kidding—Mindy Jo."

I laughed.

"Thanks for coming. I knew it."

"Knew what?"

"I knew I could count on you."

The basement floor was covered with a dingy area rug. James Wallace was standing next to the washer-dryer, one foot on a piece of electrician's tape on the red carpet as he leaned over it and launched a dart at the board on the far wall.

Hadley returned upstairs to help her mother and said she would call us when dinner was served. James Wallace handed me one of his remaining darts, a high-quality amateur set made of titanium, and slurred, "Clothes sit double stars damask." *Closest to the bull starts the match.*

I put down my beer and made a lucky shot.

"Well, I reckon you're starting."

On my next three darts, I made two more lucky throws, and one that wasn't too unlucky.

"Good show." He nodded without looking at me, lumbering slowly to a chalkboard next to the washer-dryer, and recorded my score with his shaky hand.

I removed the darts from the board and handed them to him.

Again, he stood at the line on the carpet, leaning forward. He was throwing with his left hand, which trembled so much that he used his right arm to steady his upper arm. He groaned each time his throws went wide, then staggered to the board to remove the darts, passing the darts to me, humbled.

My next three shots, which I threw in rapid succession, were also lucky, and I began to feel guilty about my good fortune—a series of flukes, I swear—around James Wallace, whose hands continued to tremble as he threw. Upstairs the doorbell sounded and I could hear footsteps rumbling above as Sheila's other guests were greeted.

We continued playing, and soon my lead on James Wallace had become insurmountable. In spite of the deficit, he continued to compete with a glossy, determined shine in his eyes.

"How do you like it here?" I asked him as my darts continued to find their marks. I raised my voice and repeated my question.

James Wallace didn't say anything, and I assumed that I wasn't speaking loudly enough. I could hear Sheila's voice, which sounded urgent and upset. As I mentioned earlier, my experience with Thanksgiving dinner was atypical, and I didn't know what to expect in a non-immigrant household. I thought at first that Sheila was yelling about something that had burnt in the oven, but the voices were coming from the front of the house. I looked to James Wallace, but he seemed preoccupied with the game and ignored me. I took his calm demeanour as a cue.

Although I could only hear Sheila's voice, the yelling from above persisted. It grew louder and fiercer, and I make out another voice—a male voice. Then I heard Hadley's voice, low and hushed. I turned again to James Wallace, making sure he saw me when I spoke: "Is everything okay? Maybe we should go upstairs."

He nodded as though to say he understood. His face was red from exertion, his shaking hands gripped tight around the darts. "My game is poor. Not much competition for you, I'm afraid," he told me. "In my day, I used to hold my own. But I suffered this stroke three years ago, and it's not quite the same." He rubbed the corners of his eyes. "Haven't been quite the same since. Now I'm poor competition. No match for you. I'm no match. Not anymore. I used to be better. No match."

The yelling grew louder, then it stopped abruptly. I pointed up the stairs to James Wallace, to indicate I was going up.

Out of the basement, I turned into the kitchen, which was empty, the gleaming turkey on the counter next to a serving dish and an electric knife. I heard Sheila's voice, now subdued, coming from the front of the house. I followed the voice until I saw her standing at the open door, gripping her own fat arms and shivering in the night, speaking to someone outside.

"For the last time, I'll call the police," Sheila said. Her voice was wobbly and hesitant. She sounded like someone threatening to jump off a bridge. "I swear I will if you don't leave."

I took a place next to Hadley, who stood behind her mother at the door like a frightened puppy. At the same time, her face was more determined than her mother's and set in a scowl—I'd never seen her so (maybe this isn't the right word) *ugly* before. There was hatred in her face. Scattered on the steps leading to the door were a dozen roses. The paper wrapping, held together by a piece of raffia, lay empty on the lawn. Outside, standing under the amber streetlights on the sidewalk, was a priggish-looking man with a goatee who wore glasses and hair down to his shoulders. His hands were shoved in his pockets, and when he spoke, steam rose from his mouth. This was Sheila's ex-husband, Arnie.

"I won't leave," he insisted. "If you won't let me into your house, then you should come outside so we can speak."

Sheila stood by the door silently. She looked to both of us with a sombre expression, then to her former husband, her forehead creasing as she began to waver.

With her eyes moistening, Hadley put an arm on her mother's shoulder and attempted to talk her down. "You can't do this," she said. "You can't do this."

Sheila turned from the door and Hadley exhaled. Sheila reappeared slinging her arms into her coat.

I wanted to console Hadley, but could only pat her on the back, as though she needed to burp out her sadness. Sheila put her hand on her daughter's cheek. "We're just going to talk," she told her. "I won't keep dinner much longer." As she stepped outside, she closed the door behind her.

"Oh, *fuck*." I'd heard Hadley curse before—she wasn't a priss like Cindy Arau, but now it came out of her with a wrenching, seething anguish, like she'd stepped on a nail and knew she was feeling only the first stage of pain. She slumped against the door, and as she began to weep her voice rose as high as a child's. "They're going to get back together, and it'll be like it used to be," she said. "You don't know what it was like." She looked up at me with such helplessness and sorrow that I felt it ripple in my own chest. "I mean, they don't belong together. The two of them fight all the time."

I took a step toward her. "I know things will be fine, I swear."

She put her arms around me and wept against my pullover sweater. "Don't make promises you can't keep," she said. Her hair had an apple scent and her grip was so fierce that I needed to hug her back with the same strength.

When I let go of her, James Wallace was entering the room glowering imperiously, displeased that dinner had yet to begin. Hadley smoothed her face and tried to explain the delay, but he couldn't hear a word until he remembered to turn on his hearing aids. I realized he had grown his white hair long to cover them over.

CHAPTER SEVEN

MY MOTHER EMERGED through the sliding doors of the Arrivals gate wearing soap-plate-sized sunglasses and the collar of her cashmere jacket turned up like an incognito movie star. With some strain, she pushed a cart piled perilously high with her luggage, shopping bags, and ugly, brink-of-bursting, taped-up suitcases she'd borrowed from my grandmother to pack gifts and other dried goods—black mushrooms, ginseng, shoes—that she could never bear leaving Hong Kong without. I waved to her from behind the barrier, and she kissed me on the cheek when we met.

Taking command of the cart, I led her to the parking lot. "How was your trip?"

"I doubled my body weight," she said, removing her glasses and folding an arm on her barely noticeable stomach. Her eyes were skittish and damp, but otherwise she looked healthy, at least more than she had when she left. There was now colour in her face, which had filled out from ten-course restaurant meals with her mother, her three brothers, her nieces and nephews, and other relatives. She had been gone almost two months, and it was now late November. "But I'm glad to be home. I want to get back to painting, back to teaching. And I've been worrying about my plants, too."

What could I do? I lied about the plants. First, I'd forgotten to water them; then I overcompensated by watering them furiously.

We found the Saab, and I loaded its trunk—and then the back seat—with her many suitcases. On the top rack of the cart, next to her handbag, was the bronze Grecian-style container—which looked like both a vase and a metal water bottle—that held my father's ashes.

"I decided I wanted him here, close to us," she said. She took the ashes into the car and carried them on her lap as I pulled out of the parking stall. "Is that selfish?"

I followed the arrows to the parking-lot exit, inching the Saab behind another driver waiting to pay the toll. "Not at all."

"I like talking to the ashes, too."

"Okay, that's weird."

"I don't expect you to understand," she said, digging out change from her bag as we approached the toll booth. "I need to be reminded that this part of my life is over—the big important part. If I don't keep his ashes around, I'll just imagine he's off somewhere, getting into trouble." The sky was the colour of dirty bathwater. At midday, the horizon was a prudish blue and the city was coated in a smoky, autumnal light. Leaves were trampled flat against the sidewalk. Once we left the parking lot and got onto the highway, fine drops of rain began to fall from the dirty sky. I let a layer of drops collect on the windshield before turning on the wipers.

I looked at the container. "What do you say to him—to it"—the word "ashes" was plural—"to them?"

"I mostly complain to him about the weather, I tell him about your grandmother's operation. What I always did."

"Are you okay?"

"We need to look after each other," she told me. "I'm going to be different now. I'm better. I looked after your father, didn't I?"

"That's true."

"It's not too late for me to be your mother, is it?"

I shrugged, not really sure what I could say—or what I could say truthfully. Then I mentioned that I was used in a magazine photo spread for new Asian designers and had appeared in a full-colour print ad for a discount menswear chain. Neither job paid money, but it was editorial experience.

We crossed the bridge and took a winding off-ramp into the city. "Have you seen much of that girl?"

"Claire hasn't called."

"I don't mean Claire."

I winced, knowing that the moment had arrived. "Yeah, I see her a lot. She's sweet."

My mother shifted uneasily in the car, her pretty face marked with unease. "Why is it that you're drawn to her?"

"What do you mean?" I asked.

"Does she remind you of your father?"

I thought about it for a moment. Sometimes when she laughed, I could see him in her eyes. But I said: "The resemblance isn't overpowering."

"So she takes after her mother?"

"Not really," I admitted. Then I told her how much Hadley liked her paintings and this complicated the light in her eyes. "Do you want to meet her?"

She looked at me as though I was joking and then, when she figured out that I wasn't, shook her head.

"Still, I always wished you could have a sister. I thought it might help you understand women better."

"You mean I don't?"

She smiled and shook her head. "You take after your father. When we first started dating, he insisted on kissing me with his eyes open."

I groaned. My mother's openness about her relationship with my father and physical intimacy was atypical for a Chinese mother and, to be explicit myself, always made my testicles retract into my pelvis. In this case, I was mortified but also curious. "Why would he do that?" I ask her.

"He said he liked looking at me," she told me with a dreamy smile. "I would worry he'd find a blackhead on my nose, but part of me thought it was romantic and goofy. Anyway, I thought it might have helped you if you had a sibling. Maybe you wouldn't have been as clueless if you had known Hadley earlier."

I reminded her that my father had two sisters.

She tilted her head, her eyes drifting back. "All right," she said finally. "What are you saying?"

"I might still have been clueless even if I had grown up with a sister."

"You're right." My mother looked at me as though I was a drowning man refusing a lifejacket. "You can't help it."

Thinking about my mother made me wonder whether Hadley's character would darken as she grew older, the way some skinny women filled out as they aged or settled down and bore children. Usually, when it came to the destiny of their body shapes, there was some telltale signal: thick ankles or a full face. I wondered what signals my mother gave off when she was younger, and looked for them in Hadley. Some people valiantly fought this predetermined figure, the same way others tried to starve and work out their sadness, but it didn't seem easy.

The more I got to know Hadley, the more I began to wonder whether she hadn't already begun that struggle. One afternoon, after a water polo practice, she came to meet me at the record store.

"Are you okay?" I asked as we stepped outside. She seemed distracted.

"Okay," she parroted senselessly. She was wearing her overcoat with the collar turned up, a red felt boa, and green mittens. "Krista and I got into the program."

"Which program?"

"You know where we build the wells?"

"Oh, right."

She groaned. "Don't you ever listen?"

"I'm sorry."

"I got the letter of acceptance today. They're going to send me to Guyana in June, during the rainy season."

"Is that better than the other season?"

She ignored my question. "My mom thinks I should be more worried about getting into university, but I don't think it'll be a problem. My grades are good, and I know which universities I want to attend. Oliver left me some money before I died, so I won't have to borrow from my mom or take a loan—which means I can go away. In fact, I'm only applying to schools in the east."

Kernels of disappointment popped inside me. "You sound eager to leave."

"I wish I could leave for Guyana tomorrow."

"What's the rush?" I asked her, now trying not to sound as though I felt abandoned.

Again she groaned impatiently at my question. "Well, I hate living with my mom."

"Is she back with her ex-husband?" I asked her.

"It looks that way. They're going into counselling—like they haven't done that before—and then they're doing a trial reconciliation. I can't stand her. She's such a bag."

"She's not so bad."

She stopped abruptly on the street. "I wish you would quit defending her," she told me. "You know *nothing* about her. Just because we have the same father doesn't make you my brother."

"I never said I was," I said, weakly.

"Good."

"What's the matter with you?"

She hesitated. "I was spun three times in practice."

"That's a bad thing, right?"

"Yes, it's the most shameful thing that can occur in water polo."

"And that's why you are in a lousy mood?"

"No, I'm not. I'm just tired of you butting in."

"Sorry."

She shook her head. "You shouldn't speak about things you know nothing about."

"I wasn't implying that I did."

"It's not as though I had a perfect, well-adjusted upbringing like you did. I didn't attend a fancy private school. I didn't have a father; I didn't even know who he was until I was fifteen. And my mother can be such an idiot—the kind of garbage she puts up with from jerks—she pays their bills and makes excuses for them when they let her down. And I can't tell her that, because she always jumps to their defence. She never takes my side. That means I have to watch out for myself."

As we stopped for coffee, I was dumbfounded, mostly because I'd never met anyone who could envy my childhood. I couldn't argue with her; even if I didn't know it at the time, I'd had it good. At the coffeehouse, Hadley and I ordered Americanos and toasted bagels and took a table. We sat in silence until Hadley bit a hole at the bottom of her little plastic cup of creamer and squirted a stream of cream into her coffee.

"Huh?" I said.

She smiled a little. "It's a water-polo thing. When you get

chlorine in your eyes, the best thing to do is squirt creamer in it."

"Really?"

"Yeah, and another water-polo trick is to put Vaseline on your ankles so they're harder to grab."

At the counter, a pack of slouching, slender teenage boys were ordering beverages and baked goods. All of them, except for Liam, retreated to a table in the room at the back. Dressed in a purple fleece jacket and black track pants, he approached our table and pulled up a seat. He had a long face, and his rubbery chin gave him a soft, gentlemanly appearance. His gaping smile and his strut were gone. He spoke with a contrite lilt, both hands wrapped around his cup of coffee.

"I was hoping I'd see you here," he said. "Would it be all right if I sat down?"

Hadley sighed.

"I won't be too long." He sat down. "My name is Liam," he said to me, offering his hand.

I shook it and introduced myself.

He looked at the both of us. "Are you two related?"

"Yes," I said.

"I didn't know you had a brother. Half?"

"What do you want?" Hadley asked with snap.

"You won't return my calls."

"Yeah?"

He looked at me. "Could we talk alone for a second?"

"No."

"Okay, then, I just want to say I'm sorry. Is that what you need to hear?" He stood up from the table. "Stop acting as though you're so much better than me. It's like you won't let go."

"*I am?*"

"You're the one who makes a big deal out of it by refusing to talk to me." His eyes grew dark. "It disrupts the team."

"Yeah."

"It's not about you and me."

I was surprised to see her back down. "I know."

"Well, I guess I'll see you at my party, then." She watched him go into the back room, then wrapped her scarf around her neck, took her half-finished bagel, and stood up. I followed her outside.

"I'm sorry I was mean," she said. "Do you ever have days that are wallpapered in shit?"

"Sure."

"Liam has this way of talking that makes you apologize even when you didn't do anything wrong. His dad's this famous celebrity psychologist—he's always on the radio, telling parents how to train their kids as though they're pets—and he picked up all these mind games from him. The more he talks, the easier it is to believe anything he says. The best thing to do is to ignore him."

"He's throwing a party?" I asked her.

"Yeah, he thinks he throws the best parties." She stuck out her tongue to express distaste. "Krista wants me to go because of this university guy there she wants to meet."

"Don't go to the party."

"I wish it were easier," she said. "Sometimes I wish things weren't so confusing. Every time I feel as though I've patched one part of my life, another part falls apart. I wish everything could be more straightforward. I wish people could be straightforward. I wish that people would say what they wanted from you and give you what they say they'll give you. But I have to go to that party, because I can't avoid stuff like that."

I always felt greedy and guilty around Hadley, because not only had I unwittingly taken more than my allotted half of our father's time, but I'd mishandled it without knowing its true value, like a mom who, in a fit of tidying, throws out her child's beloved action figurines. In the first few months I knew her, she would ask me questions about him as though she were preparing for a test, and I would provide answers with the uncertainty and hesitation of an ill-prepared substitute teacher.

"What were his favourite foods?" she asked as we left for the video store.

"He liked deep-fried tofu," I told her.

"I thought you said he liked Japanese pears."

"He liked both."

There was always a moment during our get-togethers, after enough time had elapsed and our conversation had waned, when a natural opening would present itself for us to part ways; more often than not, both of us would ignore this endpoint. We'd stare at the ground until this gap passed and we had another conversation and a new set of plans. We would go for lunch and then dinner; or coffee, a movie, and then another coffee.

"What was his favourite colour?" she asked me.

"I don't know," I said.

"What was his favourite kind of flower?"

"Do guys even have those?"

"Did he wear boxers or briefs?"

"Briefs. He was old school."

Her face compressed in dismay. "Was he a morning person or a night person?"

"Both. He stayed up late and woke up early—and perky. It was deeply annoying."

"What was his favourite movie?"

"*Mary Poppins.*"

"What was his least favourite movie?"

"I don't know, maybe *Star Wars.* He resented having to buy me so many toys."

"Did he like country music?"

"Um, I don't think so. Probably not."

"Are you sure?"

"No."

"In my head, I imagined what my ideal dad would be like."

"Really?" I asked. "So did I."

Her eyes flared open. "Really? What was *your* ideal father like?"

"Oh, I don't know. It's probably different from what you'd imagine out of thin air."

"Well, I always thought he'd be someone who could fix things. Stuff would fall apart in our house and my mom would tape it up. I used to hate it when she drove to school to pick me up in her car with the bumper held on with electrician's tape. I didn't necessarily think of him as being Asian, but I guess I always thought he'd look different from my mom, in a way that would make us look like a family. No one thinks my mom and I are related, which is sometimes a relief. Did you grow up feeling different?"

"Why? Because I'm Chinese?"

"No. I mean, yeah."

"Well, there are tons of Chinese people in Vancouver; it's more like being left-handed than being an oppressed minority. People at Chinese restaurants look at me and speak in English; I think it's the clothes I wear or my haircut. But I guess I felt different, though maybe not because I was Chinese, but for other reasons. I don't like hockey, for instance. I hate people who wear fleece and hike as a recreational activity."

"That's too bad. I was going to invite you on a hike."

"I'd accept, but it wouldn't be my favourite thing to do."

That night, we rented Edmund Chew's first film, *Shakespeare's Revolver*, from Videomatica, using the account I shared with my dad. I hadn't been here since he'd died.

"You're paying for this with your credit?" the clerk asked.

"Credit?"

The clerk squinted at the screen in front of him. "There's over five-hundred dollars on it."

I turned to Hadley, trying not to think of my father, who must have phoned in the credit from the hospice.

We had seen Chew's newest film a month ago and then caught another mid-career film on TV last week. Hadley's mood perked up when I mentioned my father's connection to him. I'd told her Chew's best movies were the first four, the ones before he became super famous. Some would say his best film was *An Unwanted Glory*, his fifth feature, but I thought it was an overrated rehash of his early highlights. We rented *Shakespeare's Revolver*, which my father and Chew wrote when they were in their early twenties, about the same age I was now, while they worked as production assistants and assistant cameramen on martial arts films.

"You don't mind reading subtitles?" I asked Hadley, as I crouched over the DVD player.

She glowered at me. "I'm not stupid."

"Sorry," I said. "The movie is slow-paced."

"I know. You told me. Fifteen times."

Shakespeare's Revolver is about a cop named Tony Luk who avenges the suicide of his heroin-addicted wife on her bald-headed drug dealer, Mr Gold. Throughout the movie, Tony Luk wears a black leather trench coat, a porkpie hat, and a dark dress shirt. The Cantonese matinee idol who plays him manages, with an insouciant smirk and some kind of twinkling voodoo, to make looking like the saxophone player in a talk-show band from the eighties a state to be envied. To complement his idiosyncratic style, Luk smokes a pipe and spends his weekends listening to old dramatizations of Shakespearean tragedies on LP. Tony is accompanied by his partner, Bobby Chang. Bobby has not only saved Tony Luk's life several times in the back story, but his family adopted Luk as a child when his parents died in a car crash. The film consists of violent gun fights interspersed with Luk's affairs with trashy but wisecracking women, each with a different physical defect: he sleeps with one woman with an artificial arm, another who wears an eye patch, and then another with Bell's palsy. Eventually, Tony and Bobby seize Mr Gold's shipment of heroin from a Bangkok shipping container, but Bobby is shot and hospitalized. Breaking all protocol, Tony surrenders his badge and barges into Mr Gold's heavily secured, luxury penthouse building. He finds Mr Gold sitting in the movie room of his penthouse, eating popcorn. Mr Gold invites Tony to sit down and taunts him with details about his wife, then plays a short film in which Bobby is seduced by Tony's dead wife, who was blackmailed into the betrayal by the drug dealer. Tony kills Mr Gold, but takes no pleasure in it. He returns to the hospital right before Bobby dies and hushes him before he can attempt a confession. The film ends with Tony listening to a hammy recital of *Othello* by a performer who makes William Shatner sound dignified and nuanced.

"He looked exactly like that when he was young," I said to Hadley over the final credits. She was puzzled by the film, if not bored, and had buried her face against my arm during the film's goriest moments, like the screwdriver stabbing. "I mean, Oliver."

"Really?" Hadley asked.

"I've seen photos. He looks exactly like Tony Luk."

"So this was the film he co-wrote?"

"Yeah."

"Which part did he write?"

"The Shakespeare was all his. Chew was responsible for the violent scenes."

"Do you think he was as sad as Tony Luk in the film?"

"Nah, that's just the movies."

"Was he as romantic?" she asked me.

And then I remembered what my mother had told me a few days earlier. "He liked to kiss with his eyes open," I repeated to Hadley.

Hadley laughed. "He was a twelve-year-old."

A couple of weeks later, on what would have been my father's fifty-eighth birthday, I spent the day getting ready for my first dinner party without Claire. Did Hadley know it was his birthday? I didn't think it was worth asking. Not that it would be an elaborate affair. Only my mother and Uncle Charlie had been invited, and for dinner I was serving my shrimp-chicken curry, a dish that I could prepare if I were brain dead. Having taken the afternoon to buy groceries and a bottle of wine for Uncle Charlie, I started sautéing chopped onions in a saucepan. Cheap Trick was playing. The phone rang.

"Malcolm?"

"Hello, Vanessa."

"Oh, the usual catastrophes and failures," she answered. "I could tell you, but then you'd die of heartbreak—or carbon monoxide poisoning." Instead of bitterly false laughter, she snorted as though she were inhaling a chick pea. "Excuse me. I'm a little phlegmy today—there's a smog warning in effect."

"How can I help you, Vanessa? Is there something wrong with your kitchen sink?" In the past two weeks, I had gone to her place to install a new computer in her home office, unclog her sink, and—after a million web searches—fix her faulty doorbell. Vanessa paid me twelve dollars an hour for her handiwork and the extra hour I would spend afterwards talking to her. I was neither rude nor rich enough to refuse her.

"Actually, this is about business. I think I have some work for you—if you're interested."

"What is it?" I asked.

"There's a new lounge that opened last month, Totem, but business is slow and the place has been overloaded with mouth-breathers in sweatpants and hockey jerseys. The manager wants to re-brand the place by hiring some metro guys to hang around the bar and talk to single women."

"This isn't stripping, is it?"

"Not unless you want it to be."

"Why does everyone say that?"

"Malcolm, I'm joking. Seriously, even Marcus Schenkenberg did this kind of stuff in Milan—in his heyday, no less. It's totally legitimate."

"What's the rate?" I asked.

"He's willing to pay you and Clint eighty dollars, cash, to be at the club from nine to one, plus you get two drinks each."

"That's not bad." I could smell the onions burning in my saucepan. "Listen, I have to go. I'm getting ready for a dinner party."

"You're having people over? Splendid."

"Just my mother and a family friend."

"Your mother must be a delight."

"She is, but—"

"And are you preparing dinner?"

"Yes, but—"

"What are you making?"

"Chicken and shrimp curry."

"Seafood is divine."

I knew why she was stalling. "Vanessa, do you want to come over?"

"I certainly don't want to trouble you."

"Not at all."

"This is very last-minute. I have other plans."

"Of course."

"A ladies' night. Some cheesecake and political discussion."

"I understand."

"But I can cancel." I gave her my address and buzzer number and told her to arrive at seven.

I made dinner, cleared my kitchen table, took a nap, and brushed my teeth. At a little after seven, Mom and Uncle Charlie arrived together, behaving the way they did when my father was around—my mother politely deflecting his muzzled flirtation. It was their first visit to my apartment since Claire left.

Uncle Charlie was wearing a tweed jacket and powder-blue shirt with the top three buttons undone. "As he pulled me in a headlock, I was briefly overwhelmed by his underarm smell. 'It's fabulous Fabio,'" he gasped in an effeminate trill.

He presented me with a bottle of Maotai. "It's a Chinese rice wine," explained. "You're too young to remember it, but Richard Nixon drank Maotai on his trip to China in 1972. It was a favourite of your father's, back in Hong Kong."

"No, it wasn't," I said.

My mother looked girlish in a maroon turtleneck and cuffed

black jeans, but she parsed my dwelling shrewishly. "I had wanted to buy you some plants," she told me. "But here"—with a stingy laugh, she handed me a bathmat—"is something you can't kill."

I chose to ignore that. "Can I get you a drink?"

Uncle Charlie brandished his bottle of Maotai. "Why don't you bring me a glass?"

I poured three glasses of red wine and asked them to sit down.

"What have you been doing with yourself?" Uncle Charlie asked me. "Any career news?"

"He's been working a lot," my mother answered for me. "Tell him about your modelling work."

I showed him some pictures in my book.

"For many gals, this is wank material," Uncle Charlie said, downing his wine. "What's Claire got that's so great?"

"She's dating this salsa-dancing novelist named Seamus."

Uncle Charlie gasped. "Forget about it. Listen, this weekend"— he wagged his finger between us—"me and you."

My mother, turning from the window, shook her head. "What's this all about?"

"Nothing," I said to my mom.

Vanessa arrived shortly afterwards, her arms outstretched with a pot of poinsettias. "I saw this and I knew I had to buy it for you."

First I introduced her to my mother.

"Your mother is gorgeous, Malcolm," she said with a stage whisper. She turned to Uncle Charlie. "Vanessa Bryce, charmed."

Handing Vanessa a glass of wine, I explained that Uncle Charlie was a family friend.

"You've done well for Malcolm," he said. "You must be quite the agent."

"Well," she explained, "it's a steep learning curve—trial and error and error, I say." She tucked a lock of hair behind one ear and curled her bottom lip over her teeth. I braced myself as she let out another laugh. She took a sip of wine and winced. Her face was locked like a death mask.

"Are you all right?" I asked.

"Yes, yes," Vanessa explained. "I had some ... well, after I had myself *refreshed*"—she made a sweeping motion along her cheeks to behind her ears—"it caused some nerve damage. For whatever reason, red wine causes muscle spasms. White wine isn't usually so bad."

"I don't think I have any."

"Would you like, um, some Maotai?" Charlie asked, grinning madly.

"It's all right. This is fine," Vanessa continued. "Anyway, as I was saying, I'm pretty new to the business. My husband founded the agency."

"So you work with your husband?"

"He died last year." She took a gulp of the wine and shook her head quickly. "I'm presently unattached."

Uncle Charlie's leer was complicated by a sympathetic crinkling of his eyes. "So sorry to hear about it."

"Oh, no," she said, and with little prodding described the circumstances of her husband's unseemly demise. "Once I settled with his former partner and assumed controlling interest of the business, I figured I'd try my hand at it. I always thought I had an eye for talent."

The difference between his regular leer and the look he had on his face now, when his interest was piqued, was very minute and required the same sort of visual intuition needed to distinguish a pair of identical twins. I shielded my eyes from the harsh glare of his jaundiced face. "Well, I like what I see," he said.

A point of red appeared on each side of Vanessa's face. She took another sip from her wine and tried to maintain the same expression.

After dinner, my mother brought out a Black Forest cake from a Chinatown bakery before she excused herself to use the washroom. When the washroom door opened, I followed her into my den.

"What's on your mind?" I said.

She stood by the sliding doors of the terrace. Parting the Venetian blinds with her hands, she looked out at the streetlights.

"Nothing out of the ordinary," she said.

"Look," I said, pointing to my desk. "Your painting."

Her nose wrinkled in delight. "I painted it about four years ago, in the fall. One night, just after dusk, the moon appeared over the city. It was pretty. I paint things because they're pretty; I know I'm no great artist. I drove to Queen Elizabeth Park, at a spot above the city, and walked until I found a spot I liked. I stared at the moon until it was covered by clouds, then went home and tried to paint what I'd seen."

"I think it's pretty, too. Have you ever heard of the ancient Chinese poet Li Po? He wrote poems about wine. There's a legend about how he died. He supposedly drowned on a boat trying to embrace the moon."

"He probably died of liver disease," my mother answered. (This was true. I later confirmed it on the Internet.) My mother looked at me with her loveliest expression, I thought, a combination of urgency and tenderness, and sighed. "Promise me you won't see her again. Don't see that girl. I don't want you to see her."

"Mom—"

Her eyes grew dusky. "Just say you won't."

"Okay."

When we returned to my living room, Vanessa and Uncle Charlie were watching his sexual harassment training video.

"Have you given any thought to doing more television work?" Vanessa asked him. "You really are good. It takes tremendous skill to be so unappealing."

Uncle Charlie raised an eyebrow. "You think so?"

Vanessa dug through her handbag for a card. "Give me a call." She made the kind of face you might see in a dentist's chair and turned her head from us as she took another sip of wine, her shoulders hunching as she winced once more. "Your talents shouldn't go unexploited."

She left shortly afterwards, followed by my mother and Uncle Charlie. I put the dishes and glasses in the sink. Out of curiosity I tried some of the Maotai. It tasted like tequila cut with lighter fluid, like something that would give me testicular cancer. I watched television and, by twelve-thirty, was ready for bed. I was asleep at two a.m. when I got a phone call from Sheila, Hadley's mother. She wanted to know whether I'd seen Hadley tonight, or if she were at my house.

"I got home from my night class at eleven and Had wasn't around," she told me. "She didn't leave a message at home with Arnie. It's a school night. I mean, I'm sure she's fine. She's probably out with friends. Of course, Krista doesn't know where she is. Or if she does, she didn't tell me. And I don't have the number of Marco's parents—you don't have it, by any chance?

I swallowed a yawn and told her I didn't. I figured she was with Marco, the same way I'd spent all my time at her age with Cindy Arau.

"Well, this is getting out of hand. She's been staying out late for the past week. It's going to affect her marks. And I hardly see her as it is, between my work and night school. It's as though she's avoiding me."

I told her that wasn't true.

"Malcolm, anything could happen. Anything. She could be hurt or raped or beaten up. Who knows? I can't do a single thing. Not a single thing."

She continued speaking; I began to hear her only in fragments. "Doesn't listen to me anymore," she was telling me as I closed my eyes. "And just one night of the week I'd like it if we could eat like a family, especially now that Arnie's back in the house. Just one night. But no. Wants to see Marco or Krista—even you she'd rather hang out with than me. Tell her to get her university applications ready and what does she do? Tells me she wants to spend a summer digging trenches in … God knows where. Can't speak Spanish. If she doesn't get into university? Smart, but if her grades drop, they won't let her in. What then? Become an administrative assistant like me? She thinks life's one big party, I tell you. Maybe I should stay home more often. What do you think? Arnie says I'm working too hard. Wants me to relax, because he makes enough money. Why we got divorced in the first place. God, where could she be? What could she be doing? Nothing good. Drugs, booze, sex. Nothing good. Wait, hold on a sec. Yeah, I think she's home. Okay, I'm going to kill her. That's right. Okay, thanks for talking, Malcolm. Good night."

CHAPTER EIGHT

I CONSIDERED KEEPING my promise to my mother not to see Hadley. I resolved to be more self-sufficient. But then Hadley called and reminded me that I'd promised to drive her and Krista to the university, where the first information session for their trip to Guyana was held. A program coordinator led a short talk about Guyana, with general information about the climate and population and what to expect from the program—not only the fundraising component and the hundred hours of local community service once the project ended, but some security issues about the capital city, Georgetown, and the limit on cash each participant was allowed to bring. Most of the volunteers were a few years older than my half-sister, who would turn eighteen only a month before the program started. One member recently back from Costa Rica—a lean, tanned man with a scraggly beard—presented a slide show. There were handout sheets, crackers and cheese, warm ginger ale, and a question-and-answer period.

Afterward, at the deli in the student union basement, I bought Hadley and Krista some vegetarian Jamaican patties.

Krista looked down at her hot chocolate, clinking her spoon against the mug. "It doesn't seem like too much fun," she said.

I'd had the same thought, and was glad she'd voiced it, even if Hadley responded with a look that didn't belong on her face—the kind of rage-soaked, paranoid expression that you could use to sell pepper spray and home-surveillance devices.

"It's not a vacation," she told Krista, flatly and soberly.

"I know that."

"We'll be able to do some good."

"You're right."

"It was your idea."

"*I know*," Krista said.

"Don't chicken out on me."

"I won't."

Hadley kept watching her, the eyebrows over her large, finger-cymbal eyes knitted, until she was able to exact another promise from Krista that she wouldn't abandon her. It surprised me how shrill she was about this trip, and it hurt me that she was so eager to leave everyone behind.

"Won't you be sad to leave Marco for a summer?" I asked.

"I guess," she said.

"Were you out with him yesterday?"

"What?" she asked me.

"Your mom called me last night—late."

Hadley's face shrivelled in embarrassment. "I guess I've been avoiding Mom a lot."

Krista laughed coyly. "You can't get enough of Marco."

She responded with what I perceived to be hesitation. "Definitely. He's great."

"Is he coming to Liam's party?"

"I didn't bother asking him—do you think he wants to spend any time with Liam?"

"I guess not."

"And I'm only going because you want to meet that university guy." Hadley said this forcefully, as though we needed to be convinced.

Krista let out sigh. "He's hot," she said. "He's a swimmer."

"We're swimmers, too."

"Yeah, but he's hot."

"We have different taste in boys."

"Definitely. You like hairy guys."

"Not really."

"What about Marco?"

"He's just one boyfriend. Liam's not hairy."

"I like smooth guys." Krista looked at me when she said this.

Throughout their discussion of male aesthetics, I watched some of the female university students pass through the deli. As one beautiful woman withdrew from sight, another one appeared.

"Like what you see?" Krista asked.

Hadley laughed.

I shrugged.

"You should let me fix you up with my sister."

"What makes you think she'd like me?"

Krista started giggling. "Trust me. She likes everyone."

When I agreed to work at Totem, a preppie nightclub with kitschy pseudo-gothic chandeliers and mounted animal heads on the walls, it was to pay my own bills and to put my presence out there, but I could barely sell it to myself.

At the club, staff dressed in black jackets and cocktail dresses attended to the patrons, most of whom sat at tables or shot pool in the back. The dance floor and the bar were empty. When I arrived, Clint, my friend from modelling school, was already sitting at the bar, flirting with a blonde as she waited for a drink the colour of Windex. The blonde, who fidgeted with her hands as though she were in need of a lapdog to pet, cocked her head back and cackled, even though Clint was about as funny as a speed bump. Once the bartender arrived with her drink, she borrowed his pen and wrote something on the back of Clint's hand. As she returned to a table full of her pretty friends, she looked back at him once more and waved.

I assumed Clint had been a great kick-boxer, because his face was smooth and free of wear; or maybe he only took kick-boxing classes. From a Cree grandmother, he had inherited high cheek-bones, tawny skin, and dark eyes that, in his better moments, reminded me of Richard Gere shoulder-rolling and reaching for his pistol at the end of the 1983 remake of *Breathless*. He was broad-chested and long-limbed, and dressed in wool slacks that fit snugly around his narrow waist, a black pullover top, and a ropy gold chain around his neck. Although his vision was perfect, he wore a pair of tortoise-shell eyeglasses to add a garnish of distinction. When Clint finally noticed me, he brought the back of his hand to my face in a mock karate chop.

"Did you see that?" he asked me.

I checked my watch. It was ten minutes to eight, our shift hadn't even started. "Good work."

"This might be the best job I ever have. What are you drinking?"

"Gin on the rocks."

"Marc," he said, nodding to a bartender with mutton-chop side-burns and a ponytail. "Gin on the rocks and another grapefruit juice."

"You teetotalling?"

He sighed. "I'm on day four of an eight-day cleansing diet. My caloric intake is restricted to borscht and fruit juice. No liquor."

I asked him how he was doing, and braced myself for any good news he might have. He was, give or take a magazine spread, at the same stage of his career as I was. Between auditions, he worked as a bike courier and lived with two other people in Chinatown. He asked me about my work and congratulated me, half-heartedly

I think, on my own magazine appearance. We spent some time grousing about other classmates who had become more successful. One of them was in a commercial for an erectile dysfunction pill and had found a glitzy New York agent. There was someone else who won a part on a pilot in Los Angeles. This killed the ten minutes until our first night of work began.

The manager, Maxwell, was younger than I'd expected him to be—at most, thirty. He was South Asian, had thick, hairy arms, and ambled toward us with an unhurried, bowlegged gait. Looking us over and deeming us suitable, he shook our hands with the kind of lead-heavy grip you'd use to strangle a woodland creature.

"The bar doesn't fill up for another hour," he said over the blip-filled Top-Forty song coming out of the speakers, "so you have time to coordinate. Go and see whether any lovely ladies want to dance. Buy them a drink—drinks are free for them, you both get half off after your comps—do some close-talking, grind your crotch up to them. You can work individually or you could be like Batman and Robin, if they were heterosexual. No offence. I don't care. By the end of the night I expect you to have talked to ten women each. Whatever you do with them afterwards is none of my concern. I mean, don't physically abuse them. Not unless they're into that."

Once Maxwell left, Clint and I backed up against the bar and scouted the room for lonely women. That night, it was like searching a beach for sand. Most of them sat in groups, laughing with managed cheer over their martinis. Dread danced inside me like the flakes in a snow globe. Claire and I had been together for two years. I'd started feeling again as though I'd like to be close to a woman—my skin felt brittle from lack of touch—but as I scoped Totem, I became dizzy.

And then the blonde that Clint was talking to pulled him over to their table. Clint asked me to join him. Not seeing an alternative, I followed.

The blonde's name was Willa and, with her arm looped snugly around Clint's waist, she introduced us. "Girls, this is Clint—he's a model." The girls made impressed noises, and Willa shot them a possessive look. Before dragging Clint to the dance floor, she turned to me. "And this is Clint's friend—I'm sorry, what's your name?"

"Malcolm."

I was introduced to Lucinda, Ellen, Rita, and Carole. I was not exactly sure who was who.

"So," one of the girls asked, "what do you do?"

Not wanting to tell them I modelled and ride off Clint's hyperbole, I told them that I worked at a record store.

It was as though I'd farted. Three of these women made stinkfaces and turned their backs to me. The one remaining, Rita, was seated closest to me and most likely found me too much bother to avoid. Rita wore glasses. She had hair cut just above the shoulders that flicked out at the end and a severe, oval face. My palms grew sweaty as I talked to a woman for the first time since Claire moved out. Some of this apprehension faded when I realized Rita was extremely drunk, and short, repetitive sentences would suffice. Someone at the table ordered another round of martinis and we all got drunker as the club quickly started to fill.

"So, you like music?" Rita asked.

"Yeah."

Rita started bobbing her head to the song. I looked to the dance floor, which was now starting to crowd, and saw Willa grinding against Clint. "So, what do you think of this song?" she asked me.

I decided to be agreeable and bobbed my head, too. "It's okay."

She nodded. "It's a classic song." She took a sip of her martini and traced her finger along its stem. "What do you think of martinis?"

I had to shout over the music. "They're strong."

She nodded again. "I think they're classic. I think martini glasses are classic, too—if you look at them the right way they look bikini bottoms, don't you think?"

"Yeah."

Her eyes lingered over me and her top lip curled. "So, what do you think about connections?"

"Connections?"

She laughed. "You know, connections are when two people connect. What do you think about them?"

"I think they're—classic?"

"Me too. Do you want to dance?"

I followed her onto the dance floor half-way through a Jay-Z song I liked, and she ground her knee against my crotch like a mortar on a pestle through the rest of the song.

"You're a good dancer," Rita said, which was far from true.

Across the room, Willa looked as though she were trying to force-feed her face into Clint's mouth. Rita moved under the flashing lights of the dance floor, and I was able to get a good look at her for the first time. She was pretty, but priggish-looking. The people who moved from one personality extreme to another—from meek to boisterous, from genial to morose—were always the scariest to me. Claire was like that, a self-serious woman who couldn't stop laughing and hugging people when she drank. To stop myself from thinking about her, I forced myself to slow-dance with Rita.

"Do you think I'm pretty?" She was barely five feet tall and had to stand on her toe-tips to whisper this into my ear.

"Yes."

"Do you have a girlfriend?"

I thought about mentioning Claire, but instead I just shook my head. "How about you?"

"Yes. No. Not anymore."

I told her I was sorry. "For how long?"

"Two years."

My engagement had recently ended, and we also had dated two years, but I didn't tell her that, either. She pried her face from my upper abdomen and gazed up at me appreciatively.

"I swear I must have seen you somewhere."

I excused myself. Totem was now thick with the kind of abrasive meatheads that Clint and I were hired to flush out, but they had numbers. Retreating to the men's room, I noticed the line of women waiting to use the facilities. Passing them by I saw a face that seemed familiar, but I was drunk and she turned her head too quickly for me to confirm that inkling. And, even in my pickled frame of mind, I knew that no acquaintance worth reacquainting with would be at such a sleazy place.

The men's room was full, too, though I did not have to wait for a urinal. As I stood, legs astride, someone tapped me on the shoulder.

I shuddered, surprised, and turned around as I zipped up. It was Sandrine, my ex-girlfriend from Montreal.

"Hey," she said, lightly. "I thought it was you." She had the same old smile and the same impatience with decorum, but her appearance had changed drastically since I had last seen her, about two years earlier when she left for Toronto under deeply unpleasant circumstances. Gone were the chopped bangs she wore across her forehead, gone was the lip-ring. Her face was more angular now, and she had lost some of the soft, doughy flesh that made her as appealing as a plush animal. Her clothes were conservative but stylish, her handbag and her shoes shiny and expensive. "How have you been, Malcolm?"

"Good," I said. "Are you visiting?"

"I live here now. I found work here for two months. I was hoping to run into you—though, not in a place like this."

"A restroom?"

"No," Sandrine said, amused by how drunk I was. "I never thought I'd see you at a bar like this."

"Me neither."

"I'm here with co-workers. We're about to leave this dump."

"Me too."

A group of her co-workers—older women with marble-smooth faces—were waiting at the coat check. I wrote my phone number and e-mail address on the back of an expired membership card for the Cinémathèque. Sandrine took a step into the street to hail a cab. I glanced at the card she gave me. She worked as a casting agent for commercials.

"How's that girlfriend of yours?" she asked.

I shook my head. "I wouldn't know."

"What did you do to *her*?" she asked me.

The guilt hardened inside me like a muscle. "This time, nothing," I told her. Then I reconsidered. "Well, no one thing."

She slipped the card into her bag. "You sure made that one thing count with me."

I was exhausted, but too wired to go to sleep when I returned home and was still awake when Hadley called me at one in the morning. She was at Liam's party and had a friend with a Jeep (it was the snowiest winter in recent history) who could bring her here. I offered to drive her home, but she had missed her curfew. She was a little drunk and not in the right state of mind to incur her mother's wrath. By the time she arrived at one-thirty, tramping in snow from her rubber boots, I had folded out the futon and brought out bedding from the closet. In a box of Claire's belongings that she had never claimed, I found an oversized T-shirt in which she used to sleep.

We lay on the futon with the duvet up to our necks and watched *Mary Poppins*.

"Why was this Oliver's favourite movie?" Hadley asked me. "Did he watch it as a child?"

"Actually, he saw it when he was a teenager, but he liked the singing. His favourite character was Dick Van Dyke. When we moved to Canada, and he was looking for a job, he said he actually considered getting into chimney sweeping. My mom never really got it. She thought we had a Julie Andrews fetish."

"Do you?"

I looked at her like she was crazy, but in a funny way, I did. As a child, I couldn't help but place our family in the movie. My father was the banker preoccupied with work, my mother was the suffragette who was ineffectual at home, and I was the kids who misbehaved out of neglect. Hadley watched the film with a hard-set expression, as though she were studying an artifact from a lost civilization.

"You should call your mother soon," I told her.

"I will, in a minute," she said. "I want to make her sweat a little first."

"How was the party?" I asked her.

"Absurdly icky."

"How so?"

She stuck out her tongue. "Krista spent the whole night sucking face with the boy she thinks is so hot but really isn't. Plus, Liam was in attendance."

"You smell like an ashtray," I told her.

"Everyone was smoking around me," she said.

I didn't believe her. "How much did you drink?"

"Only a couple glasses of champagne."

"You smell like a winery."

She sniffed at me. "Well, you smell like spray tan and perfume."

"Does spray tan have a smell?" I asked her, fully serious.

The phone started ringing.

"That's probably your mom," I said, sliding off the futon.

"Don't tell her I'm here, okay."

"I can't do that."

"I swear I'll call her in the morning."

I picked up the phone and half-listened.

"This is getting crazy, Malcolm. She said she be would home by one. Never here. Spent more time over the holidays with Marco and his family than with me and Arnie. No appreciation. No respect. I have to resort to calling you and Krista. Never tells me where she's going, never says when she's coming back. Now she's teaching swimming lessons on top of water polo. And there's that whole Guyana business. Don't see her at all. When she does get home, it's after I get back from night school. She says she's studying with Marco. That Marco—it's all his fault. I thought Liam was bad. But Marco just wants to drag her down to his level. Nothing good. Follows her around and plays his guitar. Hairy as an ape. Why can't she study at home? Her grades haven't slipped yet, but they might. I had to make sure she got her university applications out. The girl can't even take care of herself, and she wants to go to school in Ottawa or Halifax? She wants to study human kinetics, do you know that?

With that brain she has, and she wants to be a P.E. teacher? Unbelievable. She could be an engineer or a doctor. Breaking my heart."

If she'd shut up for a second, I'd have told her Hadley was five feet away from me, but I never got the chance.

"For Christ's sake, I'd be happy if she became a history teacher," she continued. "So proud. Overjoyed. You don't know how important it would be for me, not having gone to university. I had to support my parents. Deadbeat boyfriends. Your father was very nice to put some money away for her education—not that he paid much in the way of her food and shelter before—but at least she won't have to go in debt. Bless your father, he was a good man. She used to come home from school, so excited about what she learned. She'd run into the house, tell me about dinosaurs or fractions. She always loved school."

As she yammered on, my thoughts see-sawed toward the idea of Christmas two weeks away, then back to my memory of the previous Christmas. As I mentioned earlier, the holidays weren't a big deal for my mother and father, but last year, for Claire's sake, my mother tried to recreate the holidays for her with a tree, stockings, even a roasted goose. There was something studied about it, as though aliens were trying to replicate a habitat for the humans they'd captured and placed in a zoo. Sitting down with my family and Uncle Charlie, who'd stapled himself to the couch next to an open bottle of Johnnie Walker Black, Claire could sense how unreal this situation was and how this effort made my father grumpy. Although she had been the one who didn't want to return to her family in Ottawa, to sit through her father's bloviations about how all the entrepreneurs of the world bank-rolled all the arts students of the world.

After chewing through dinner with monosyllabic comments and polite nods, Claire told my mother that she wanted to find a store still open that might have whipped cream for the pie she'd made. We had parked down the street. When I looked out the parlour window, the car was still there. She came back to the house fifteen minutes later, without whipped cream, and sat down next to my mother and me at the dining room table with a drawn, bleached face.

My father eased himself from his spot next to Uncle Charlie and asked Claire for a slice of her pie. He never ate dessert, not even the red bean soups that my aunts loved. He sat down and took one bite, set his fork on the plate as though he were signing a cheque, then took another bite.

"Charlie," he yelled across the house. "This is worth getting up for."

"I'm in the middle of something," Charlie yelled back.

"Well," he said, turning to Claire, "this is the first pie I've had since Malcom's mother almost poisoned me with her baking."

"I did not," my mother said.

My father ignored her. "We had just emigrated and lived in a basement. We didn't even have a proper kitchen, only a hot plate and a toaster oven. There were no microwaves back then. We were very poor. Neither of us had found a job, and our savings were running out."

"But it was such an adventure," my mother said, sighing. "We felt like explorers."

"I wanted to move back."

"You still do—"

"We were having trouble paying the rent, and the landlady was an immigrant herself, from Poland. She knew our situation and liked Malcolm's mom, so she offered to pay her for Chinese cooking lessons. But Eliza was a bad teacher."

My mother shook her head fiercely. "She wanted to learn how to cook chop suey and General Tso's chicken," she said.

My father sniffed. "You couldn't teach her that?"

"It would be like wearing yellowface."

My dad kept his incredulity in check, though it rippled on his face. "Well, she didn't want to *give* us money, so every once and a while she'd drop by with extra groceries that she bought, always by accident. A little piece of chicken. A pie shell."

My mother downed her glass of wine. "I was very young," she said, placing her hand on my father's arm. "I didn't know you had to cook the chicken first before you put in the pie shell."

"I was sick for *two* days," he said, laughing at her. "I lived by the toilet."

"You're being silly. You like to make that time seem so bad. But, admit it, some of it was fun. Wasn't it?"

"Not at all."

"Don't ruin the night."

"Okay, okay. Maybe a little."

My mother was pleased.

Claire had never seen my parents like this, the way my father could egg my mother on—the way my mother pouted until he was sweet to her. And when my father went for a second slice, she gladly offered to serve him. Even Uncle Charlie ambled back to the dining-room table.

The snow was thigh-high outside my window and still falling. By now, Hadley had fallen asleep on the futon while Dick Van Dyke was dancing with the other chimney sweeps. I turned off the TV. She was sleeping on her back, her hair fanned around her head like the points of a starfish. "So popular, never shy, always the girl who made sure the new girls didn't eat lunch alone," her mother continued. "Remember one report card that read, 'Hadley is a gift.' Still have it somewhere."

PART TWO

Pity

CHAPTER NINE

FOR A WHILE, IT seemed as though my mother had entered a period of genteel widowhood. When I spoke with her on the phone, she was preoccupied with yoga, preparing for the life-drawing class she was teaching at the community centre, and the idea of buying a medium-sized, hypoallergenic dog. She and a friend of hers, who'd also lost her husband, were talking about going to Venice. "I want a dog now," she told me. "But I don't want to leave him alone when I travel."

"I could watch the dog," I told her.

She shook her head. "When they're puppies, they imprint on you, so if you let someone else take care of him, the dog will never belong to you."

"That's not true," I said.

"When I was a child, I had a friend who went to Australia right after she got her dog. When she came back, the dog kept running away. I don't want my dog to think he has other options."

"Travel first, then."

"But then I have my class to teach."

The sadness in my mother was still evident, but now more subdued, and I felt less guilty for ignoring her request to stop seeing Hadley. But then, a few days after New Years, my mother called me, frantic and adamant that I come over immediately. I knew that voice, both terrifying and vulnerable, and I drove over. When I arrived, I found Uncle Don in the sitting room. He sat with his neck on the back of the couch and his knees spread apart, a copy of the duty-free catalogue on his lap. He looked over his reading glasses and grunted at me.

"How's it going?" I asked.

His eyes were opaque and smoky, like bottled cigarette smoke. When we were younger, he used to give my mother long, ass-patting hugs. "We're here on points," he answered. "I bought some points from a woman at my office. Her husband left her. I'm jetlagged, and we leave for Hong Kong tomorrow. The air in this city always makes me so sleepy. What's with the air in this city? It's so—so clean."

"How's work?"

"I hate teeth." He shrugged, unable to keep his eyes from returning to his duty-free catalogue. "Except for that, I get by."

"Can't you give me any peace?" my mother screamed in Cantonese from upstairs. "I've lost my husband."

"I've waited patiently. Someone needs to respect his wishes," said Aunt Mirabelle with a measured tone of voice that resembled my father's. "Where are they?"

"Go away. He belongs here."

"He never wanted to be here in the first place."

"You couldn't stand not having him all to yourself. You and your sister were always meddling."

My mother stomped down the steps with my aunt close behind. While my aunt looked weary and exasperated, my mother had that glow on her face she always had when she was arguing and had someone's attention. Throughout my father's life, she and Aunt Mirabelle always got along tensely. She and Aunt Paula doted on my father. He never screwed up in their eyes, and when he did— when he missed their birthdays or turned up late for dinners—they scrambled in search of others to blame, even if they had to take it themselves.

"Your father made a request that he be buried with the family," Aunt Mirabelle told me. "He *told me* your mother might not follow through. I'm here specifically for them."

Lately, my mother had kept the urn with my father's remains behind the couch in the front window, as though it were a dog waiting for its owner to return. My aunt had been stomping around the house looking for it, and it was right there behind my uncle. Aunt Mirabelle tried appealing to me. "I just want to follow your father's wishes to be with our parents. It's important for me, and for your Second Aunt, that he be with his family."

"We are his family," my mother said in a whisper. "Malcolm and I." It was clear she was saying to me what she'd already said to my aunt. "I need him here."

"He spent his life looking after you."

"You could never stand that he had his own family," my mother snapped back. "His own wife, his own life."

"Now that he's dead, can't you do the one thing he asked for? It's no wonder. No wonder—"

"What are you suggesting?" my mother growled.

My aunt had turned to her husband for support, and while he offered nothing but his frowning presence, she must have been looking hard enough at him to notice the urn behind him. She almost leapt across the room for it. She took the urn, bundled it in her arms, and announced to her husband that they were leaving. Uncle Don stood up on cue.

He nodded at me. "The rental car we have has a funny smell," he told me. "They better give me a discount."

My uncle went to hug my mother, but she thrust her hand at him and showed him the way to the door.

My mother disappeared upstairs. I was surprised she had given up so easily. I heard her talking to someone, her tone of voice breezy and nonchalant. "I knew it when she called," I could hear her saying. "I knew what she was after. Doesn't take no for an answer. Relentless. I don't know how you two could ever be related. Paula, too. The three of you are so dissimilar. Maybe that's why you were all so close." She came down with a blue tin that once held Danish butter cookies. "I knew she wouldn't leave without you. She'll probably be in Hong Kong when realizes what's in that urn."

"What's in the urn, Mom?" I asked her.

She looked up at me, surprised I was there. "Oh, nothing really. Just sand from a school playground. A little kitty litter, too."

After our run-in at Totem, I was ambivalent about seeing Sandrine again. In the New Year, when she got back from Toronto, we agreed to meet for a movie on the second Friday of 2009. To complicate matters further, I'd asked several discreet questions about her work and learned that, among other projects, she was preparing a new spring menswear campaign for her store. If she still didn't hate me, she could help me with my career.

Sandrine was on my mind when I met up for beers with Vanessa, who had been strangely silent over the holidays before inviting me out that night. As we stood outside an Irish pub waiting for her to finish her cigarette, I mentioned Sandrine and her job.

"You're saying she's an ex-girlfriend?" she asked. "Pretty girl?"

"Yes," I said.

"You like her still?"

"I'm not sure."

She stubbed out her cigarette and we returned to our pints of Kilkenny inside the pub, which served Imperial pints and had a full kitchen that made bangers and mash with so much care one felt vaguely guilty eating them. "So you're asking me whether you should sleep with her in order to get some work?" she asked.

"Well, I don't know whether she even likes me. There's a good chance she might despise me."

"Oh, just close your eyes and lay her one."

I raised an eyebrow at her and smiled. "I never knew you had such a salty tongue."

Vanessa made a sound like someone coughing out a live hamster. "Well, don't sleep with her," she insisted. "I'm not asking you to do anything you feel is wrong. But don't feel too guilty about making use of those you know."

I couldn't resist asking. "Do you think she'd use me in the campaign if we did it?"

"How would I know?"

"You're an agent."

She hung her head sheepishly. "I guess."

We had another pint and played darts. Sitting at the table next to us a fiddler and a guitarist played chirpy Celtic music. As we ended our second game, Vanessa turned to me and asked if I had heard from Uncle Charlie and, if so, whether he had mentioned her.

"We were an item over the holidays," she said.

"What?" I said.

"You heard me."

I groaned. "No."

"It was my first Christmas without Harold," she continued. "And there was a leak in the roof and the refrigerator was making a funny sound at night. I started smoking again. I figured something eventful would soon occur. I was either going to meet a man or get my thighs done." She let out a wistful sigh. "I'm not saying we were meant to be a couple, or any such nonsense, but I was hoping he'd return my calls. Or my faxes and registered letters to his office."

"Sorry," I said. "Haven't heard from him."

"He seemed so nice," she said.

"Really?"

"Very sweet."

"Uncle Charlie?" I asked.

She nodded. "Sensitive."

"Come on."

"How could I not sleep with someone who wept as he recited Emily Dickinson?"

"What?"

"I only wish he would've told me why he didn't want to see me anymore. Even if the excuse he gave was rubbish—it's the polite thing to do, don't you think?" She wiped the score of the last game from the chalkboard and handed me a dart. "Closest to bull starts the game."

I had an idea. "Let's ask Uncle Charlie why he stopped seeing you."

She put her finger to her mouth, a hesitant, though faintly pliable expression on her face. "But I've already tried."

"Let's go to his house."

"You know where he lives? We normally met at the bus stop."

At first, Vanessa decided she didn't want to harass him until I force-fed her a shot of Jägermeister, which caused that exquisitely pained wince to appear on her face. I knew Uncle Charlie was going to be monumentally livid. But I wanted to get back at him for our double date with Krystal and Rayelle. We left the bar and found a cab with a driver who waited for me to slurringly enunciate Uncle Charlie's address before speeding off.

Uncle Charlie opened his front door wearing flannel pyjamas, his thick hair untamed. When Vanessa appeared at the door, his face assumed a reeling, dumbstruck expression.

He closed his eyes and yawned into the heel of his hand. "Mac, do you know what time it is?" he asked.

Obviously, he thought this was my doing—he wasn't an idiot. But Vanessa stepped forward, expecting something from him. "I wanted to see you once more."

"You look well," he mumbled, his voice forming fog in the early morning chill.

"I wasn't hoping you'd marry me."

"I'm sorry. I'm very bad at returning calls, especially when I'm busy with work," he said, looking to me smugly, to say I would get no more sincere response than that.

Vanessa continued to look at Uncle Charlie, first with disdain, but also with disappointment and tenderness. She took a step toward him and placed her hand on his cheek, then took two steps back, looked at him once more, and turned toward our idling taxi.

As we walked away, we could hear Uncle Charlie call out, his Brooklyn accent as foreign as a sitar on a cold Canadian night.

That January, Hadley had been grounded by her mother, and outside of her time at the pool, she remained at home during the week. On Saturdays and at school, and only then, could she see Marco. Hadley had no choice but to obey when Sheila threatened to cancel her trip to Guyana.

And I had no choice but to spend time with her at the pool.

"We can't take too long," she said, "or Mom—did I tell you how much I hate her?—Mom will throw a fit. Well, she won't mind so much if I'm with you. She likes you a lot."

"Really?"

"Don't seem so pleased. She says you remind her of Oliver."

"And that's good?"

"I guess."

I stepped into the pool until I was in waist deep.

"Let's try putting your head underwater, okay?"

I nodded hesitantly.

"Okay, go."

I crouched in the water and put my head under. After only a second, I was standing up and gasping.

"Let's try that again."

I tried again and became less afraid. Then I learned to tread water, keeping my hand on the edge of the pool, and then on my own for a few seconds.

"You're doing a great job."

To show how naturally buoyant people are, she helped me onto my back and let me float in the water. Guiding me forward, she put her hand on the back of my head, her face above mine.

"Okay, start kicking."

I started moving forward and she let me go. I hesitated for a moment, but managed to stay afloat.

"Look at you."

After we changed, I drove her home. Outside, the rain turned into pellets of hail smacking against the windshield. We were listening to a local folk singer on the university radio station.

Hadley turned to me, in her hoodie and sweatpants. "You look preoccupied, Malcolm."

"I'm supposed to meet up with an ex tomorrow. The woman I was seeing before Claire."

"Like on a date?"

"No. Well. I don't know."

"So, it ended messy, like me and Liam, right?"

"Um, sort of. Things went down." I trailed off in what, I thought, was a pointed manner.

"What happened?" she asked anyway. "Did she sleep around on you?"

"No."

"Did she steal something from you?"

"No."

"Did she secretly tape the two of you having sex and show it to all her friends?"

"Actually, it wasn't like that."

She nodded gravely. "I see." She paused. "What did you do?"

"I don't want to tell you. I don't want you to hate me."

"That's impossible," Hadley said. "But she wants to see you anyway?"

"Yeah."

"Have you apologized to her?"

"Not yet."

We arrived at the front of her house, where I let my hand-me-down Saab idle. "The first thing you should do before you even sit down to meet with her—before you even say hello—is apologize to her. If she wants to see you, then she's willing to forgive you."

"You think?" I asked her.

She nodded, one hand on the door handle. "Definitely."

"Thanks for the advice. What do I owe you?"

"Your undying gratitude."

I was aware of Sandrine Jennings weeks before we were introduced. The first time I saw her, she'd been drinking Long Island Iced Teas at a bar with some friends that I knew from my dorm. The back of her canary-yellow tank top was damp with humidity, her breasts jutting out absentmindedly. She had an eyebrow ring and a nose piercing that she was already phasing out. She was not exactly luminescent—it wasn't a glow that came from her—but her face was perpetually flushed, as though she were teetering between amusement and outrage. There was a gaggle of men spiralled around her—boyish men who wore tight, kitschy t-shirts, burly, hairy guys in hockey jerseys, sophisticated, sneering men, and forceful, foultempered men. Men old enough to be graduate students and boys like me. She treated them equally, like comic foils, each of them a potential punch line. Her drunken eyes seemed to swim independently of each other, and as she threw her darts, one foot would leave the floor as though she were being kissed. Holding her cigarette above her shoulders, she flaunted her pale, slinky hands. She saw me sitting with my friends, always silent while they chattered. She glanced in my direction as though daring me to approach her. I didn't have the opportunity until months later, when someone introduced us at a party.

"You look like somebody who says what they mean," she told me. "I'm someone who says mean things."

Not knowing it was a line that she'd used in the past, I had the immediate impression that she was Dorothy Parker reincarnated with body piercings and a cocaine-induced twitchiness. We spent three hours talking. Early on in the conversation, I needed to pee, but wrenched my legs together and held it because I didn't want to surrender my audience with her. At first, our discussion was safely impersonal. We talked only about school, books, and bands, as we conducted due diligence on each other's taste. I told her that I was listening to a Brazilian singer-songwriter named Caetano Veloso. I was impressed that she knew about him.

"That's pretty sexy stuff," she said. "Is that what you listen to when you bring girls to your room?"

"Sometimes," I said, not wanting to mention Cindy Arau. "It's maybe too obviously sexy. You'd be trying too hard."

This observation seemed to pique her interest in me. "Yeah, I think the best kind of music for hooking up is stuff that makes you happy and want to smile, not the kind that makes you depressed or swoony. Fast hard music, good dance music."

"The romantic stuff is for stressed-out moms taking bubble baths," I said.

"So, you're not a romantic? I see you as one of those guys who spend hours making mix-CDs for girls with no taste. That's not true?"

I tried to laugh it off, but she had decided I was harmless. I suddenly knew how it felt to be a kitten or a box of mini-muffins. If our conversation had run its course, at least I could get up to pee. "It's true," I told her. "You've figured me out."

"Don't pout, Malcolm. I wouldn't kick you out of bed for making me a CD," she said. "What was the last movie you watched?"

"*Mary Poppins,*" I told her after hesitating.

She laughed. "Really?"

"I was back in Vancouver with my dad. It's his favourite movie."

"My dad likes James Bond movies," she told me.

"Connery or Moore?"

"He likes Roger Moore," she said, looking sheepish about her dad's Bond preferences. "But he didn't think George Lazenby really got a fair shake."

"Are you close to your dad?" I asked her.

She hesitated, looking at me as though I were a gap between buildings that she wasn't sure she could safely leap across.

"I worshipped my dad," she confessed.

Sandrine grew up outside Montreal, but when she was ten, her parents divorced. Her mom got sole custody and found a job in Toronto. They lived in a dreary basement apartment and would eat macaroni and cheese every other day. The first few months she was preoccupied by overwhelming homesickness and misery and called her father constantly. When he wasn't home to answer the phone, she would watch *Octopussy* on DVD.

She moved back to Montreal for school and to spend time with him, but he had remarried and was busy with a new family. Every month, she would go to his house for dinner, but these gatherings were stilted. Her father was far more comfortable with her half-siblings than he was with her. It slayed her.

"I need to pee," I blurted out as she talked about her father.

The switch had flipped. She drew her wineglass to her mouth and returned to her earlier, more sardonic self. "Are you asking me if you want me to watch?" she asked. "You're more interesting than I suspected."

At the end of the night, we exchanged phone numbers. Afterward, going home alone, I was afraid to sleep out of a senseless fear that my good fortune would flee in my dreams.

I would've waited longer to see her again, to be cool, but she woke me up the next day and insisted I come over for pancakes. I rode my bike to her house and she answered the door in a pink polka-dot housecoat, a cigarette in her mouth. In the kitchen, her four housemates were already eating blueberry and banana pancakes and drinking champagne from jam jars. The roommates nodded amiably at me, then resumed their private conversation.

"Are you hungry?" she asked me.

I nodded.

She gave me two pancakes and a jar of champagne. I started eating while she took the last remaining seat in the kitchen—a foot stool by the counter.

"Are you always up so early?" I asked her. "I was sleeping when you called."

"Yeah. I wish I could sleep in. It's not good for my reputation to be seen up and awake before noon."

"Have you already eaten?" I asked her.

"Yeah, but I like to watch people eat. I like the noises people make when they eat. It freaks them out to be watched like that."

Her roommates cleared out and we did the dishes while listening to Paul Anka on an oldies station. She wanted to walk in the park and then go thrifting, but I had made plans that morning with Cindy Arau, who was becoming increasingly depressed about the cold and the weight she'd gained since moving. Eventually, her depression would lead to our break-up and her return to Vancouver at the end of the term.

"Still with your high-school girlfriend, right?" she asked me.

I wanted to admit anything but the truth.

"I don't get involved with guys with girlfriends," she told me. "We can be friends, though." She fingered the purple fleece sweater I wore underneath my ski jacket and shook her head in disgust at my khaki cargo pants. "These clothes would look good on you if they weren't so ugly."

Beleaguered with work, Sandrine cancelled our Friday movie, and we made plans for Saturday instead. I had the feeling she wasn't completely sure she wanted to see me. Eventually, when we did meet for lunch, we talked so much that I couldn't finish my chicken salad sandwich. It had always been that way with her.

Our conversations lurched sideways into tangents and associations. Before running into her at Totem, I hadn't spoken to her in nearly three years, and we spent much of our time together remembering almost everything that had happened between us. We kept talking in order to avoid the thing I needed to apologize for. Sandrine listened patiently to my stories about my father, my-half sister, and my ex-fiancée. Not that I expected to speak at length about any of them, but I did. In the past two-and-a-half years, she had met and broken up with a boyfriend, found a job she liked, and moved to the UK. After working as an intern at a design house in London and, realizing that her kooky designs no longer appealed even to her own tastes, she found herself drawn to the marketing side of the industry. She was hired for her current job, finding faces for print campaigns and television commercials in Vancouver, through a family friend.

"Do you ever think the old version of yourself would hate the current version of yourself?" she asked me.

"The old version of me would throw a brick at the current version," I said. "Then again, it's because of you that I wanted to be a model."

She hoisted her eyebrows. "I wouldn't want to be responsible for wrecking your life."

I had brought some of my clippings with me, but she changed the subject before I got a chance to show them to her.

"You've changed a lot," she told me in a way that suggested she was holding back something else. "I didn't see it last month at that club, but you have." She paused, as she pondered the new me. "You're older."

After this extended silence, I knew I needed to bring up the thing that had come between us. "I haven't asked you about it—"

"It's okay," she said. She took a sip of water to draw out the moment further. "After I left Montreal, I went home and stayed with my mom."

"I remember."

"She was cooler than I thought she would be about it. She helped me deal with it."

The words stuck together in my mouth like caramel corn. "I've wanted to apologize for that since I saw you a month ago," I told her. "But I thought it might be too little, too late. How I behaved was unforgivable. It was so bad, I don't how I can make up for it. So I wasn't going to say anything."

"You don't need to apologize, but I appreciate it. It was a good thing, actually. It showed me there were consequences to *your* actions."

Neither of us had plans for the rest of the day, and neither of us wanted to be alone yet. Having decided to see a movie, we took a bus downtown and walked into the film five minutes late. Sandrine had forgotten how I was at movies, and she kept shushing me in the dark.

"Wasn't that guy in that movie where he played the heavy breather?"

Shush.

"I'm going to get some Twizzlers. Do you want anything?"

Shush.

I returned from the concession stand. "Do you want some?"

"No."

"I mean, I think to myself it's funny, ha-ha funny, but why am I sitting here thinking this and not laughing?"

Sandrine jabbed me in the ribs, and we laughed for the first time since we'd entered the theatre.

It had been a habit of my father's to talk through films. Since he saw every movie he liked about five times on average, he wasn't too afraid of missing anything. Movies were truly social outings for him. He'd ask me about my classes, my life. Of course, I was so annoyed by his bad manners that I resolved never to behave like him. The trouble was that when people rebel against their parents, they often do it unwittingly on their terms. I thought I behaved beyond reproach by talking through movies *less* than my father, but that was still enough for me to annoy all of my friends. One exception was Hadley, who was used to watching movies with Oliver Kwan. The two of us would sit in the front row away from everyone and chatter without interruption. Since my father had died, I probably talked a little more.

"You just couldn't shut up?" Sandrine said on the street afterwards. The last time she said that, about four years ago, she hadn't been so good-humoured. I had told her that all her friends were boring and pretentious—and wondered why they were all men who made eyes at her. She fumed at me, mocking me for using the expression "making eyes," and then we had angry, mutually disrespectful intercourse in the bathroom of a Thai restaurant. We always found ways to be spontaneous and reckless. "Do you feel like dinner?"

"Sure."

"Can you cook now?" she asked me.

I nodded. "More or less."

She was house-sitting for friends of her parents, who had retired ten years ago at forty-five and now travelled. They were presently on safari in Kenya. Their four-story condo was in a row of condos looking onto False Creek with shiny hardwood floors and skylights. The house was filled with vintage furniture—space-age lounge chairs covered in cantaloupe-orange wool, a round teak-

and-glass coffee table. Beside the leather couch was a freestanding metal ashtray in the shape of a Zippo lighter, about three feet tall. We had bought groceries.

"There's wine around here, if you want," she said. She looked out of place in the kitchen, as if she was afraid to touch anything. "I don't drink anymore."

"What happened?" I asked, assuming some tragic accident must have caused such a choice.

She leaned against the island counter so that I could see the curve of her back. "It's not really my kind of thing."

We ate dinner and drank juice at a glass-topped aluminum table. Before the meal was finished, she asked to see my book, which I'd brought in my messenger bag.

"These aren't bad." She leafed through them quickly. She smiled politely, but I thought the dullness in her eyes betrayed her disinterest. "You have this tortured thing down pat."

"I never thought of myself like that."

"Do you want me to show these to my boss?" she asked. We had begun clearing the table. She shook her head. "I can't promise you anything—"

I watched her rinse the flatware and load the dishwasher. "Don't go out of your way."

She let her mouth hang open. "Is that why you were so eager to get together?"

"No," I said. "Not at all."

She looked up at me, curious about what explanation I might have.

Taking a seat on the leather couch, I flipped through a copy of *Artforum* until she returned with a teapot and two mugs on a tray. She poured the tea and took a seat in the orange lounge chair. The glass coffee table and its W-shaped legs stood between us.

"There's something about you that's different," she said.

"We've talked about this already," I replied. The chamomile scalded the roof of my mouth. "What do you think it is now?"

"You're not as nice."

"Sorry."

"I'm more perceptive now that I'm sober," she said. "You were probably my nicest boyfriend. At least to begin with."

"Is that a compliment?"

She raised her mug to her face and nodded into it. "Not much of one."

My mother offered me fifty dollars a week to model in her six-week class at the community centre. "It'll be fun," she said. "You get some work, and you won't feel as guilty for not spending time with me." Work was still coming slowly, though I did appear on an afternoon talk show to model new underwear for a local designer. Vanessa said it would be good exposure, almost like editorial work. I considered taking acting lessons, but waited too long to sign up. The money my mother gave me was enough to quit my job as a professional idler at Totem, so I accepted her offer.

Although there was no gender or age restriction for her class, every one of her thirteen students were women in their sixties or seventies. Some of them were members of a retirement community down the street who used the centre frequently. They sat in chairs huddled closely around the centre of room, their sketchpads on their laps and charcoal crayons in their hands. I disrobed in the community centre change room and stepped onto a small platform in a classroom in the basement. I found myself quite comfortable standing there naked.

My mother stood in front of me and introduced herself to the class. She'd adopted a different persona as a teacher. She had dressed down, in a black sweater over a skirt and dark tights, and spoke with a measured, practiced tone that I had never heard her use before. "Thank you for coming," she told them. "Over these six weeks, we'll be looking at various aspects of life-drawing."

Early into this preamble, one woman who been sitting closest to the door removed her sketchpad from the easel and tried skulk away. My mother called out to her.

"Are you double-booked?"

The timid-looking woman turned to her, smiling apologetically. She was more shabbily dressed than the others, in a denim jacket and a T-shirt emblazoned with an arctic wolf, and seemed to have come alone. "I'm sorry, I really am," she said. "I don't think I belong here."

"Is this your first art class?" my mother asked.

"Yeah."

"But you've drawn before, right?"

"Yeah, how did you know?"

My mother shrugged. "I have a good sense of these things," she told her, with that same reassuring voice that she used to start the class. "I can't tell you what's art or what's not art, but I can tell the kind of person who loves to draw and paint. And I can tell, without even looking at their work, which students take this class just for fun and which students take it because they see an opportunity to renew an old love and to be with people who share this obsession. This course could be a waste of time for you. But you might be able to better decide after this first class."

The woman stepped back from the door and took her place behind the easel as my mother gave her first lesson on gesture.

"Gesture is an essential element of figurative drawing," she told the class. "Before we can get to contour and dimensionality, it is necessary to understand composition and proportion. Gesture-drawing is also a great warm-up for artists, in the same way that musicians practice scales or dancers stretch on their barre."

My work was movement-oriented and not concerned with facial expression. I had to find a centred feeling, a stillness, in becoming the object of representation. Aiming to be a surface and submitting to interpretation, I wasn't sure whether I thought less or concentrated harder; I only knew I had to not so much escape myself, but lose track. It was like spinning in a chair until losing your balance. Or the way your thoughts become groggy nonsense as you relax before sleeping. At some point, when the work went well, I could step away from my body and see myself as others did. I literally walked away. There were imperfections, of course—no one is perfect—but, more importantly, I felt true.

"Try to react to his motions without hesitation," my mother told the class. "He doesn't have to be moving around to have motion. The motion is in your pen and how you perceive the lines of his body coming out from it."

My mother would occasionally turn back and asked me to repeat one motion with my right arm, holding it to my chest, then flinging it out. Imagine someone throwing an invisible Frisbee or rehearsing a soliloquy from *Hamlet*. Because she had adopted a different manner, it wasn't as uncomfortable as it might have been being her nude model. I could detect a note of vindication on her face, as though she had been waiting to show me this side of herself. Maybe this calmness and authority was, above all else, her natural condition, which motherhood and marriage had masked and eroded.

Next she asked me to fall to the ground, arms outstretched and

legs bent in the shape of an upside-down number four. I was a
cloth doll that had been tossed onto the floor. Then I lay with my
feet crossed, one leg bent with a knee in the air, the other one flat
against the floor. I had one hand folded across my head and the
other spread to the side. I looked like a goalie sprawling to stop a
forward deking wide on a penalty shot. Finally, I turned my back to
the students with my legs astride, my neck and back crumpled forward as though I were recoiling from a gunshot. One hand I folded
across my stomach, the other covered my brow—here was someone
overcome by intestinal pain.

Their charcoal pens scraped across their pads. My mother hov-
ered around the room, arms folded, scrutinizing each student's
progress.

"Don't worry about drawing his likeness, just try to capture his
essence in one line."

"Imagine his limbs and torso as though they are shaped like
cylinders."

"You're drawing his head first when you should be more concerned about the motion. His head's unimportant."

"You might consider positioning your sketchpad vertically,
and keeping it an arm's length away. That will help you with your
foreshortening."

"Try to picture his body as a skeleton, a collection of bones holding up his flesh."

There was quiet chatter among the women and some giggling.
Finally, one of them—a woman in her seventies with hair the colour of pink champagne—raised her hand.

"Yes?" my mother asked.

"May I ask you about the handsome young man standing before
us? Is he by any chance a relation?"

"Yes," my mother said. Her pedagogical aloofness dissolved in a blush. "Everyone, say hello to my son, Malcolm. He's very helpful."

CHAPTER TEN

A FEW DAYS AFTER I saw Sandrine, Hadley showed up at my house a little after midnight, a school bag on her back and a rolling suitcase in tow. She didn't seem upset so much as cranky and tired.

"Did I wake you up?" she asked me.

"No, no," I said through a yawn. "Are you okay?"

"Yeah," she said meekly. "My mom and I got into a fight. I showed up at home after my curfew. I was at the library and then Krista's, but my mom thought I was lying and forbade me from seeing Marco. I was really pissed. I picked up one of those ceramic animals she collects—her favourite one, the deer—and threw it against the wall. She's really pissed at me. Can I stay with you for the night?"

"Of course. Let me set up the futon."

Hadley looked at the futon in my living room. "I can sleep here."

She followed after me as I fetched bedding from a closet, then helped me carry the futon into her den. "Does Sheila know you're here?"

"Yeah, she insisted on driving me," Hadley said. "I can see if Krista's parents will have me tomorrow."

It was so easy. She needed to stay with me, and I was only beginning to realize how desperately I wanted someone around. For both of us, the only matter remaining was not appearing too grateful—not revealing how badly we both needed the same thing. She looked around the nondescript den, perhaps imagining her things in it.

"We could hang a bed sheet here to give you a little more

privacy," I told her. "You want me to clear some space on my desk for your laptop?"

"Are you sure I won't get in the way?" she asked.

In the past few months, I had lost my father and my fiancée. I was failing to advance in an industry that I still felt half-embarrassed to be a part of. I was paying most of my bills with a credit card and had debts that seemed better suited to someone with a drug or gambling addiction. The only hesitation I had about Hadley staying with me was that she would find my neediness, which she must have already sensed from a distance, overpowering at close quarters and take flight.

"I hope you *do* get in the way," I told her. I wanted her in the way, like a safety net comes between a high-wire walker and the hard ground.

During her first couple of weeks with me, Hadley wasn't around as much as I thought she'd be. I couldn't tell whether she was very busy or simply giving me space. Of course she had water polo, school, and a boyfriend. Occasionally she would call to say she was studying at Benny's Bagels or the library, which made me think of Claire. She got home late, but still full of energy. After she finished her homework and called Marco, I'd make hot chocolate and we'd watch TV together until she fell asleep on my futon. A couple of hours would pass before she crept to bed.

I adopted Hadley's routine, and by seven-forty-five each morning I'd be making oatmeal and listening to the radio while she showered. It was a relief to find her home when I returned from work or an audition, to share meals with someone. Krista, Hadley, and I went ice skating. Marco brought over his guitar and we played Black Sabbath songs. Hadley, Marco, and I went Go-Karting. If my life were a film, this part would be a montage set to sprightly music.

An example of our domestic arrangement would be as follows:

One evening, upon her return from water polo, she brought home a bunch of assorted flowers for me.

"Any special occasion?" I asked her. I didn't have a vase so I placed them in a one-litre beer stein—a gift from a friend who'd purchased it at a steakhouse in Hoboken.

"I'm sorry I yelled at you last night," she told me. She'd yelled at me for not turning down the music when she was studying. "I think shouting is my new inside voice. I need to practice speaking normally."

"I'm glad you're putting up with me."

"Am I annoying you?"

"No."

"Krista's parents said I could stay with her."

"No, no, it's okay," I told her, trying to conceal my fear she would leave. "Do you want to go out to eat?"

"No, I've been feeling tired lately. Let's order in."

"Do you want to rent a movie?" I asked her.

"Okay, but I owe them seven dollars in late fees. I forgot to return *Superman III* and *Ugetsu* by nine p.m."

We ordered a pizza and rented *Barfly* with Mickey Rourke and Faye Dunaway. We ate on the futon and watched the DVD twice, talking through it each time.

"How do you think," she said, "you'd have turned out if you hadn't grown up with a father?"

"What do you mean?"

"Just say, when I was born, if Oliver decided to live with me and Sheila, and left you and your mom alone?"

"My dad wouldn't have left my mom. Not ever."

"I'm just asking you to pretend."

"Fine," I said, pausing to think. "So, if my dad left my mom when you were born, I think I'd have grown up faster. It would have broken my mother's heart, and I'd have been angry at him. I'd be less carefree—even less carefree. I'd have taken better care of my mom. And I probably wouldn't want to be a model. I'd try to do something practical like law or engineering, so I could save up money to hire burly men to rough him up."

"When I first met Oliver, I was fourteen," said Hadley. "I wasn't sure how I'd feel about him. If he had tried to be my father, I would have laughed at him. The first time we met we went to the aquarium. It was so cheesy, I thought, hanging out with this strange Chinese guy who seemed to smile at everything. 'Hadley, look at this jelly fish,' he'd say. 'Hadley, those otters are kissing.' 'Hadley, do you want a plush dolphin?' But he grew on me. He was like a big kid, smiling at everything. I was the cynical one. And I wondered what my life would be like if he had lived with me and my mom. I'd live in a house with a swimming pool like Liam. And I'd know how to speak Chinese."

"But I can hardly speak Cantonese."

"Well, I'd have learned it better. I'd get to go to a private school with carpeted hallways. And my mom would dress better and wear less makeup, and she wouldn't have dated losers and married a jerk and bore like Arnie. My mom and I would fight less. And I would be sent to really cool summer camps that would let me go horseback riding and design video games."

"You'd be spoiled and bratty and selfish."

She agreed. "I still wish I had a father," she told me. "I envy you."

Here is another example of our domestic arrangement:

I was sitting in my armchair, halfway through *Tender Is the Night*, when she walked into the room looking like a girl in her mother's clothes. She was wearing high heels, a gauzy pink dress with lace trim, and a baubly turquoise necklace. Her hair tumbled down her back in wavy curls.

"Are you getting ready for the prom?" I asked, half-seriously.

"I want you to show me how to walk like a model."

I shook my head. "I don't do runway." At school I was told I was not tall enough for the New York or Paris catwalks.

"Just teach me how to walk. Should I slouch? Or should I keep my head back?"

"There's no one way to do it."

I moved my shoe-rack from the front hallway and made her walk from the door to the end of the living room, stop for a moment, and then turn back. I didn't have any dance music in the house, so I put Al Green's version of "Oh, Pretty Woman" on my stereo.

"Wait until I tell you," I said, waiting. "Go!"

She came wobbling forward on her heels, swinging her hips exaggeratedly. Her head and her curls swung right and left.

"So, what did I do wrong?"

I couldn't help laughing until my eyes were wet. "You didn't even walk in a straight line. I thought you had taken gymnastics."

She looked at me, hands on hips, with only a hint of a smile. "What else did I do wrong?"

"You have to walk naturally, but with confidence."

"I don't know how to do that!"

I decided we would walk together, in step, and then turn in opposite directions before we hit the wall. "Are you better at turning left or right?" Sadly, I asked this with utter sincerity.

We walked down my apartment hall a dozen times before we were in step. By now, it was no longer her idea of fun. "Some good work today," I told her. "But we should bring accessories to change into if we really want to simulate real-life conditions."

Hadley was at my house when I received a phone call from Claire. It was only a few days after Hadley had taken residence in my den, and I didn't hear the ringing from the shower. After coming out of the bathroom, I found a Post-It note by the phone.

Claire called. 10:30 a.m.

Hadley was checking her e-mail in the den. I waved her note in the air.

"What did she have to say?" I asked.

She didn't look up from the screen. "She wanted me to say she called. And that you could call her back if you like."

"She didn't say why?"

"Uh-uh," Hadley said. "To be honest, she sounded surprised when I answered the phone."

"Do you think I should call her?"

She nodded. "Don't feel you have to prove anything. Don't pretend you're angry when you're not."

"I still want to talk to her."

She raised an eyebrow. "Are you sure?"

I didn't know what Claire had to say to me, but any of the possibilities made my head swirl. "Maybe not."

She nodded. "Think about it."

By the end of January, barely two weeks into her stay, Hadley was starting to wear. She said she was unhappy about the strain her extracurricular activities had placed on her, and I had no reason not to believe her. Because she would not consider dropping out of the Guyana program, she decided she would have to give up either

Marco or water polo. And she didn't want to disappoint her team or disrupt its chemistry. Even so, considering that she'd left her mother over her boyfriend, I was surprised by her choice. For the first time since I met her, I saw an unflinchingly ruthless side to her.

"It's not as though I want to break up with him," Hadley told me. She was finishing her oatmeal before she left for class. "I'm just going to tell him that I need some time apart."

I took her bowl, rinsed it in the sink, then poured myself a cup of coffee. "I guess your mom was right about Marco," I said, with a grim puff of laughter. "He is a distraction."

"Don't be mean," Hadley said. "I like him a lot, but it's not as though we're going to get married or anything."

"Okay," I said without conviction.

"It's not going to be easy."

"I know."

"It's not like I'm dumping him for some other guy—some asshole."

"Yeah, that would be cruel."

"Malcolm."

They broke up on a Monday, a hectic day for me. First, there was a shift at the record store, then an afternoon at my mother's life-drawing class when she was teaching contour. For this class, I sat on the floor, one leg sticking straight out, the other folded in front of me. My hands were in my lap. At first, my mother didn't want her students to look at their papers as they drew.

"Concentrate on the subtleties of Malcolm's face—his nose, his eyes, the shape of his mouth. Imagine your pencil tracing Malcolm's body. Make sure you capture the angle at which his arms are bent and the curve of his calves. Don't worry if the lines don't meet. The details are what matter."

In later sketches, her students would be allowed to peek at their sketch pads. But what remained most interesting to me were the introductory sketches. In one of them, my face was round as a pizza and my nose was where my forehead was, but the eyes, the posture of the figure, looked familiar. In other sketches, I recognized the shape of my feet or the curl of my mouth. I saw myself as a collection of body parts, of lines and circles, taken apart and reassembled without proper instructions.

It was six p.m. but already dark when I entered my apartment building. I had opened my mail box when I saw Marco lumbering down the stairs. He wore a blank, colourless expression on his face.

"Oh, hey," he said. His hands were in the pockets of his dark jeans and his shoulders were hunched.

"How are you?" I asked him as I pulled mail from my box.

He shook his head sadly.

"You okay?" I asked.

"I suppose I might not see you for a while," he told me. His chin trembled.

I could have asked him what he was talking about, but I saw no point in pretending.

"It's only because she's busy," I said. "That's what I think."

He shook his head. "That's not it."

"Why do you say that?"

He shrugged. "It's not been the same for a while."

"You two will still be friends."

"Maybe, maybe not."

We shook hands and wished each other well. I took the stairs to the third floor as I usually did. Walking up, I sorted through the four or five pieces of mail I received that day. All of them were bills except for a letter. There was no return address on it, but the handwriting was unmistakable. Standing on the third-story landing, I opened and read it as though it were another eulogy.

January 26, 2009

Dear Malcolm,

I completely understand if you don't wish to remain in contact with me. Nor am I surprised that you did not return the phone call I made to you last week.

But if you wanted to hear from me, please accept my apologies for not writing sooner. Aside from the usual assortment of mixed feelings, I have also had a lot of school work. I hope things are well with you, that you're in good spirits.

The reason why I called you, and the reason I'm writing you now, is to inform you that Seamus and I are getting married. This may or may not be difficult for you to accept—I don't wish to be presumptuous—but I wanted you to know about it through me. You remain very dear to me, Malcolm, and I wish, eventually, that all of us could become friends. Obviously, you and Seamus did not meet under the best of circumstances. It's possible that time will allow us to overcome this rocky start.

Again, I hope this letter finds you well. Please send my regards to your mother.

Yours fondly,

Claire

The hurt I had felt over Claire had disappeared sometime last year—or had I been fooling myself? I read this letter twice more, in the hope I had skipped some vital clue, a hidden message.

Once I was in my apartment, I took the letter directly to my room and read it again on my bed. The apartment was still and quiet when I heard a whimper from outside my door. I stood up from the bed to look for Hadley. She was at the desk, sitting in my office chair and staring at my mother's lugubrious portrait of the moon. I put my hand at the top of the chair and swivelled the seat until Hadley, soggy with tears, was facing me.

"It's so hard," she said. "So hard."

Around the time that my own home filled up with Hadley, the house I grew up in went on sale. I wasn't surprised that my mother made this decision. After all, she had too much room. There was no need for three bedrooms, a two-car garage, a soundproof basement lair from my guitar-playing days, or a home office. Besides, the mortgage was too high for her to pay down comfortably on her own. By the end of January, she listed the house with a real-estate agent in the hope of selling by the summer and began looking at condos and co-ops downtown, where she kept her studio. (She never really liked the studio she'd had built in the garage.) Although I was not shocked by her decision, its inevitability felt like yet another blow I had to endure.

My parents bought their home in 1991, just after I started grade four. Our neighbours were professors and architects. As real estate prices rose in the 1990s, the teachers and librarians who retired and moved to the suburbs or their island cottages were replaced by computer hotshots and accountants. From the front yard, obscured by bushes and an overgrown cherry tree, our house resembled a wood-shingled milk carton—a small, kid-sized carton.

"Won't you miss your garden?" I asked, nursing the hope that she might reconsider.

She shook her head. "It's just too much trouble for me these days." She wanted to concentrate on painting. "I don't know how I found the time to garden for all those years. With a job, housework, a child, a husband. How did I find the energy?"

I didn't say anything about her coping strategies. Over the kitchen sink, beside a jade-leaf plant, my mother kept her husband's ashes, which were still in the biscuit tin.

"I'll find a place that you'll like," my mother said to the tin. "It'll have a lot of light and a spare room for Malcolm."

"Are you serious?" I asked, looking at the tin.

"It makes me feel better."

"Are you pretend crazy?" I asked her. "Or the real deal?"

"You would know the difference."

Around the same time my mother put her house on the market, Vanessa, my agent, abandoned her fixer-upper. In her words, it had become a death trap. While alive, her ex-husband had kept the house from falling apart, but evidently these measures were stop-gaps. And now the steps leading to the back entrance had rotted. Plaster fell from the ceiling. The furnace worked erratically, so the house was muggy in the summer and chilly in the winter. The basement was roach-infested. The contractor she brought over to examine the extent of the decay was so overwhelmed he needed to sit down.

"I asked my neighbour if he still wanted to buy the house," she told me. "He thought he had me over a barrel. He told me that the housing market wasn't what it had been—not in this economy. And he's right, but he wanted to give me $80,000 less than I'd paid for it."

"And you didn't fold."

"No, I didn't." She wiped the miso gravy from her face. "He only got me for $30,000 less."

"Good, good."

We were finishing our weekly lunch at a vegan restaurant in Kitsilano. Though Vanessa still paid, in the past month we'd abandoned any pretence that our meals were business-related. I had a bowl of curry squash soup, which, Vanessa told me, had been a favourite of her husband's. "He took his salsa classes nearby," she said. "Occasionally we'd meet here for lunch."

"My mother is putting her house up for sale," I said. "Maybe you should take a look at it."

When Vanessa said something silly or pathetic I now neither cringed nor plotted ways of disassociating myself from her. The opposite occurred; I wanted to protect her. This might sound patronizing—after all, she was almost my mother's age—but I wanted to shield her from others—the contractors, the other models, the industry people—who snickered when she was out of earshot. My most horrendous new fear was that she might realize what a fool she was.

As she mulled over the idea of another home purchase, her eyes grew dewy and wistful. "I'm not so interested in owning a home."

"Why's that?"

"The truth of the matter is that Harold and I bought our home to start a family. Harold, it appears in retrospect, was only trying to amuse me. And now I seem unattached, um, indefinitely. And, well, maybe it's time for me to look at smaller places."

"Vanessa, I wouldn't give up," I started, but stopped mid-platitude.

"You know my mottos for life," she told me. "If at first you don't succeed, fail fail again. Fail fail harder. Trial and failure. Fail and learn." Even her laugh—which sounded like the mating call of a scavenging bird—had become familiar. She waved down our waiter and signalled for the cheque. "But I have my limits."

"For someone who looks at others—"

The waiter brought our bill.

"It's all right, Malcolm," she said, exchanging the receipt for a twenty-dollar bill. "It's something I've accepted."

"You don't seem to realize you're a catch."

"Thank you, Malcolm." She stood and put on her jacket and wound her scarf around her neck. "I doubt I would make a good mother."

"When does that stop anybody?"

She shook her head. "My clients are my children. Any baby I'd have would seem pudgy to me now."

I smiled. "I'm proud to be your client."

She jabbed her finger in the air. "That reminds me. I have heard through reliable sources—on the Internet—that Edward Chow is filming a commercial in Vancouver."

"You mean Edmund Chew?" I asked.

She snapped her fingers. "Yes, I'm terrible with names. Anyhow, I made some calls, and there is a part open. You mentioned you had a personal connection to him, didn't you?"

"Well, through my father," I said. "But I don't think it could get me anywhere."

"What about your former paramour? The one who works in casting?"

I followed her outside, trying to absorb the news, wondering whether Sandrine would help me. As we walked to her car, Vanessa froze in terror. I waited for her to explain.

"It's him."

I looked up the street. "Who?"

"I can't face him." She cowered behind me. "He's coming down the street."

"Who?"

"I'm liable to slap him."

"Who?"

"Harold's male lover."

"The one he was meeting when—"

"Yes."

"What does he look like?"

"Very good-looking. Young."

"Really?" I'd seen pictures of Harold, and he was flabby, bald, and middle-aged—far from sexy.

"A gold-digger. He persuaded Harold to buy him expensive clothes, a massage chair, his own tanning bed. Harold even gave him my jewellery. I don't even have my own engagement ring! I'm thankful the handwriting analysis proved that the second will was a fake."

Across the street people hurried along in the cold. Between a used furniture store and a ski and snowboard shop was a doorway that led to the second-floor salsa studio that Claire—my ex-fiancée and a trust-fund beneficiary—went to. A nostalgic feeling rattled in my chest. Then I saw him. Sauntering down the other side of the street and turning into the door, unmistakably smug and floppy-headed, was her new fiancé, Seamus.

CHAPTER ELEVEN

It was in February, when the mornings were so dark that one could forget waking, that I finally learned what had been troubling Hadley over the past few weeks.

The day had started late. Because Hadley had slept in, I did too. Jolting out of my room and chattering like a monkey, I rolled her off the futon, where she had been swaddled in a duvet, and was drooling into her pillow. I clapped my hands.

"Just give me a moment." She rubbed her temples. "I'm exhausted."

"Okay, but it's eight-fifteen."

A resolve set on her eyes, and she put her hand on her mouth as though she were gagging.

By eight-thirty, the oatmeal was getting cold, and I was already dressed. Hadley was still in the bathroom.

"What's keeping you so long?" I said at the door.

I heard her turning on the faucet as she called out: "Ready in a second."

After another five minutes, she emerged with her hair in a po-nytail and toothpaste smudged on her chin. She looked pale and a jittery, carrying her oversized knapsack into the car.

"Are you sick?" I asked her.

She shook her head. "I don't think so."

"You may have caught something. Why don't you call in sick?"

"I'm already falling behind."

"I'll turn the car around."

"We can't go back," Hadley shouted. "I have too much to

do today." At the next stop light, she tried to soften her anger. "You worry too much, Malcolm. You know what I do when I get worried?"

"What?"

"I think about someone who cares about me, I think about the last time I was with that person. When I do that, my face feels warm. I feel safe. And then I realize it's not so bad."

Before she stepped out of the car, she kissed me on the cheek and told me to have a calm day.

I went for a forty-minute run before going to the record store. Work felt like a marathon measured in millimetres. I sat at the register and read another page and a half of *Tender Is the Night*. I decided to phone Sandrine at work. We hadn't talked since our night out. Upon hearing my voice, she sounded apprehensive.

"Are you in the middle of something?" I asked.

"I'm not supposed to take personal calls. My desk is right next to my boss, but she's away now."

"Are you making a good impression?" I asked.

"So-so," she said with a nonchalant noise. "By the way, I showed her your clippings."

I barely avoided squealing. "What did she say?"

"She hasn't gotten back to me yet, but she didn't toss them out. We're still fine-tuning the spring campaign. Something might turn up."

"I like turnips."

She groaned. "You're better than that."

I related Vanessa's gossip about Edmund Chew and the possibility of a role in his new commercial. "You remember me talking about how my dad knew him, right? Do you think you could help me?"

"What would that accomplish?" she asked.

"I don't know. Want to grab a drink and talk about it?"

"I don't drink."

"Right. What do you do with someone who doesn't drink?"

"You'd probably go for a hike in this city."

"I don't really want to do that."

"Me neither. I'd rather drink."

"You don't drink."

We made plans for next week. By the time my replacement arrived at work, thirty minutes late with a flat bicycle tire to blame, I had likely missed Hadley's game. Still, on the chance of meeting her for dinner afterward, I drove to the aquatic centre at the university and waited for her by the changing rooms. I watched her teammates trickle out, one by one. When Krista appeared, I waved.

"Hi," she said, looking caught off guard.

"Who won?" I asked.

"We got cocky."

"Is Hadley in there? Did she leave already?"

She put her hands in the pockets of her track pants and shrugged her shoulders. "Hadley wasn't feeling well."

I knew it. "Do you know if she went home?"

"I think she had an appointment."

"Okay, thanks. I'll go home. Can I give you a ride anywhere?"

She shook her head and I turned away. Outside the aquatic centre entrance, Liam stood with a bag slung over one shoulder. The lit end of his cigarette brightened. When he saw me, his mouth curled wickedly.

"Where was Hadley?" he asked.

"She's sick."

"We missed her today. Tell her that."

"Sure."

"She's really a great girl."

"Yeah, I know."

"I blew it with her."

"Really."

"She's got a temper."

"Sure."

"She won't listen to me. I didn't think she would get together with Marco like that. It was a surprise."

"What do you mean by that?" I asked.

He shrugged.

"When I met her, she seemed so pure."

I watched him take a lingering drag on his cigarette. He looked intelligent enough to pass a job interview and impress future in-laws, but not smart enough to impede his own impulses with second-guessing.

"Do you want one?" he asked me.

I shot him an appalled look, not because I didn't smoke, but because he was trying to win me over.

"Sorry, it's a bad habit." He threw the butt to the ground and smiled, pleased with himself. "I've got a lot of those."

My dad succeeded in quitting smoking when I was twelve. He had turned forty-five, the same age his own father had been when he died of a heart attack while walking up the stairs from work. (My Aunt Paula would discover his body when my grandmother sent her to look for him; later on, when she was twenty-nine, she would marry a seventy-five-year-old billionaire who died two weeks into their marriage. "My luck balanced out," she told people.) This milestone, paired with the recent death of his own mother, prompted my father to reshape his lifestyle. For three months, he went running, cut back on his horse-playing, resumed work on his screenplay, ate salads, helped me once with my homework, went out less often and, most drastically of all, cut out the cigarettes that were his extra appendages, the habit that punctuated his conversations and broke his social outings up into a collection of appearances between breaks.

He slapped a medicated patch onto his arm, chomped gum, carried around a pen to gnaw on while he sat in his editing room, and grew a belly from his panic overeating. My mother, who'd spent years pleading with him to quit, hiding his cigarettes, forcing him to smoke outside, throwing out deadlines and ultimatums, watched him give up smoking with forced cheer.

With that gone, she was pushing against air.

"I don't think he's quite right," my mother told me, not wanting to say what she was suspicious about. "He's trying to be someone else, but I don't know exactly who."

For the next two weeks, I watched my father scrupulously. I wrote down what he ate (mostly fish, vegetables, and tofu) and wore (horizontally striped golf shirts on the weekends), what time he came home (normally around eight) and went to bed (around eleven), and his general mood for that day (mostly irritable). My mother was right. It was as though he'd undertaken these extreme measures to distract us.

"I'm surprised," my mother said, half smirking, before my dad took us out to dinner. "Are you trying to win a bet?"

My father had lost almost all the weight he'd put on after giving up smoking. His skin had softened, and there was colour in his puffy face. We went to the Malaysian restaurant he went to on his birthday. After he ordered, he said he had news.

"News?" my mother asked.

"Well, potentially."

"What is it?"

He explained that he had been talking to a friend in Hong Kong who wanted him to work on a police serial. He asked my father to write and direct some episodes, and thought we should move back to Hong Kong with him. I could attend an international school and take classes in English. "You'll love it there," my father said. My mother would be closer to family. We could keep the house for a year and see how we felt. If things went well, he could find more directing work.

My mother glowered at him.

"So many of our friends have done this already," he said to her as our chicken skewers arrived. "Why are you so attached to this place?"

"This is where we live."

"I don't want to wonder."

"You deserve better."

"I did not say that."

"Why don't you move without us?" my mother asked angrily.

"I thought about that."

"You did?"

"It wouldn't be the worst thing. I would visit."

"This is what you wanted all along, isn't it? You suggest we move back, but what you truly want is to move back by yourself."

"I need to try this."

"This is about Edmund Chew."

"No."

"You think if you were like him, without a family holding you back, that you could have been the one loved by everyone?" my mother asked. "We never held you back. The reason why you never made a film like Edmund Chew is because you never had his ability. We're not the reason why you failed. We're only your excuse."

My parents would argue about this for days, the issue unresolved until my father's friend called to say the writer-director they'd originally wanted, their first choice, had become available after all. My father kept running for a few more weeks, kept eating salads for a while longer, but eventually the old habits all returned in a way that was both more intense and more muted. Now, he took his time, relishing each cigarette as though it might be the one to do him in. He would turn his cigarettes between his thumb and index finger as though he were winding a watch.

I hurried home, my head filled with ugly thoughts. I knew Hadley would be there. She was watching television and eating microwave popcorn when I returned. She had hung a bed sheet on a clothesline to give herself some privacy. I pulled the sheet aside.

"Where have you been?" she asked, reaching across the futon to turn on the desk lamp. She was in pyjama bottoms and a white, men's undershirt. There was haggardness in her eyes. "I didn't go to the water-polo game. I might have the flu."

"I just stepped outside."

"My mother left a message on your answering machine," she said.

"What did she have to say?"

"Probably wanted to complain about me—you know, the usual."

"I should call her soon."

She giggled. "I think she's got a crush on you."

I sat down at the edge of her futon. "You would tell me if there was something wrong with you?"

"Of course."

"Are you pregnant?" I asked.

"No," she told me.

"Then why have you been behaving so strangely?"

"What are you talking about?"

"Are you pregnant?"

"No, I swear."

"What is it, then?"

"I have the flu. They told me to rest."

I didn't say anything. I sat there and waited for her to tell me the truth. "I might take a couple of days off from school," she said, changing the channel. She got up from the futon and returned the empty bowl of popcorn to the kitchen. "Can I get you anything?" she asked. I remained silent. "I'm pretty tired. I think I'm going to bed. Okay?"

I heard water running in the washroom sink. The water stopped running. She came out with tears dribbling down her face.

"What do you want me to say?" she asked. "What do you want me to do?"

"It's your decision."

"Well, I was talking to the doctor about it. He told me to think about it. I have a few weeks to decide."

"You're not going to have it?"

She wiped her eyes with the heel of her hand and let her mouth fall open incredulously. Her voice was raw and husky. "I'm too young. Do you think I'm old enough to have a baby? Do you think I could support a baby and go to school?"

"You could give it away."

She didn't seem to hear me. "I don't have any choice. I don't."

"What about Marco?"

She didn't understand what I meant. "He's my age."

"But is he going to help you do it? Is he going to help you pay for it? Is he going with you to the clinic?"

"I don't know. I haven't told him."

"Maybe he should know."

"There's no point in upsetting him."

"He did this to you."

She shook her head quickly. "No."

"Don't defend him."

She shook her head. "*No.*"

"You mean—"

She nodded. "You don't need to know."

"Tell me."

"It doesn't matter."

"*Who?*"

"I don't want to tell you."

"Should I guess?"

"I don't care. Go ahead."

"Was it Liam?"

She shook her head. "It doesn't matter."

"When did it happen?"

"I don't know. It was an accident."

"What do you mean by that?"

"I didn't mean for it to happen."

"Are you saying—are you saying—"

"It's my fault," she said, glumly. "It's all my fault."

In my disappointment, I edged away from her until I was standing at the far end of the room. "What happened, then?"

She looked me square in the eye—her face flushed in anger, then resignation—until I could no longer bear it and turned from her. Then I heard her say quietly, "I got carried away."

Maybe it ran in the family, in our bodies. Maybe we all carried irresponsibility in our blood, a deadbeat gene.

Sandrine and I had been dating, on and off, for over two years. Our relationship was often mutually tortuous. I was still mourning the loss of Cindy Arau and her family. And for someone who could act so nonchalantly about relationships—"Nearly half of all marriages end in marriage," she liked to say—she harped on me for not holding her hand in public.

I was obsessed with the men she'd already slept with and paranoid about what I saw to be her fickle heart. And then there was the cocaine, which she used to perk herself up after drinking too much beer. It made her reptilian. When she was coked up, her gaze would pass over friends and strangers like a supermarket checkout scanner, everyone she saw given a value based on their looks or their status. Entire nights would be ruined or derailed while she waited for her dealer to arrive at her apartment.

Still, I loved her. With Cindy Arau or Claire, I needed physical intimacy to feel as though we were in sync. That wasn't the case with Sandrine. Sex with her was like the resolution to a decent detective novel: necessary and satisfying, but not quite as fun as the build-up.

Much of the time, when she wasn't doing coke, Sandrine and I acted like we were high on a drug the two of us alone had discovered. One week we decided to dress alike, wearing matching colours and outfits, even finding a Christmas sweater set, which we wore in February. We threw a party that was themed around the colour white: we dressed in white, draped the couches in bed sheets, and served powdered donuts, White Russians, and Wonder Bread sandwiches. We were always irresponsible in tandem.

Ironically, Sandrine's pregnancy didn't arise from one of those occasions when we'd been careless about birth control. There'd been quite a few of those, and a couple of close calls, after which Sandrine went on the pill. She got pregnant when the antibiotics she was taking for a urinary-tract infection cancelled out the contraception. Like Hadley, she had been cranky and pale for an entire month, and I had begun to nag her about seeing the doctor. I thought she might have a virus. And that I might catch it.

A week or two before she discovered her pregnancy, a couple of friends and I began planning a trip to New Orleans. We'd be gone about a month with extended detours in Austin and San Francisco. Sandrine was intending to join us until her home pregnancy test turned out positive. We sat on her bed staring at the results.

To say I behaved poorly would be an understatement.

"How could you do this to me?" I asked her. "You should have checked the cold medication for side effects."

"Don't be a dick."

"You're going to get rid of it, right?"

"Yeah, I think so."

"You think so?"

"Well, it is a big deal."

"You need to think straight."

"You're half responsible for this, too, you know?"

"Am I?"

We didn't speak for several days after that. She told me it might be better if she went to the clinic alone, and that I should go on my road trip. I wasn't blind; I saw opportunities in that period that would have allowed me to behave properly. Instead, I went away on my trip; when I returned she had taken leave from school and moved back with her mother. We spoke twice over the phone. She assured me she was doing well but wasn't returning to Montreal. "You should get on with your life," she told me. And so our great love affair was snuffed.

The day after I learned about Hadley's pregnancy, I saw Sandrine again. Because she was working late, we found a coffee bar filled with students studying in front of their laptops next to their open textbooks. I sat in a high chair facing the street window.

"Hey, mister."

She was wearing thick black glasses, a floral dress that she had winterized with dark tights and a cardigan, and soft black leather boots.

"Having a shitty day?" she asked, taking a seat next to me.

"Good guess," I told her.

"Is it about Claire—her engagement?"

A mutual friend of ours from Montreal, who was supposed to be a bridesmaid at the wedding Claire and I had planned, was coming into town next month for her wedding to Seamus. Even though it was being held on short notice, three hundred guests were invited—many of whom were being flown from Ottawa and Montreal by Claire's wealthy father.

She raised her chin and looked me over, with a half smile flickering over her face.

"I miss picking out clothes for you to wear," she told me. "Don't take it the wrong way. Take it the right way."

I didn't want coffee; I wanted a drink. "You weren't an alcoholic, weren't you?"

"Not then, but once I stopped doing drugs, I ratcheted up my cocktail intake. I guess I need a hobby, like bocce ball or slot machines. What do you think?"

"Anything but salsa."

We left. Outside, the street was quiet. The dry air smelled like boiled cabbage. I pressed my hands against my ears until they no longer felt numb.

"Well, I have some good news for you," Sandrine told me.

"I'm listening."

I was looking at her and envying the knit cap with earflaps that she had pulled over her head. "My boss liked your clippings. She says you have a fresh look."

"Does she have a spot for me in the department store campaign?"

She shook her head. "She can't use you for that. But it's better. She can get you an audition for the Edmund Chew commercial. She's been working with the team in Hong Kong. Are you happy now? You got what you wanted."

We went back to her house-sit. Sandrine entered the security code, and the lights of her borrowed house were activated by motion detectors. Placing her cap on a hook by the door, she removed her boots carefully. Before I was asked, I slipped off my shoes and put them neatly in place. The lights trailed us as I followed her up the stairs to the main floor, going down the hall past monochromatic canvasses and souvenir portraits of poor Latin American children, up another set of stairs, unlit, and down a corridor and through a pair of doors to the master bedroom.

The windows of the bedroom offered a view across the Creek, the water oily and thick as yogurt. The night sky was black, veined with streaks of blue. The room felt airless, its objects untouched for months. The bed frame was made of black wrought iron and looked as if it had been fabricated from recycled prison bars.

"I usually sleep in the guest room," she pointed upstairs. "A single bed."

"I need to wake up early tomorrow," I told her.

Taking a sharp breath, she sat on the bed and told me what was on her mind. "I haven't had sex in a year. You better be good."

"I'll be better than average," I told her, sitting next to her. "I'll give you the standard-plus package."

"Why do you think we're trying this again? I did a good job forgetting about you."

"You can still back out," I said.

For the first hour, we held each other's hands and then lay down in a chaste embrace. Slowly, we became less shy. Sleeping with Sandrine was like revisiting your hometown after being away for a year. Nothing drastic has changed, but you're still amazed to be back—amazed that this body or place has gone on without you and not vaporized in your absence. And what has changed, however minute, is unduly fascinating.

She had switched perfumes and filled out, her hips more womanly than I remembered. She seemed less impulsive in the way she moved—she didn't, for instance, dig her fingernails into my back to startle me. Every gesture now was deliberate and telegraphed. She kept her eyes trained on me as though she were reading a graph.

Afterward, as we lay in the bed, I told her about Hadley's pregnancy. "This time, I'm going to behave the right way," I said. "I won't let her go to the clinic by herself like I did with you."

"Malcolm—"

"I'm so sorry, so sorry about how I behaved."

"I know you are," she said, putting her hand on mine. "If you were the pregnant girl and I was the dude, I'm not sure if I would have acted much better." She paused. "Listen, I didn't tell you everything about the past."

Then she told me she'd had the baby after all.

CHAPTER TWELVE

IN THE DAYS AFTER learning about her pregnancy, I became pre-occupied with Hadley's decision to have an abortion. I was more polite, but less kind.

Hadley noticed. On non-practice days, she zipped back home from school. She decided the television rightfully belonged to the living room and vanished into her sleeping space lugging Victorian phonebooks like *Vanity Fair* and *Bleak House*. In the living room, while watching television, I'd hear coughing from her room, but nothing else. She didn't talk on the phone. She read and studied, and the lamp in her den went out before ten. In the morning, she woke up early, leaving without waking me.

One night I called her to dinner. There was no reply. I repeated myself and approached her room, pulling back the curtain when she didn't answer again. On her bed she sat cross-legged, highlighter pen in hand, textbook open in front of her. She removed the head-phones from her ears.

"I made dinner," I told her.

She nodded with the docility of a chastened prisoner. "Sure."

For several minutes, we chewed and slurped at the kitchen table.

"I'm doing laundry tomorrow," I said at last. "Is there anything you want washed?"

She murmured, readying to refuse my offer, but stopped. "I'll leave some clothes in the hamper. Thanks."

"When do you see the doctor again?" I asked.

"Next week. Tell me again why you want to go with me?"

"I don't know," I said, taking our dirty dishes to the kitchen sink. "It's something I want."

"Okay, then." As I ran the faucet, she lingered by me, hands planted on her hips, chewing over some worry. "I'm cancelling my trip to Guyana."

"Why?"

"I've got too much to do. I've lost interest."

"You'll regret it."

The phone rang, Sheila calling. Hadley spoke quickly, threading her responses into her mother's breathless monologue. "Hey," she said. "Yeah, can you believe it? It's me. He's here. I decided to pick up the phone. I don't know—I figured I should talk to you. No, I don't hate you. No, I don't. I don't. How have you been? How are your classes? Yeah. Okay. Sorry to hear about that. You—you—you sound really busy. He fell—again? I know he would hate being in a home, but what can you do? I guess. I don't know. Well, he's old; maybe it's for his own good. Who knows? Okay, busy. A little tired. Things are good. Yeah—he told you that? I thought I was too busy to have a boyfriend. Yeah, okay, you said that, too. *Congratulations.* We're still friends. Mom. Mom. Listen to me. Okay. Okay. *Okay.* I've been studying every day. I can put Malcolm on the phone and he'll tell you that. Haven't heard from any universities yet. I think all the letters would be sent to your address, anyway. You haven't gotten anything? No, you are not allowed to open my mail. I said no, *even if.* Yeah, I know some send them early. Still, it could be a few more weeks. Yeah, I know. Thanks. Yeah, I'm not sure about Guyana. I'd still like to go, but it may be too much trouble. Yeah, you said that, too. I'm thinking about it. Malcolm is good. He's working, going to auditions. Haven't seen him as much. No, he hasn't thrown me out of house yet. No, he does the cooking. Because he wants to. Yes, I help clean. No, I don't leave his milk out. Don't say that—don't say it. Okay, okay. I miss you, too. Mom. Mom, I don't know when—or if—I'll be coming back. Well, I mean exactly what I just said. You know I'm going away for school. I can't talk too much longer. Malcolm needs to use the phone. Okay, miss you, too. Maybe we can go for coffee next week. Okay, sure. Yeah. Me, too. Malcolm's saying he has to use the phone now. Okay, bye. Bye. I'm hanging up now. I'm hanging up—bye."

On our way to the clinic, tiny flecks of wet snow fell and splattered against my windshield. We sat in the car silently as the wipers made a squishing noise. Hadley had an appointment for an ultrasound. She was pale and sleepy and jittery, and sat with her head against the side window.

"I'm sorry you have to come with me," she said.

"I asked," I reminded her.

"Then you like pain."

"I was in shock that night I asked you about it."

"It's okay. I was lying to you."

"Dad used to have a short fuse, too. Sometimes I remind myself of him when I'm upset."

"Really?"

I nodded. "It didn't always happen, but he would sulk when we didn't share his enthusiasm. When I was thirteen, he forced me to go on an Alaskan cruise. He told me to look at the whales—I refused to look. He asked me to play shuffleboard—I didn't want to. I sat in my cabin and played Game Boy instead. Finally, at dinner, he told me he would pay for my flight home in Fairbanks. I didn't accept his offer, but for the rest of the trip he wouldn't look at me."

She didn't say anything.

"He was right to be angry with me."

"Remember when I said that he never talked about you?" she said. "I wasn't telling you the entire truth. I once asked him what you were like."

"What did he say?" I asked, trying to conceal my curiosity.

"He said that you were smart and talented, he was proud of you, but that you worried too much about offending people or saying the wrong thing. He worried it was his fault."

Of course! *It was his fault.* "But why aren't you like that? You're his daughter, too. Why aren't you full of self-doubt?"

"Maybe it was my upbringing."

The women's clinic was on the hospital's third floor. Inside, we followed the coloured lines on the floor until we reached two thick glass doors. At the entrance, Hadley spoke her name through an intercom before we were allowed through. A nurse, who sat next to a black-and-white monitor flashing different security shots, handed Hadley a form on a clipboard and pointed to a room down the hall. The room was self-consciously cozy. There were plush blue sofas, two overstuffed armchairs, and violet wallpaper. You could fall asleep here, but you'd have nightmares.

The nurse standing at the door called for Hadley.

"Do you want me to go with you?" I asked.

She shook her head. "The doctor's just going to figure out how far along I am—it's nothing."

"I wouldn't mind asking her some questions."

She turned to the nurse, then put a hand on my arm. "Malcolm, I'll give you my pamphlets."

My mother glowered at me when I arrived late for her class. The subject of her last life-drawing lesson had been drawing hands and feet. She passed around a book filled with anatomical sketches by Leonardo. Then she brought out another book, one with Escher's *Drawing Hands*. A right hand holding a pencil is drawing the shirt cuff of a left hand, which, in turn, is drawing the right hand's shirt cuff. I sat at a table in a tank top with my right hand palm down on a pillow while her students huddled around me, heads cocked, to scrutinize my hand. Then they stepped back as they sketched.

"There is no shortcut to drawing hands. The best way to learn how to draw hands is through practice, hours and hours of it." She let out a self-effacing sigh. "It's very easy to practice at home.

"Look at Malcolm's hand and try to imagine it first as though it were covered with a mitten. Draw only the outline of the hand. If you are approaching Malcolm's hand from an angle, try to add some dimension to the palm and keep in mind how important the knuckles can be.

"There are three joints for each finger and two for the thumb. Imagine each joint as a cylinder."

I had smooth, flat, square hands, and my palms were the same width from base to top. My mother asked me to turn over my hand so that the class could sketch my palm. Years ago, a friend had given me a palm-reading book, which I read in one hungover afternoon. One's love life was represented by a horizontal line that could start beneath the index or ring finger and curved past the pinkie. Mine started below the index finger and was long, which meant I would have a happy, stable love life. If the line had started under my ring finger, it would mean that I was selfish and romantically obtuse. If it was short, it would signal a disinterest in romance. The two strong horizontal lines underneath my pinkie indicated I would be married twice, but since there were no intersecting lines, I would have no children. My line of fame ran vertically from the bottom of my palm to beneath my ring finger. It ran strong and clear, which meant I would be satisfied by my recognition, though below my ring finger, the line broke into a fork, which suggested that this success might be of questionable merit.

The life line curved around the thumb. My life would be long but shallow, which meant it would lack vitality. The horizontal line running from the bottom of my palm was my travel line. It intersected with my fate line, which ran vertically underneath my middle finger. This signalled that any journeys I would take would alter my life. Any other vertical lines crossing the travel line would augur danger. I didn't believe in the wisdom of palmistry, but the idea of one's body telling a story wasn't farfetched to me.

Sandrine wanted me to buzz her up. We'd made dinner plans near my house and she insisted on stopping by.

"This is the girl you used to date?" Hadley asked. She was in her pyjamas with her laptop, instant messaging with Krista.

I nodded.

"Not the one who bought the condoms?"

"You know it's not her."

She smirked. "Sorry."

I waited by the door for Sandrine and waved at her as she approached from the elevator. Hadley shut her laptop and introduced herself to Sandrine. "Sorry I'm such a mess."

"That's okay," Sandrine said, stepping back so she could take in my half-sister and myself at once. "I know you're busy, but I wanted to say hello."

I turned to her. "Rocks off yet?"

"What kind of brother are you, Malcolm?" she asked me. "Do you share your toys?"

"Well?" I asked Hadley.

Hadley clutched the laptop against her chest. "He's pretty good." She paused. "You know what? I kind of wanted to see what you looked like, too."

"Really?" Sandrine asked.

"I wanted to know whether you were as cool and pretty as Malcolm said you were," she said, with a twinkle like my dad's. "I thought maybe he was exaggerating."

"Obviously, bullshit runs in the family."

Sandrine invited Hadley out to dinner with us, but she declined. We went to the same Greek restaurant I'd gone to with Hadley's water-polo team, and talked about the audition for the commercial, how I should prepare, what I should bring.

"How many people are auditioning?" I asked her.

"A few dozen, which isn't a lot."

"Why do you think I have a good chance?"

"I don't know. You fit their description of what the director is looking for."

"Edmund Chew? What's he like?"

She shook her head. "He's supposed to show up for the auditions."

It was only when we were comfortably into our meal and had exhausted all other topics, that we lit on the big one.

"So, do you still want to meet him?" she asked.

"Yeah, of course."

Returning back from Montreal, Sandrine decided she couldn't go through with an abortion. She'd actually known right away, but I confused the issue, which was why she sent me on my road trip. Once she was in Toronto, her mother helped arrange for an open adoption with a couple who couldn't have children. Sandrine transferred to a fashion school in Toronto and completed her coursework while she waited for the baby. Her mother accompanied her during her labour, which had been quick and all natural. The open adoption would allow her to see the child, a boy named Felix, every couple of months. She'd moved west partly because her child's adoptive parents had recently relocated nearby to the Island.

It had never crossed her mind, Sandrine told me, to raise the child on her own. "My mother offered, but she had too many issues with her own health to bring up my baby," she said. "And I didn't want to grow up so fast." Even so, it was Felix's presence in the world that made her stop drinking, get a new hairdo, and start a career. She didn't want him to be the biological offspring of a wastrel—two wastrels.

"How about next month?" she asked me.

"When exactly?"

"It's up to you. Kurt and Joanna are pretty easy-going."

"Just let me know and I'll be there."

Since arriving in town, Sandrine had yet to visit her child because of work and then the holiday season. And since we became reacquainted, she wanted to unload the news on me first. I had the feeling that she had taken up with me again so we could share this experience and take from it the same kind of rueful joy—the kind of pleasure that burns.

Hadley was ten weeks pregnant and had another six to go before an abortion grew risky. She set an appointment two weeks after the ultrasound, but let it slip—she didn't know she had to make a confirmation. Water polo and an overdue essay took precedence the next week, and she postponed again. By early March, I grew worried she would wait too long.

"You're running out of time," I said. "The doctors have busy schedules."

"I know that."

"Well, it's important you find the time. All the spaces could be filled in a couple of weeks. You know, all that spring fever."

She wrinkled her forehead at my bizarre logic.

"I think you should get it done next week."

She nodded, sitting in front of the television and eating cereal—all she ate now was oatmeal with a little honey and corn puffs—in an extra-large T-shirt and black track pants—the clothes she wore at home, at school, in bed.

"Malcolm?" she asked.

I nodded.

"What if I say I can't go through with it?"

"We've talked about this," I told her.

"I could give it up for adoption," she said.

"What about your trip this summer?"

"I'm only eighteen—I can put it off a year."

"If that's what you want to do," I said flatly. I had resolved not to put any pressure on Hadley.

"I don't know. If I did have it, would you help me out?"

"What are you saying?" I asked her.

"I'm thinking out loud—tell me."

"I'd do whatever I could," I told her at last.

"So you're saying you'd help me?"

"It's only hypothetical—"

"I want to know."

"Of course."

"We could do it."

"I've already told you what I think."

"I could have it," she repeated.

"We've been through this."

"I know."

"Then you'd have to tell your mother," I said.

She let out a miserable groan. "Is there any way I could avoid her for another seven months?"

I laughed.

"Fine," she said flatly. "I'll make an appointment tomorrow morning."

"Don't behave like a kid."

"What do you mean?" she asked, whining.

"You're acting as though you have no choice. You can do whatever you want. Don't behave as though I'm pushing you around."

"You are."

"I'm not."

She took my hand and placed it on the bottom of her belly and pushed—I felt a hardness. "It's filled with blood here. In the ultrasound, you can actually see it. Its body, its head."

I looked her over coldly, pretending that her belly didn't scare me. "Nothing I haven't felt before."

She made an appointment for the following week. In the days preceding it, I read her brochures and conducted web searches. I borrowed library books. I read about abortion history—the years it was legalized in different countries—and the ages of consent in each province and state. In an attempt to desensitize myself, I forced myself to look at pictures of embryos that anti-abortionists toted around during their protests, the foetuses like birdlings with their pink skin and beady eyes. I read chat forum posts about what muscle relaxants and antibiotics she might be on, how she might react afterwards, and what I should say to her.

Based on my research, I told her that she should bring an extra pair of underwear and some pads. Hadley shuddered at my suggestion. My interest seemed unnaturally exhaustive to her, but it was the same thing I'd done when my father got sick. Then and now I read and researched until my eyes hurt.

Krista had insisted on coming as well. She arrived at our door festively attired, as always, in clogs and a tube top, her lips glossy and shocking pink. The two of them shared the back seat on our way to the clinic.

"There's nothing to worry about," Krista said. "My sister says it's a breeze."

"Has she had one?"

Krista shook her head. "But she has a lot of friends who have. They say it's not painful at all—not compared to having a tattoo."

Hadley laughed. "Maybe I should get a tattoo afterwards."

"Of what?"

Hadley thought about it. "Since I'm half-Chinese, maybe a Chinese symbol. Like the word for love or compassion."

Krista nodded enthusiastically. "Those are cool. Or how about a Celtic knot on your ankle?"

"That sounds lame."

"In Montreal," I said, "I knew someone who had a picture of Axl Rose's head tattooed on his back."

"Who's he?" they asked.

"Never mind."

"We should get tattoos when we go to Guyana," Krista suggested, "instead of buying key chains."

"Are we still going?" Hadley asked.

"My dad will send me to a juggling camp if I don't go."

"*Ew.*"

"I wonder if there are tattoo parlours in Guyana."

"Forget it," Hadley said, forcefully. "Do you know what the HIV-infection rate is like down there?"

"So maybe we should get tattoos here."

"We could get our hands henna-ed instead."

"But what about the pain?"

We waited again. Hadley and Krista sat in the armchairs on each side of the long coffee table. I took a seat on the couch next to Krista, beside a couple who were speaking Cantonese. I could understand maybe half of what they were saying. The boyfriend looked my age and had a curly quasi-pompadour. He wore a Hugo Boss sweatshirt and black jeans and smelled like cigarettes. As he waited, he checked his iPhone for messages. His girlfriend seemed about three or four years older than him. She was tiny, with maple skin and round eyes. In a nasal, hectoring voice, she explained to her boyfriend, again and again, where he should have parked his car.

The nurse called Hadley's name. We followed her to the door and watched her shuffle away. The entire procedure would take about two hours, which included the mandatory counselling session.

"Do you want coffee?" I asked Krista. "Or something to eat?"

Krista put down the magazine she had been reading, glaring at me as though I'd suggested letting Hadley take the bus home.

"I'm not hungry," she said finally. "You can go, but I want to be here in case she needs someone."

"I'll stay."

We tried to make small talk.

"So which schools did you apply to?" I asked.

"You sound like my dad," she said. "I'm taking a year off, then I'm enrolling in a jewellery-making course. I might go to university, but not until I'm older—like twenty-one. Hadley says your big shoot is tomorrow."

"It's an audition, but yeah."

"Are you excited?"

"I've been too worried about this thing. I mean, I know it'll be okay, but still I can't think about anything else."

"Me, too."

"She seems ambivalent—I wonder why that is."

"You think?"

I looked at her cross-eyed. "I don't know—could it be—I mean …" I shrugged. "If there's anyone else involved—"

Krista's face stretched with the astonishment of someone who had uncovered another person's secret agenda. "What exactly are you asking, Malcolm?"

"What do you know?" I asked.

"So you don't know?"

"Do you?"

"Uh-uh. She wouldn't tell me who it was."

"It's not important."

"If it was, she'd tell us."

We sat in silence. Another couple arrived, a man and a woman in their early thirties who spoke a Slavic language and behaved with disquieting nonchalance. The woman nodded off on the couch. Her boyfriend tried picking dirt out of his fingernails. The nurse appeared at the door again.

"Hadley wants to see you," she told one of us.

I stood up, but she shook her head and nodded at Krista instead. They disappeared down the hall before I could hand Krista the pink polka-dot underwear and the extra pads I had brought for Hadley.

I checked my watch. It was ten in the morning—there was another hour to go.

At the nurse's desk, I told her that I was going out for a cup of coffee. Following the lines on the floor, I reached the elevator and pressed the button for the main level. Once there I wandered around looking for the cafeteria, which was in the hospital's basement. Once I found it, I checked a clock on the wall. There was another forty-five minutes before I was needed upstairs. The thought of spending more time in the waiting room filled me with dread, and without a destination in mind, I walked aimlessly until I left through the sliding doors to go outside.

In the past week, the weather had gone from being clear and almost balmy, with an apricot glow at sunset, to a late-winter snowstorm that turned to grey slush overnight. Now, in mid-morning, the clouds had the iridescence of soap bubbles. The rain dropped steadily but in spurts, shifting in minutes from drizzle to downpour and back. I followed the driveway until I was past the parking lot attendant's booth and onto the sidewalk skirting the hospital. The cars made shushing sounds as they sped by me. When the rain grew heavier, I stood underneath a bus shelter until it subsided several minutes later. Starting out again, I reached a cross street and turned in, so that I was still on the edge of the hospital grounds.

Halfway down the north side of the hospital was another entrance, whose sliding doors opened for me. I walked through the reception area to the far elevator, around the corner. Once I got to the fourth floor, I walked down a corridor. My father's room had been on the right side of the hall, the second door from the end. It was empty, though one bed was unmade, with a paperback lying spine-up on it. At the far end was the window out of which my father used to stare. I sat by the window in an armchair facing the front door. Turning in the chair, I could see the mountains in the background—they were blue-green and had a translucent quality, like panes of stained glass. Across the street, two women entered a public tennis court wearing shorts and T-shirts—people were so eager for spring that they dressed for it in advance. I didn't remember the time elapsing, but I watched long enough for the tennis players to switch ends and grow sweaty.

The washroom door opened and a pale, compact man in his eighties wearing blue pyjamas stepped into the room. He walked with a cane and carried a newspaper in his other hand.

I stood up from the chair. "I'm sorry."

"What's the matter?"

"This was my father's room last summer."

His chest rose and sank, and he looked at me gruffly. "But he's not here anymore?"

"No."

He let my answer sink in. "When did he die?"

"In September."

"I'm sorry."

"I didn't mean to intrude," I told him. "Why are you here?"

"Do you really want to know?"

I looked at the floor.

As he took a seat at the edge of his bed, he let out a sigh. "You can stay here for a while. I'm getting a little tired, but I won't be napping for another fifteen minutes, maybe half an hour."

I checked my watch. "I should go."

"Are you all right?" he asked me.

My mouth was dry and my throat felt sore when I swallowed. I removed some gum from my pocket. "I really have to go. I have to pick up my sister."

I'd begun to leave the room when I heard his voice again.

"You dropped something."

And with his cane he picked up a pair of pink polka-dot underwear from the floor.

By the time I returned to the Women's Clinic, soaking from rain and dabbing my brow with the underwear, Hadley and Krista had been waiting fifteen minutes on the plush couch. The two of them gaped at me—half in relief, half in resentment.

"What took you so long?" Hadley asked.

"I went to visit someone."

Hadley and Krista exchanged glances. "Who?"

I shook my head. "No one you know."

Hadley was pale and wobbled when she stood. She looked at me with her eyebrows fused together, then brushed some wet hair from my forehead.

"You look," she told me, "as bad as I feel."

CHAPTER THIRTEEN

EDMUND CHEW DESPISED airplanes. He had a sister in Vancouver whom he wanted to visit, so he set his commercial here to shave off a few travel days. It would be the last of three minute-long, standalone commercials for an Italian car company, each specifically geared for Asia, Europe, and North America. The first two commercials featured global movie stars, were shot over a week on vast Hong Kong soundstages that needlessly recreated outdoor settings like Roman street markets and Angkor Wat, and went so far over budget that Chew, who was bankrolling a divorce with the commercials, needed to approach the final commercial with the frugality that characterized *Shakespeare's Revolver*.

I sat in the lobby of a community playhouse with a dozen men. Our ethnicities were a scramble, and though we were about the same age, we all possessed an unpolished look. I recognized one slack-jawed redhead from Videomatica, who concentrated on his copy of the script while drinking a bottle of root beer. Another auditioner was reading the latest issue of *The Economist*. None of us acted as though we would get this job.

Over an hour passed before an assistant uttered my name. I was asked to stand in front of the stage, where a camera had been pointed. Behind a set of monitors sat a few people in rumpled, handmade suits who worked for Edmund Chew. There wasn't any actual acting in the commercial, which played to my strengths. The dialogue came in voice-over, read by another actor. I would be pictured driving and staring languidly ahead throughout the commercial. And yet I was asked to read aloud the lines that Chew had written himself. I stood on the stage with my copy of the script, which I had mostly memorized, rolled up in my hand and tried to follow Sandrine's advice and offer an affectless, unpracticed reading.

"The worst thing would be if he was someone unlike me—a physical opposite. She will be drawn to him and then repelled by him. He will be artless and tactless. He will lie to her. It will pass by in moments. They will live a counter-life together," I said onstage, my voice growing louder as I settled into the room. "The only thing worse would be if he was my mirror image. She will be repelled by him, then drawn to him. He will be empathetic and sensitive. He will reveal my weaknesses. It will last for at least one lifetime. They will live the life I shared with her together."

While I auditioned, a figure appeared from the back of the room and whispered into the ear of one of the Armani-suited assistants. I didn't expect for them to make a decision immediately, but I was given the part as I stood.

They'd call. It wasn't something I needed to wait for; it was something I could expect.

In the two days following her abortion, Hadley did little else but sleep and eat. She wouldn't return phone calls—not from her mother, not even from her water-polo coach or Krista. When I was finished work, we played Scrabble and watched *Mary Poppins* three times over. I allowed her two days away from school, but insisted she go back to class afterward.

"If you're still feeling bad," I suggested, "let's find someone for you to talk to."

"Maybe I have mono."

"Sure you're not depressed?"

"It's not like that," she replied. "I feel groggy."

"The procedure could have affected your immune system," I suggested. "You could have an infection."

"Can I stay at home?"

"Why don't you go just to school in the morning, and if you feel sick, call me and I'll drive you back."

She agreed, and managed to get through the day. Upon her return, she refused dinner, crashed onto her futon, and slept until the next morning when I roused her. As she got herself ready, I made oatmeal and poured a glass of milk for her. She sat at the table in a confetti-patterned thrift-store sweater and sweat pants, then took her bowl of oatmeal and threw it on the floor.

"I didn't mean to do that," she told me.

I went for my broom while Hadley picked up shards of bowl from the floor.

"I want to start feeling better soon."

"You will," I said.

"I can't stop thinking about it. It's all I can think about, Malcolm. Not only what happened, but being in that room, the doctor, the tools she used. I can't concentrate on school, on picking a university, on going away this summer. There's nothing else in my head. I didn't think it would hurt so much. Before it happened, I'd thought it would feel the way it did when my wisdom teeth were pulled out; the doctor would put me under, and I would wake up with holes in my mouth. But it felt so much worse. It felt like the doctor was ripping something from inside of me. She took something out of me that didn't want to be taken away."

I put the broom down and sat with her until her breathing slowed to normal. Then, in my cupboard, I found a white coffee mug with "Claire" written on it in black lettering and asked her to throw that, too. I winced, anxious about my damage deposit, when it chipped the plaster off the far wall.

One night she called out from her sleep. Usually I slept naked, so I got into a T-shirt and my boxer shorts before checking on her. She was sitting on the futon, her eyes wet.

"Did you have a nightmare?" I asked.

She nodded. "I'm driving a car from the back seat and I can't see out the window and my feet don't really reach the pedals."

I lowered myself onto the futon and eased my arm around her. "I have that dream all the time. Many people do."

"I can't go to sleep," she announced.

"Are you still afraid?"

"No. I was thinking about something."

"What?"

"I was thinking whether you still hate me."

"No, never."

"You were angry with me. It made me sad."

"You're being melodramatic."

"You were upset at me. I wasn't the girl you thought I was."

I kept quiet at first. "I was upset, though not at you. I was worried. I wanted to look out for you."

"You make me feel safe."

"Normally, I'm the one looking to be taken care of."

"You know who you remind me of?" she asked me. She didn't wait for me to guess: "Mary Poppins."

In April, Charlie Branca demanded that I meet him. "It's your fault," he told me when I arrived at his neighbourhood sports bar. "I can't get that woman out of my head."

A few weeks after Vanessa and I confronted him, Uncle Charlie saw her again. "I wanted to apologize the only way I know how," he told me. "With my clothes off."

I didn't know what to say.

"To be honest, I wasn't used to being with a woman like that," he continued. "So sober, so quiet."

"Quiet?"

"She doesn't make a peep."

"Really?" I asked in disbelief.

"She's so quiet, it drives me crazy."

I groaned, but still couldn't help myself from imagining the act. Eventually, Uncle Charlie told me that he had scared Vanessa off.

"I told her I loved her and wanted to have a three-way," he told me.

"Which part of that scared her off?"

"I was pushing it with the three-way," he said, downing his rye and ginger and ordering another round for us. "She won't talk to me. It's been two weeks now. I need to do something to get her back."

It had almost slipped my mind that Uncle Charlie had been, like Vanessa, betrayed in marriage. I barely remembered his wife, Ling, but was told that Charlie had been, as he might put it, a true nipple-twister. Since I knew him, he related his trysts with forced, almost dutiful, cheeriness, with the look of someone who'd committed a crime years before and was coming home to a police car in his driveway. With Vanessa, he'd found someone whose own personal foibles surpassed his own, who had a mulish capacity for humiliation, and who was unlikely to rob him while he slept.

Uncle Charlie made me promise to mention him the next time I saw Vanessa, but that wasn't necessary. She and I met at an Italian restaurant, and when my mushroom pizza arrived, she burst into tears.

"Why did you have to order a pizza?" she wailed. "It just makes me think of rape. And Charlie." She dabbed her eyes with her napkin. "I was thrown off by the request for group sex. Harold and I only did that later on in our marriage, and even then it was mostly him and other men. Sometimes I'd get out of bed and knit. But why did he have to say he *loved* me?"

"I think he meant it," I said.

"That's the trouble. I was getting used to his shiftiness, his casual lying—the stains he left on my sheets. To be honest, I liked how he leered at other women. Even before Seamus, Harold spent most of his time staring at men's crotches. Sometimes I'd stuff my jeans just to get his attention. But, the truth is, I don't even know if I can trust my own feelings. I was once completely in love with Harold, and he gave my own wedding band to his male lover."

I was instructed by Vanessa to wish Charlie well, and nothing else. Charlie, however, refused to play along. He decided he would propose to Vanessa anyway. He asked me to come with him to find her a ring.

"Don't you think this is stupid?" I asked him when he picked me up in a black Mercedes leased by his company. "You ditched her a few months ago. Now you want to marry her?"

He looked me up and down. "Well, no, Mac, I haven't sat down and thought this through and realized that I'm doing something that's outwardly foolish. Jeez, don't you think I'm old enough to make my own decisions? When someone your age does something, it's stupid. When someone my age does the same thing, it comes from a fucking wellspring of prudence."

We stopped in front of a high-rise and stepped out of the car. At the entrance, he swept a card and entered through the lobby, which had the leather and burgundy tones of an upscale steakhouse.

"Where are we going?" I asked in the elevator.

He swiped a fob for the top floor. "We're getting the ring," he said.

We stepped out of the elevator and went down a long granite hallway before stopping at a door. Charlie handed me a pair of surgical gloves and a hairnet before covering himself up as well. With a set of keys, he opened the door to a penthouse suite with twenty-foot-high windows overlooking the city. I was almost dizzy looking out at the skyline.

"Who lives here?" I asked Charlie.

"Seamus and Claire."

For some time after learning about Seamus's connection with Vanessa's husband, I sat on this information. I admit it, I wanted to see Claire fleeced and heartbroken. A few weeks passed, and with her wedding fast approaching, I'd decided to make a phone call. The first two times I called her, I got her voicemail. I left two messages saying I had important news and that I needed to speak to her. I waited another week. Finally, I left a rambling, hurtful message that outlined Seamus' relationship with Harold—the seduction at the salsa class, the relentless phone calls, the promises of undying love, the gifts, demands for bigger gifts, the broken marriage.

Two weeks later, I learned from an online photo album that they were married in a lavish ceremony at a downtown hotel. Blue was her favourite colour. The table settings were calla lilies and roses cradled by delphinium. The three-tiered butter-cream cake was hand-decorated and topped with fresh lisianthus. The bride wore a Grecian wrap gown with Chantilly lace and draped chiffon. The groom wore bespoke seersucker. Everyone who commented on the photo album agreed they made a gorgeous couple.

Of course I felt greasy about sneaking into the suite, but these feelings were overpowered by my throbbing curiosity. As I stepped inside, I saw the pictures of Claire snuggled against Seamus, who glowered into the camera. The place was dominated by a wide bright living space with an orange sectional couch, a shag throw-rug, and tear-shaped armchairs. None of it was to her taste at all. Why did she bother to reclaim her things from her apartment when all of it had been replaced?

"How did you get the security card and the keys?"

Charlie paced around the living area, almost frightened by the view. He retreated back into the kitchen. "The security guy in the building and I go way back," he said. "I taught him how to read."

"Why do you need me here?" I asked.

"I don't. I figured there might be things you'd like back from Claire. Or maybe you want to shit on their bed. Use your imagination."

Uncle Charlie turned into the master bedroom where he went through the drawers, looking for Vanessa's original engagement ring. "You mind checking in the other room?" he asked me.

The other room was Seamus's office. His desk was surprisingly small, with room only for the laptop that sat on it. Notes, tacked directly into the plaster, covered the entire wall facing the desk. I turned on the laptop and waited for it to boot.

"What if it's not here?" I asked.

"What do you mean?"

"What if he sold off Vanessa's jewellery? What if he gave the ring to Claire?"

"Just keep looking."

I turned on the computer and looked for the most recent files.

I found a file titled "Future Prize Winner.doc." I'm sure Seamus had backed up and printed out his new novel; maybe he'd already submitted it to his publisher. But by the time Charlie had located the ring, with a blue sapphire cut chunky like a cough drop, I had deleted the file anyway.

"Take a dump on their bed," Charlie suggested. "I'll give you some privacy."

The concept for Edmund Chew's commercial involved a man following his lover in his car after she leaves his apartment to see another man. The nature of the romantic relationship between the man and the woman is intentionally obscure: you're not supposed to know whether this man is the husband or the cuckold. He follows her across a bridge and through several city backdrops as the voiceover plays.

In publicity stills, Chew was always pictured in wrap-around sunglasses and a black leather jacket with the collar turned up. He was known for making on-the-fly revisions to scripts and driving the starlet models who worked for him, by turns, horny and livid. In person, Chew was a short, plump man with an oily mass of side-swept, ink-black hair who wore tight jeans, a rumpled blazer, and smelled like stale cigarette smoke—just like my dad. He introduced himself to me in the trailer I was given.

"I am very excited we found you for this part," he said in halting English as he shook my hand. "Tell me about yourself. Your parents are from Hong Kong?"

"Yes," I said, straightening out the collar of the tuxedo-shirt I wore open-necked with a mauve jacket and matching pants. "My father knew you. Oliver Kwan."

He smiled. "Ah, yes," he said after a slight pause. "We worked together. How is he doing now?"

Something inside me plunged as I learned that my father's intense recollection of his time with Chew had not been reciprocated. As his proxy, I felt embarrassment carpeting my skin like hives.

"He died of cancer in the fall."

"You must be tired of people saying they're sorry," he said. "Or do you take pleasure in that?"

"My dad said he helped you write *Shakespeare's Revolver,*" I blurted.

"Some people thought sharing a dinner table was collaborating." He squinted up at me. "You look like your mother. Maybe that's what I responded to."

An assistant pulled him outside. Then I waited another hour until filming commenced. In a nearby condo, we shot a scene with the woman playing my lover, an actress-model named Cordelia whose features were scalpel-etched, except for the full candy apple of her mouth.

This scene, conducted without dialogue, was shot at a brisk pace. A professional driver handled the shots of the car in city traffic and across the Burrard Street Bridge. Like all Chew's films, the commercial was shot at night. It made sense for Hong Kong, a city that blushed with neon, but in Vancouver, the street scenes and moonlit vistas needed to be cherry-picked in tight frames. I sat in another car, towed by a truck with a camera mounted on it, as the photographer caught the reflection of the bridge lights against the windshield.

"I want you to look like someone who's used to feeling bewildered," Edmund Chew told me at one edge of the bridge. "You're playing someone who finds familiarity in his disorientation. It's the routine that you find shattering. But, of course, all this takes its toll on you."

Absorbing this direction for a moment, I settled on the kind of dully blissful expression I wore when I used to smoke vaporized hash in my first year in Montreal.

The commercial ends with Cordelia, the love interest, stepping out of her car—in a black shift dress and heavy diamond earrings, her hair in an up-do—to be greeted by my double. The betrayal that isn't a betrayal, a betrayal that's self-induced or really only a self-betrayal, was a continuous theme, a creative tic, that ran throughout all of Edmund Chew's films. This scenario was a laughably obvious example of that trope.

The scene would be filmed twice, once as my character pulls up in his Italian sports car, and once with me greeting Cordelia, who looked like Cindy Arau stretched out in a funhouse mirror. The commercial ends with two images: the love interest turning from one version of myself to see the other version, then the second version of myself, the one in the car, calling out to her.

Chew knelt in front of the car, which was parked within eye-shot of the hotel entrance in which the love interest would emerge from the car. "Let's make this easy, okay?" he asked. "I will play the stand-in for you, the version of yourself that receives the woman. The camera will be fixed on your expression as you speak, though of course, you will not be heard in the commercial."

"What should I say?" I asked.

"Say what comes to mind," he said, tossing his head jauntily. "It could be something appropriate to the situation. Don't pretend you're Ibsen or anything. Watch my expression when you call out to me. That's how I want you to look."

I waited for the love interest's car and my car to be towed. I thought of betrayals that weren't betrayals, the betrayals that were self-induced, the betrayals of the self, the self-betrayals that were felt by others. Had my father been a victim of Edmund Chew's treachery, or had he allowed himself to be back-stabbed? Was he a back-stabber himself? The camera started rolling. The truck pulling my car started moving. As I moved, I thought of the fuzzy circumstances surrounding my parents' coupling, the nameless other man involved, and so I pictured myself as my father, then I pictured myself as Edmund Chew, betrayed and betraying. And then I remembered what my father told me in the hospice, the non-sequitur shared by him and Chew that appeared in his film, and as my car approached the love interest approaching Edmund Chew, I uttered those words:

"What time is the late show?"

I watched Edmund Chew's face and tried to follow the ripples of recognition that he'd successfully hid from me earlier in the evening, and then the sorrow, the hostility, the resignation.

It's never too late for the late show.

That month, Hadley returned home to be with her mother, who had grown disconsolate after her reconciliation with Arnie failed. Sheila yelled, then she pleaded. She promised to be less strict, less critical, less nosy. And there would be no more Arnie, not ever again. They had been apart for almost three months, and not only did Hadley realize how much she missed her, but she knew her mother would crumble on her own. I knew that feeling.

"I've seen it happen before," she said, packing her bags. "She can't handle being alone."

We returned my futon to the living room, and I found myself alone again. I walked around in my underwear and left half-eaten cans of Beefaroni in front of the television. Clint came over to drink beer. Sandrine and I saw each other a couple of times a week, though both of us felt uncertain about that. Four times a week I ran through the endowment land trails. I played basketball, poorly, on Thursdays at the Jewish Community Centre, and continued swimming lessons with my sister.

Hadley rejoined the water polo team in time for the provincials in the second week of the month, where her team finished fourth. I saw her between practice and school once or twice a week in the weeks leading up to her birthday, April 22nd. On the day she turned eighteen, we went for lunch at my favourite diner, Helen's Grill on Main Street, and shared a chocolate milkshake.

"How do you feel?" I asked.

"Old—like I have to be an adult."

"Wait until you're my age."

"Twenty-five is ancient."

"I'll be twenty-six in July."

She gasped. "I'll miss your birthday."

"Give me a call."

"I don't think there's a phone where I'm staying."

"Write me a letter."

"But it might come late."

"I'll understand."

"I'll think about you all day on your birthday."

"July twelfth."

"I knew that."

It was then that I gave Hadley a digital camera.

"I thought it might be good for your trip," I told her. "If you already have one, you could exchange it for a travel alarm-radio or rechargeable batteries."

"Thanks, now I can take pictures instead of being in them."

"Just like Dad."

She took photos of me standing in front of an empty lot across the street. "Malcolm, I want you to make it with the camera," she said. "Give me more passion."

I turned away from her then faced her with the pose I planned to use for the cover of a romance novel—once I lifted more weights—and made kissy faces at the camera.

"Now I want you to act sad."

I dropped my face into my hands. When I removed them, my bottom lip was quivering and my eyes had rounded. I looked at the camera, then to the ground, as though I was weighed down by a sadness so heavy that I could no longer hold my head up.

"Beautiful," she said, kissing the tips of her fingers. Then she tapped the side of her head. "Now pretend that you're thinking really hard."

I put my chin on hand, wrinkled my forehead, and made my eyes narrow and inward-looking.

"Give me the camera," I told her, after her last shot.

"I told you—I don't like photos."

"We'll ask someone to take a photo of the two of us."

A curly haired man with wire-frame glasses who was passing by agreed to take the photo. It was remarkable how fussy, how dictatorial, strangers could be when handed a camera. He adjusted the lens, took a few steps back, then stepped forward. He asked us to get closer together. He told me that I should smile more. He told Hadley not to slouch.

This would be the only photo of me and Hadley, who would die in an accident in Guyana that summer. I stood with my arm around her, the exaggerated, plankton-catching smile on my face held so long that my jaw ached. Next to me, my darling sister stood at attention, her eyes fixed forward.

CHAPTER FOURTEEN

SPRING VAULTED INTO SUMMER. The commercial was released in mid-May. I never actually saw it on TV, but friends mentioned they noticed it a couple of times mid-way through a legal drama. It was released online and viewed 10,000 times in its first week.

I was now working regularly. There was a print ad for a perfume and another magazine spread touting state-of-the-art beachwear. It seemed as though every week Vanessa called screaming good news until her voice grew hoarse. She seemed more amazed by my success than I did, and it buoyed her own confidence.

Having gained some momentum, I decided to start my career in commercial work. Vanessa arranged a dozen auditions for me, the first eleven of which I performed miserably. I'd walked into the casting offices, confident from my recent winning streak, sweating brio, and tanked. Didn't this kind of production run in my blood? My line readings were overemphatic or garbled, my movements stiff. The Chew commercial wasn't a typical experience.

I should have known that commercial acting was a skill, something altogether different from catalogue or magazine work. I got serious and enrolled in an eight-class seminar, where, working from advertising copy, I practiced vocal technique, product handling, and physical presentation. The advertisers, I learned, were interested in someone who could achieve the image they wished to present, and there were skills—an ability to modulate one's voice, a level of eye contact—necessary before one could speak and stand with conviction. At my twelfth audition, I landed an ad for a local Credit Union.

"Have you considered acting?" Vanessa asked me at brunch. She was wearing her engagement ring on her right hand. If Uncle Charlie remained in counselling for three more months and his surgery was successfully reversed, she would relocate the ring to her other hand.

"That would be a lot of work." To be honest, I'd started to feel that there was an early expiration date to this work for me. A year ago, being photographed was something I needed to do. It gave me purpose. Now I felt like, soon enough, I'd be searching again.

She nodded. "I thought you had an interesting look when I signed you, but I didn't think you'd make much of it. A lot of young men go into the business thinking they're good-looking, they can make some money, but then they grow bored or easily frustrated. Take Seamus, for instance—he gave up right away."

"If I didn't seem serious," I said, "then why did you take me as a client in the first place?"

"You know me." When she laughed through her nose, she produced a muffled, wheezy noise. "I like challenges."

She'd been laughing much more, and I figured the best way to cancel out the noise was by laughing equally as loudly. Even so, my laugh could not match hers.

"No," I said, with a booming shout, "you can't resist a lost cause."

"Then that makes me the lost effect."

On my twenty-sixth birthday, I went for a walk along the Seawall with my mother. Waiting for me at home was another letter from Claire.

July 9th, 2009
Dear Malcolm,

Happy Birthday (assuming this letter arrives on time)! I hope this finds you well and celebrating with friends and family.

I'm also writing you to ask for your forgiveness. Not just for the callous way that I called off our engagement, but also for my failure to respond to your calls. (In case you're interested, legal proceedings have already begun. His whereabouts remain a mystery.)

I'm writing in the hope that we might get together for a meal or drinks. I'm leaving town in a few weeks and will be there until the fall. I wouldn't be shocked if you refused to see me. But if you want to talk, I'll be around.

Yours,

C.

I waffled, reading over the letter until it was rumpled before I decided to write back. There were half a dozen drafts. My final letter, the one that was sent to Claire, went like this:

July 16, 2008

Claire,

If I didn't want to hear from you again, I would not be writing you this letter, but reading your handwriting and looking at your stationery makes me feel lousy—physically ill. For a really long while, I didn't know how I felt about you … I didn't how I felt about the way you left. First, I panicked and thought I'd lose my mind. I was so sad I couldn't eat or sleep. Then, like two days later, I thought I didn't care at all, couldn't care less what happened to you. I was furious with you. I didn't know what to think because of my father. It was difficult for me to deal with both things at the same time.

There really isn't a point to this letter, I'm just writing what falls into my head, because everything else I've written sounds so fake. If you were here I would tell you how much I cared about you, even though there were times when you seemed to be making all the effort. I didn't say enough, I acted too slowly. You were right. And when I asked you to marry me, I didn't take it very seriously.

Sorry again for this rambling letter. You were right to have left me, but I can't forgive you for it. Does that make sense?

Yours,

Malcolm

Three days later, I picked up the phone and heard Claire's voice. She sounded mumbly and hesitant, like she had awoken in the middle of the afternoon, and we had one of those conversations where every banality and pleasantry was called forth.

Flummoxed, entranced, curious, whatever—I agreed to her suggestion that we meet for coffee in the early evening. I arrived a few minutes early and waited on the street as she approached. She had lost so much weight that her features not only stood out in greater relief, but seemed to have enlarged on her face. Her deliberateness, a single-mindedness that she exuded with every stride, had dimmed, and she seemed not so much to walk, but to drift in the breeze, her face like a lollipop on her emaciated body. We bought French vanilla coffee to go, walked to a park near my house, and sat on a bench staring at an empty duck pond.

She was sleeping on a couch in a friend's apartment, had decided to delay her final year of law school, and was considering a move back to Ottawa, where she would live in her parents' pool house.

She lifted the lid from her cup and took baby sips. "I learned a lot about myself. Do I sound self-involved saying that?" She lowered her head and sighed. "When I was with you, I was very insecure. And I'm not saying that to blame you. I've always been that way."

"So have I."

"Well"—she tried to hide her displeasure—"maybe in a different way. My insecurities made me work harder. I thought if I worked hard enough, I would make up for my weaknesses. Of course, it was much more extreme than self-improvement. If I studied hard enough, no one would know how stupid I felt. If I exercised, if I did enough salsa and skipped meals, then I might not feel so ugly." She looked me over. "I always wished I could feel as good about my looks as you do."

"That's not true."

She nodded. "You might worry about everything else, but not whether other people think you're good-looking.."

"Did it really matter to you?"

"Well, what did you mean in your letter," she asked, "that you didn't take your proposal seriously?"

"I said it because I wanted someone to take care of me. I thought we could get married and I wouldn't have to act any differently."

She moved farther away on the bench. "You didn't love me," she said plainly. "Not the way the way I wanted you to, not the way you were supposed to. You felt safe around me, because I was plain-looking." I tried to deny it. "Say what you like. I was angry at you. I wanted to hurt you. I thought I'd sleep with Seamus to hurt you, because I knew you hated him. He told me things that I wanted to hear from you, but which you didn't say because you were thought-less. No, you weren't thoughtless, you were lazy. You were lazy. You didn't work hard for anything. We got engaged because you didn't want to involve yourself with anyone who was hard to get."

The friend she was staying with lived nearby, and I offered to accompany her there. As we walked, she asked me if I was seeing anybody. I lied and said I wasn't, partly to protect her, but mostly to spare myself. I didn't want to confirm her worst suspicions about me—that she was like a bus shelter that I stepped inside while waiting for Sandrine's return.

"I've been meaning to ask you about something," Claire said to me. "Who was that girl you were with who followed me into the supermarket?"

"That's a long story."

"I saw you on the street that time and was waiting for you to say hello. When you didn't, I just kept walking. I was having a bad day. Seamus and I had gotten into a fight over money; the last thing I wanted was to speak with you. I figured you felt the same way, but then that girl you were with started following me around in the supermarket. I noticed right away. She wasn't a good spy. Finally, I turned to her and asked her what she wanted. She said she was a friend of yours. I asked her why I didn't know her. I thought it was strange that she was so young. She told me that you'd met only recently, through a mutual friend, and that she thought you were a good guy. She wanted to know if I'd really thought over our break-up. It was such a point-blank question, especially coming from a stranger. And it made me angry. I wasn't angry at her, though. I was angry at *you*. I felt all alone, and there you had this girl who would risk embarrassing herself to ask about our relationship. It seemed so unfair to me that you should have someone in your life. How did you get so lucky?"

"I never thought of it that way," I said. "Did you actually buy a box of condoms?" I asked after a pause.

Her face blanched. "That's none of your business."

Hadley and Krista left for Guyana in late June, just days after graduating from high school. They were going to the southwest corner of the country by the Brazilian border and would be gone for five weeks. After receiving training on health issues in Georgetown, they would travel by boat along the country's many rivers and discuss nutrition, malaria prevention, and HIV risk with the Indigenous peoples of the sparsely populated inland.

"I thought you two wanted to dig wells," I remarked to Hadley, a few days before she left.

"We did," she spat out with disappointment, "but that was the ten-week program. Krista only wanted to go away for a month. Besides, it costs another thousand dollars to go for ten weeks—neither of us could really afford to build an aqueduct."

"You have to get ready for school, too."

She nodded. She was enrolled to study human kinetics in the fall at Windsor University in Ontario. "I'll be back in time to register for my courses online."

"How's your mother?" I asked. "I bet she's sad you're leaving."

"Are you sad, too?"

"Absolutely broken-hearted."

"Liar," she said.

"You look happy."

"Do you think so? I guess I am. For a while, I wasn't so sure. I guess I was unhappy because of how badly Mom and I have been around each other. But she's been super-nice to me lately, on account of me going away. Do you know she bought me a Spanish phrasebook? Like I haven't tried telling her that Guyana was a British colony—she doesn't believe me. We've been doing everything together. We're like sisters—just like you and me."

Because her project site was so remote that it was difficult to send a letter, I didn't expect to hear from her until she returned. I wouldn't have had the time to reply, anyway. In the first weeks of the summer, I was preoccupied with work and acting lessons. After the afternoon I spent with Claire, after clearing away my bad feelings toward her, I found myself able to be with Sandrine without reservation. In the fall, Sandrine's house-sit ended, and she moved in. We sometimes invited friends over for barbecues or late-night drinks, but preferred time alone. We killed afternoons with absent-minded, unimaginative sex and stayed up talking. While the nights were still warm, we sat outside on the balcony in lawn chairs and listened to revellers stumble home on the weekends.

Whenever I wanted something, I remember feeling that I could have it. My imagination contained a catalogue of objects that could be purchased with effort and perseverance. I began to realize why people accepted growing up. In return for the possibilities of youth, with its countless revisions and inexhaustible do-overs, one played to one's strengths and accepted the outcome. I had actual professional prospects, even if I already felt like I wanted a new profession. I had a new girlfriend, who was my old girlfriend but calmer. I had thirty-five minute runs through the endowment lands and weekly basketball. I had met Felix.

Afterward, although there was no reason for it, I felt guilty that I had been so happy at that time. If only I had been more concerned about Hadley and had persuaded her not to go, she would still be here. As it was, I encouraged her to go and, when she was away, I was too busy to worry about her. Why should I worry? She was with her best friend and involved with a reputable organization. Five weeks wasn't a very long time, and we would have a few weeks to spend together before she went away to school. I was so preoccupied with myself that when I received the phone call from

Sheila in August, I didn't fully understand at first. I listened to her blubber on the phone, then hung up. It came so suddenly that I felt as though it could be undone if I concentrated hard enough.

That night, Sandrine asked me questions about the accident, but I didn't have any answers.

"You're in shock," she told me. "I want to give you your space."

She kept talking because she didn't know what else to do. I yelled at her, then apologized. She didn't say it, but she wanted me to be more demonstrative. We each drank a beer while we watched a desultory hour of reality television, then she told me she was going to sleep. I thought about seeing Sheila, who had invited me over to her house when she'd told me the news. She'd be awake and would want to see me, but I couldn't see her because it would be overwhelming. I knew I felt only a fraction as badly as she did, but I didn't want to have to console her. Nor did I want to be consoled. Sitting on my futon in my unlit living room, I felt as though I was receiving an angioplasty, as though a balloon was being inflated inside of me, pressing against my chest and making it hard for me to breathe. I tried to ignore it as if I was trying to overcome seasickness or a cramp.

Eventually, I lay down next to Sandrine on our creaky double bed, trying my best not to wake her. Normally I jostled her as I burrowed a place into unconsciousness, but now I lay on the edge of the mattress on top of the covers, measuring my breathing. I was exhausted but tense, like a kettle that's been boiling so long that it's almost run out of water and is rattling on the stove. I dropped one foot on the floor, then the other, and stepped out of the room.

Sandrine stood in the doorway in a T-shirt and a pair of flannel pyjama bottoms.

"You want to go for a drive?" she asked me.

She took my keys and we drove east to the edge of city where the highway began, then all the way to western edge, looping around the university before turning south through blocks of tree-lined residential streets, then back north. "I don't drive enough," Sandrine told me. "Especially at night, when there's no traffic except for police cars and raccoons."

"My dad liked humming along to the radio," I said. "People who drive without music or the radio on, they always make me nervous."

"When I was pregnant with Felix, I would get on a bus and go from one end of Toronto to another, then back. I was depressed and fat and hopeless, and it was nice to feel like I had somewhere to go."

"I wish I were someone who could act upset."

"It used to piss me off. I wanted a reaction from you," Sandrine said. "I just wanted to know you cared, but the more I tried to get a reaction from you, the quieter you got—it's like you're in some kind of trance."

"Do I still piss you off?"

"Sometimes. I don't think you'll change. It's how you are."

"And you're okay with that?" I asked her.

"If everything else stays the same, then I'm okay with it."

Eventually, I asked Sandrine to take me to Queen Elizabeth Park. We left our car on the side of the hill by the restaurant where grandmothers were taken for brunch, and we walked along the edge of the glass-domed conservatory until we found the place where my mother did her late-night painting. We sat holding hands on the low stone wall that separated the viewing area from the tree-covered hillside. In the foreground were the roofs of homes, beyond that, another band of trees that looked almost purple in the light of dusk, then the unlit downtown skyline, with the mountains of the North

Shore in the background. My mother's painting had captured this view earlier in the evening, when it was dimmer outside and the moon fuller than it was now, half swallowed by the cloudless sky. I closed my eyes and reimagined this scene with a darker sky and a moon fattened until it was as round and bright yellow as an egg yolk, because I preferred that picture in my mind.

She'd drowned. Krista had been there, on the shore. They were four weeks into the project, travelling along the rivers on a creaky wooden boat with a small outboard motor. The area surrounding the rivers was lush and green, and on the banks brown-skinned Amerindians washed their clothes. They were part of a group of fifteen volunteers who spent a few days in each village helping teach workshops to community leaders or assisting local doctors and dentists set up makeshift clinics. The work could take seven or eight hours a day in the humid weather. Every day after finishing, they went swimming. Guyana is a Taino word for "land of many rivers," and the water followed them everywhere. In any direction from a village there was a river or a waterfall.

She and a few others were swimming in a river near the base of a waterfall. In order to avoid scraping their feet on the rocks of the river floor, they were told to wear sandals in the water. Hadley's old sandals had a weak Velcro strap that would often come undone as she swam. Krista saw her stop in the water to adjust the strap, her body keeping her afloat. The water would sometimes run fast and occasionally push someone under. It looked as if her other shoe began to slip away, and when she reached for it, she sank under the water. Running along the shore, Krista saw Hadley holding her sandals. Each time her head bobbed above the water, she swallowed more water. It's been suggested that she might have bumped her head on a rock. Her head no longer broke through the surface, and by the time Krista could reach her in the water, she was no longer breathing.

But I'm not sure if I heard the story correctly. Because if Krista had been there, she would have jumped into the river and rescued her. Perhaps I only think Krista was there because I had heard the story through her. Maybe it was another project member on the shore, someone who couldn't swim, who witnessed her sinking. Or maybe Krista didn't dive into the water, maybe she had turned her back or was distracted by some guy, and by the time she noticed Hadley, it was too late. Knowing exactly how it happened doesn't matter to me. Please forgive my incuriosity.

I won't say much about the funeral, because I hardly remember it. It came less than a year after my father's, and it was at a church that was filled with her high-school acquaintances who scribbled their condolences on a banner that stretched out on a table in the foyer. At Sheila's insistence, I sat with her and her father in the front row and spoke after an opening prayer and hymn. I was better prepared than I had been last September.

"Hadley and I shared a father, but we didn't meet until last year," I told the audience. I was wearing a pin-striped suit I'd bought the week before. "And though we didn't know each other a long time, we caught up quickly. As you all know, she was big-hearted, caring, and poised. She loved water polo, watching movies, and animals—even the ones she was allergic to, like long-haired dogs and horses. When she laughed, you had to laugh too. I can't begin to tell you how smart she was. I don't mean she was a great student, but she knew things without having to learn them. Both of us grew up as only children, but she was the one who taught me how to be her brother. I envy every one of you who knew her longer than I did, and I can't say how much I'll miss my sister."

In 1989, Sheila Wallace met Oliver Kwan on the set of a commercial for the Swiss Chicken Lodge, a chain of family-style restaurants. Since moving from Ontario with a boyfriend, Sheila had worked part-time jobs in restaurants waitressing and at a downtown bar checking coats and making sure no one was using drugs in the men's room. She was twenty-four, tall and curvy with thick strawberry-blonde hair, bold eyes, and a perfect smudge for a mouth. Her friends had suggested she was good-looking enough to model. Her boyfriend called a few agencies on her behalf. Eventually, he found someone who thought Sheila might have potential as a spokesperson or a commercial actress. This agent arranged an audition for a commercial directed by my father.

Alongside the glistening rotisserie chickens, Sheila was the star of my father's Swiss Chicken Lodge commercial, the camera tracking her wholesome figure in a peasant dress as she carried two steaming platters of chicken dinner toward a family of five.

The commercial was filmed on location in the early morning before the mall connected to the restaurant opened its doors. My father seemed intimidated by her, startled at the sight of her in her lace-up front, his hands fidgeting along his jacket pockets in search of his cigarettes. Throughout the shoot, he said very little to Sheila, relaying his instructions through the assistant director.

For whatever reason—no respectable reason, I'm assured—Sheila was intrigued by him. During a break, she followed him outside where he was smoking in the mall parking lot behind a trailer. He looked at her, expecting a question about her performance. She asked him for a cigarette, though she didn't normally smoke.

He handed her one and a pack of matches from his jacket pocket. "Aren't you cold?" he asked her.

"I can stand it," she said, flashing her front teeth before placing the cigarette in her mouth. "Why are you so quiet?"

He smiled. "I'm thinking when I work."

"About what?"

"Work."

"It's my first commercial—how am I doing?"

"All right. You have a nice smile."

She thanked him. "Is there anything I could be doing differently?"

"Have you ever worked as a waitress before?" he asked her.

"I still do."

He lifted his eyebrows. "That surprises me. You're holding your chest out a little too much."

"I thought that's what you wanted to see."

"It doesn't look safe."

They kept talking until they were called back to set by the assistant director. The more my father talked, the more he laughed like a child, the closer he drew himself toward her.

Later on, they would meet in the afternoons or early evenings, conducting their affair in motels and at her basement apartment while her boyfriend was working nights at the paper mill. When they finished, he would walk out the door with an easy stride. Yet he wrote her mash notes. When she brought up her boyfriend, a topic she introduced to put everything in its place, he grew sullen. He made increasingly reckless alibis to see her. He concocted a business trip, and they drove to Long Beach to stay at an inn near the water, and they both cried when they boarded the ferry home. She returned from the trip and broke up with her boyfriend.

"It was his idea to have a child," Sheila told me forty-five minutes into a late-night phone call. It had been four days since the funeral, and though Sandrine had been startled awake and then fallen asleep again, I was still up, watching TV and drinking peppermint tea. "We let ourselves become careless. He wanted a daughter, too. You might not want to hear this, but he was getting up the nerve to tell your mother how it was. Things had soured.

"He was not pleased when she was fired from her job, all she wanted to do was draw those terrible paintings of hers—oh yes, I've seen them. I heard about it all. The longer we carried on, the more I heard about it. Every time he tried to tell her, she threw a tantrum. She smashed her hand through a window once. She threatened to do things to herself, but what did it was when she promised to take you away from him forever. You were the one who kept him away from us, and, before I met you, I resented you for it.

"Your mother thought she'd won. She even made him promise not to visit Hadley when she was a child. Your mother wanted him to pretend she never existed. I can't help thinking how it might have been different if he had left her, anyway. I've been wondering for eighteen years. We would have been safe. She would have been safe. She was such a good girl, Malcolm, wasn't she?"

I was quiet.

"Are you there?" she asked after a while.

"She was a very good girl."

CHAPTER FIFTEEN

A YEAR AFTER MY father's death, my mother sold her house and purchased a two-bedroom condo in a Yaletown high rise, a unit in a glass-and-steel structure from which the boats on False Creek looked like white, wing-tipped shoes sliding on a conveyor belt. When I arrived at the house to collect my own things, she was barricading herself with boxes wrapped in packing tape.

She hurried me upstairs. "No fooling around now," she said, one hand pushing me from behind. "The movers I hired charge by the minute."

My mother showed a look of frantic determination. My childhood home had been polished like marble. The floors were mopped and buffed, the windows scrubbed so they reflected starlight, the washrooms sanitized and freshened. The empty rooms I passed bore the new, optimistic smell of an elementary school in the fall.

"Here's your chance to collect your junk," she told me. "Don't ruin my fresh start."

The only boxes that didn't have Chinese written on them were those labelled "Malcolm." I held each one of them to my ear and rattled them like gifts. With an exception or two, I didn't hear anything familiar enough to save from donation.

As her movers trucked furniture to her new place, we spent the afternoon shepherding extra boxes—my father's clutter objects—into a storage space in a part of Chinatown that smelled like old dishrags.

Two days after the move, I heard from her unexpectedly. She was demanding to look through my boxes.

"I'm looking for your father."

At my door, she threw herself on me, sobbing until my shirt was damp. In her most lulling voice, Sandrine guided her to a chair and poured her a cup of tea. She sat at our kitchen table, her eyes darting between us. The last place she remembered seeing my father's remains was above her kitchen sink.

"And you went back to the house?" I asked her.

"Of course—do you think I'm stupid? It wasn't there. I checked my apartment, my car. I checked everywhere. I called the movers. I asked the real-estate agent. I even called the police. It's my fault."

I shook my head. "Maybe it's not worth the bother."

My mother's eyes felt like fishhooks tearing into me. "He gave everything to you, and you're not even concerned about where his remains might be?" she said in Chinese, so Sandrine wouldn't understand. "They could be flushed down the toilet for all you care, and you don't. And all because of that girl."

"What are you talking about?" I asked her in English.

"You promised me you wouldn't see her again."

I shook my head.

Her voice was low and deliberate. "I wish I had never given birth to you. I wish you weren't my son. I wish you had died inside me before you were born."

She knew I would do anything to keep Sandrine from seeing her that way. We tore through the boxes I kept in the den, but only uncovered old report cards and comic books. We then drove down to the storage space and went through dozens of boxes, a job that took seven hours to complete.

There wasn't anything my father wouldn't keep. In the smelly locker, we found copies of his favourite movies, binders filled with production notes, treatments for seven abandoned features written in Chinese, income-tax receipts, movie stubs, and yellowing newspapers. Even amidst all his trash, my father's remains somehow escaped her grasp, and to this day my mother treats their disappearance like a final rebuke from him.

"It's your fault," my mother said to me. "If only you'd kept your promise to me, I wouldn't have been so distracted." My mother slapped me across my right cheek. "Why do you treat me like I'm trash?" The next time she slapped me, pain splashed down my jaw. "I'm glad that girl has died. I'll never have to see her face again. I hate you. I loathe you. What have I ever done to deserve you?"

She turned and went outside. Before I joined her to take her home, I removed an item from one of the boxes. It was in a manila envelope lodged between a stack of other papers. Collected in the envelope, I guessed, were items taken from his body before the cremation. Along with his water-resistant watch and his wedding band, there was the bracelet given to him by his daughter. I took it with me, then wore it myself for a few weeks, then put it somewhere I'd never lose it.

First my father, then Hadley, played through my mind in a loop. Everything I saw reminded me of them, and every reminder felt barbed. Now, a year later, I'm writing this not so much to have a permanent record, but simply to remember, to stir the memories I do have, before they clot and dry in my head.

I haven't told anyone about it, out of fear, but I saw Hadley after her death. By this, I mean I imagined seeing her. I would see someone who shared a feature with her or wore an item of clothing she'd owned, and a glitch in my brain would create an illusion. The most unsettling time was when, after lunch on Granville Island, I was making a phone call and glimpsed a woman leaving the ladies' room; she had my sister's glossy, shoulder-length hair and love-bitten complexion. Catching my stare, the woman scowled like a Rottweiler.

Another time I saw Hadley in a supermarket. She was in hiking boots, khaki shorts, and a blue cotton blouse, pushing a shopping cart. I watched her turn at the end of aisle and followed her to the produce section.

This woman was taller than Hadley, wore her hair differently, and was several years older—about my age. The nose on this woman's face was completely wrong, and she had the knotty, scratched-up legs of a hiker. But her large brown eyes were deep and still, and their resemblance to Hadley's was eerie enough to make other dissimilarities irrelevant. I found myself thinking how she might have been in a few years—if she had grown older, perhaps she would have cut her hair and given up swimming pools to traipse across forested hillsides. She would be finished her undergraduate degree, and perhaps she'd be at teaching-school, as she'd planned.

A few days later, on Main Street, I saw someone who shared the same build as Hadley, wearing the same overcoat my sister used to own—and about the same age. I watched her, unwilling to inhale.

I wasn't the only one who noticed this resemblance. Standing by a car on the street was a small man with a goatee flecked with grey, wearing a leather jacket. He'd been putting quarters into the meter when she emerged onto the street. A sick, anxious look—maybe, I thought later, it was a guilty expression—flashed on his face. He turned from her back to the meter, but couldn't resist looking at her until she disappeared from view. Then he crossed the street into a sandwich shop.

Only when I had returned home did I realize that that was Arnie, Sheila's ex-husband. Things Hadley had said about him crossed my mind, and I leapt to some conclusions that I will never be able to prove. These thoughts visit me like unwelcome guests, yet I can't turn them away.

Sandrine and I missed our ferry. It was early August, a few days before I learned about Hadley. We were on track to make the boat, but a car accident on the highway slowed us down. Sandrine called our child's adoptive parents to tell them we'd be two hours late. We parked our car in the line-up for the next ferry, then went to the terminal and bought cheap sunglasses and coffee.

"Are they upset?" I asked her.

"No, they're cool," Sandrine said. "I made sure they were cool before I let them have my kid. If I could choose my own parents, they'd be Joanna and Kurt." She was wearing a white tank top and denim shorts. Her hair was tied in a pony tail. "The trouble is, they're double-booked two hours from now. They're supposed to be at another kid's birthday party at the water park. So we're going to have to meet them there. They gave me an address."

"Is it okay I'm coming?" I asked. I was dressed in a golf shirt and pressed khakis, to make a good impression.

"Yeah, they want to ask you about your family medical history. Plus, they saw your ad online."

Finally, a voice instructed drivers to return to their vehicles. Once aboard the ferry and parked, we sat on the deck while seagulls swooped above. Some teenaged boys drinking beer from brown bags were checking out Sandrine. As the ferry entered open water, Sandrine got cold and we relocated inside next to a couple of German-speaking backpackers who were busy making sandwiches from a loaf of bread and a jar of Nutella. I was getting impatient.

"Who does Felix look like?" I asked Sandrine. "You or me?"

"It depends," she told me. "When he was born, he looked eerily like you. The second time I saw him, at four months, he was more like me. The last time I saw him, maybe six months ago, he looked like my grandfather did when he was working on a model ship. Felix was playing with blocks, and they had exactly the same look of concentration."

As we disembarked from the ferry, Sandrine punched the address of the park into my GPS. They lived a few minutes outside the Victoria city core among small but well-tended houses with tree-shaded lawns in front of them. We finally approached a large park with a swimming pool. We parked. I popped open the trunk so Sandrine could retrieve the present we bought for Felix—a toy guitar that made squealing electronic sounds. I had picked it out over Sandrine's objections: "Joanna and Kurt are going to hate us."

It was hot and dry, and the park was full of children gathered around the water park. Farther out, people lay on beach blankets reading books or playing soccer shirtless. We headed away from them toward a picnic table near the pool that had silvery balloons tied to it at each end like a four-poster bed.

A dozen sets of couples, all of them about a decade older than me and Sandrine, were gathered watching their young kids. I looked for Kurt and Joanna. According to Sandrine, Kurt was tall and Nordic, with a thick beard and deep-set eyes that made him seem both saintly and demonic; Joanna had an olive complexion and was rail thin. He was an engineer at a solar-energy company; she taught elementary school.

Right before meeting Felix, I wondered who I would see in his face. No one's face belonged completely to one's self. And no face contained beauty unto itself. It took other people to bestow beauty; it took others to superimpose their memories and desires on each feature.

It was Joanna who noticed us approaching. She ran over to Sandrine and hugged her, then clasped both her hands around mine.

Felix sat on Kurt's lap, wet, with a towel wrapped around him, watching the children in the water park splash and holler. He was a fat, brown-eyed two-year-old with hair the colour of a chocolate milkshake. As we drew closer, Kurt waved at us and turned his boy on his knee. I thought Felix had both caution and wonder on his face. When he caught sight of me, the boy's eyes flickered and his mouth drew back in the shape of a hello.

ACKNOWLEDGMENTS

I'd like to thank Shyla Seller, Brian Lam, Martha Magor, Derek Fairbridge, Chloe Chan, Peter Darbyshire, Susan Safyan, and offer my gratitude to the Canada Council for the Arts and the BC Arts Council for their assistance.

While I came up with the idea for the Ninja Pizza commercial in Chapter Four on my own, it should be noted that various funny folks have already uploaded viral clips with similar concepts onto YouTube. Type "Ninja Pizza" into YouTube. They're all definitely worth a click.

KEVIN CHONG was born in Hong Kong in 1975. He is the author of a novel, *Baroque-a-Nova*, a music memoir entitled *Neil Young Nation*, and a forthcoming memoir on horse-racing. His writing has appeared in the *Globe and Mail*, the *Walrus*, and *Chatelaine*. He lives in Vancouver.

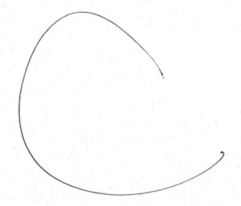